P9-APT-611

Employment Is Murder

Employment Is Murder

Daniel B. Brawner

Five Star • Waterville, Maine

First Edition
First Printing: August 2004

Published in 2004 in conjunction with Tekno Books and Ed Gorman.

Set in 11 pt. Plantin by Ramona Watson.

Printed in the United States on permanent paper.

Library of Congress Cataloging-in-Publication Data

Brawner, Daniel B.
    Employment is murder / Daniel B. Brawner.—1st ed.
        p. cm.—(Five Star first edition mystery series)
    ISBN 1-59414-189-4 (hc : alk. paper)
    1. Mythologists—Fiction.   2. Golf clubs (Sporting goods)—Fiction.   3. Los Angeles (Calif.)—Fiction.
    4. New Age movement—Fiction.   5. Unemployed—
Fiction.   6. Smuggling—Fiction.   I. Title.   II. Series.
    PS3602.R395E395 2004
    813′.6—dc22   2004046973

Employment Is Murder

Acknowledgements

I would like to thank my mother, a great mystery fan who has always believed in me and to my dad who taught me the value of hard work and a good story. Thanks to my writers' group: Joe Curran, Emory Gillespie, Barbara Lau, Amy Shuttleworth, and Mary Ann Taylor, all terrific writers, whose insights have been of immeasurable help. Thanks to the gifted astrologer Maggie Anderson (Astromaggie.com) for her technical assistance.

Chapter 1

"How about this one?" Kenny said, folding the newspaper in half. " 'Wanted: Goodwill ambassador for aggressive, mid-sized hazardous waste plant. No experience necessary. Must be able to speak clearly through a gas mask.' "

Simon closed his sky blue eyes and, sitting in a lotus position in the middle of his kitchen floor, cleared his mind of earthly distractions and filtered for the essential truth of the ad, as a migrating whale filters for plankton.

While he was waiting, Kenny made himself a triple-decker peanut butter sandwich. By the time Kenny had polished off the rest of the yogurt and washed down some kind of tofu granola bar with two glasses of milk, Simon had opened his eyes.

"So which is it, swami," Kenny asked, "thumbs up or down?"

Simon said, "I feel that the money might be good. But there is trouble in the office."

"Something green and glowing in the water cooler?"

Simon frowned. "I sense the employees suffer from a feeling of mythic detachment."

Kenny chewed his peanut butter and swallowed hard. "Well that would do it for me," he said. "That and those pesky tumors. Try this one. 'Before you say no to mortuary sales, consider this exciting, recession-proof career. No sales rejections. No credit turndowns. Late nights and a positive attitude a must.' "

9

Simon folded his hands. "They're about to lose their lease and the secretary has been embezzling them blind."

Kenny shrugged. "I don't know how you do it. You're the only person I know who reads help wanted ads like they were tea leaves."

"It was in the Sunday *L.A. Times*."

"And what are you now, zero for three this year?"

Simon got up off the linoleum. "How was I supposed to know that photographic inventory job was just a front for a burglary operation?"

"And what about the job selling solar-powered street lights?" Kenny reminded him.

"It sounded environmentally responsible," Simon said.

"Yeah, well, you're lucky your lawyer convinced those nutbars at the city of Evergreen that having their street lights on only during the day would make it easier to spot UFOs."

"There have been sightings . . ." Simon began, but stopped with a look of admonition from his friend. "I wouldn't be doing this at all, you know, if it weren't for Amy. I get a hundred and fifty dollars a month and free rent for managing the apartments. I don't need a regular job. Steady employment interferes with my quest for self-actualization."

Kenny leaned his 300-pound frame against the refrigerator, tilting it slightly against the wall. "First of all, gainful employment is not a death sentence. Lots of people work with hardly any ill effects. A job can be a good thing. I know. I've had dozens of them. Besides, Amy doesn't care if you work or not." He scrunched up his disproportionately little nose. "She thinks you're cute."

"After her parents meet me tonight, they'll think I'm a bum."

"Who cares?" Kenny said. "In a couple of years, Amy's law firm will make her a partner; you can get married and let her take care of you." He pawed through a cupboard. "Haven't you got anything else to eat in this place?"

Simon picked up the paper and started scanning the help wanted ads. "Try some of that stuff in the refrigerator in the blue Tupperware."

From what Amy had told him, her parents had been a little overprotective of her because they always thought of her as a problem child. She had been small for her age and very pretty, but her parents felt she was somehow not quite feminine. She climbed trees, argued with adults, and played war games with her Barbie dolls. When Amy was in first grade, her mother received a call from the teacher saying Amy had gotten in trouble. Her mother was sure Amy had been caught stealing—her mother had an obsessive aversion to stealing. But the teacher assured her that was not the charge.

"Mrs. Castor," the teacher began slowly, "your daughter has been in a fight."

"Oh, my God! I thought she got along so well with all the other little girls."

"She didn't start it, Mrs. Castor, but she did break the boy's nose in two places."

And so it went. Other children had friends—Amy had allies. Other children played—Amy trained. By the time Amy was a freshman in high school, she had the sincere respect of every boy in her class. But no dates. The situation suited her fine, but it worried her parents to distraction. They gave her ballet lessons (just made her tougher), drama lessons (sharpened her debating skills), and art lessons (she drew devastating cartoons of her enemies).

Her father said in despair, "Is there nothing this child cannot turn into a weapon?"

Somehow, they decided, instead of sending her to summer camp, to send her to cooking school—one of those chic, extravagant affairs that advertise in the back of gourmet magazines. Amy loved it. At the end of the summer, she came home with an impressive repertoire in haute cuisine. On holidays, she dazzled the relatives with one of her masterpieces. Occasionally, she would even bring a boy home to sample her cooking who, to her mother's exceeding joy, inevitably began seeing Amy in a different light. Amy, on the other hand, could never take seriously anybody who loved her for something so trivial as her cooking.

Amy met Simon when she worked as a law clerk for the legendary prosecutor Maxwell "Maximum Sentence" Strickland. The case involved a multi-level marketing scam: selling organic minerals allegedly derived from primeval forests, promising the participants a long life without cancer or gray hair and wealth beyond their wildest dreams. Simon was the defendant's star salesman. He testified that most of his customers were under forty and therefore not prime candidates for cancer or gray hair anyway. However, he became suspicious when he walked in on the company president, Skip Arbite, filling gelatin capsules for his secret "organic minerals" with a mixture of No-Doz and cherry Kool-Aid.

Simon turned the matter over to the authorities, not so much because the customers weren't getting a profitable business opportunity—some were making piles of money. And it was not because the stuff didn't work—many reported they hadn't felt so energized in years. What bothered Simon was that the company promised its customers a miracle of ancient wisdom and gave them cheap chemicals instead. When the jury looked into Simon's earnest blue eyes and listened to him talk about the power of real miracles and how wonders were all around them if only they could read the signs, they were all ready to follow him anywhere. Amy, whose daily associations consisted almost entirely of hardcore criminals and attorneys, thought Simon was the most innocent person she had ever seen.

When the trial was over, Skip got five to seven at San Quentin and Simon got Amy. Simon was won over with Amy's unwavering sense of right and wrong. And her chocolate cheesecake.

"Ever since I got out of college," Simon spoke into the newspaper, "I have felt the cold vacuum of consumerism, sucking me toward the dark vortex of debt and despair. All this time, I've chosen to live outside the tempting glow of capitalism's campfire light. But now, I must descend into that forsaken world and do the best I can." He sighed. "For love."

"Or you could always go back and finish your doctorate in comparative mythology." Kenny stood suddenly transfixed beside the open refrigerator, Tupperware in one hand and fork in the other. Finally he spoke. "Do you know what this is?" he whispered.

"I think it's Kalbanierenbraten mit Kartoffelklassen," Simon said, glowering at the want ads.

"No, it's heaven," Kenny said reverently. "Pure heaven." Again, he launched into the Tupperware. "If you and Amy ever broke up, it would be the saddest day of my life."

"Listen to this. 'If you truly have a sense of mission,' " Simon read with great significance, " 'if you seek something more from work than just a job, don't pass up this opportunity of a lifetime. Call Going Platinum today.' Did you hear that? A sense of mission!"

Kenny scraped along the side of the plastic container with his index finger and licked it off. "Sounds like a straight commission sales job to me, partner. I'd say pass."

"Well, I wonder what the great Joseph Campbell would say?"

Kenny rolled his eyes. "Here we go again."

Simon strode across the kitchen floor, becoming animated. "You know what I think he'd say? I think Professor Campbell would say, 'Follow your bliss!' That's exactly what he'd say. When, as a young graduate student, Campbell met the Hindu mystic Krishnamurti, he could have gone right on studying European mythology. But he didn't. He followed his bliss and pursued Eastern mythology with a passion. When he was a poor but ambitious college instructor, Campbell was offered a chance to knock out a quick book on world mythology and make a couple of bucks. Do you know what he did?"

"He followed his bliss?"

"That's precisely what he did. Although he didn't get one penny more from his publisher, he took five years and wrote *Hero with a Thousand Faces*."

Kenny snapped his damp fingers. "Going Platinum! Say, isn't that those guys dressed like gangsters who sell platinum-plated golf putters on late night TV?"

Simon was pacing now. "A sense of mission! I have a feeling about this one, Kenny. This is big! This one was made for me."

"It's like they saw you coming."

"If all I wanted was a job, that would be one thing. But I have a calling I can no longer ignore. Remember when we were kids and I fell out of that oak tree that had been hit by lightning?"

Kenny chuckled. "Somehow, you landed on your head, square between the horns of that mean Angus bull we'd been teasing."

"What were the odds of that happening?"

"One in a million, partner."

"One in a million," Simon echoed. "Remember, I was knocked cold? And when I came to, that monstrous black bull was standing over me. I knew then and there I had been touched by the hand of the Eternal."

Kenny giggled. "I still can't believe you kissed that evil son of a bitch on the nose!"

"I had nothing more to fear, from the bull or anything else. I had only to wait until I was called by destiny. Ever since then, I have had a sense of mission."

"But like you said, you don't really need a job. You're only thirty-five."

"I've been saving myself all these years."

"Like a virgin bride," Kenny added wistfully.

"I'm calling Going Platinum right now!" Simon reached for the telephone.

"Couldn't you just let the FBI handle it this time?" Kenny blurted out. "I mean, I know you don't go deliberately looking for trouble when you apply for a job. I'm sure you have the best of intentions. I don't know how you do it, but when you get a job at a bank it turns out they're printing their own money. When you go to work at a supermarket, it seems the meat department has a deal with the local veterinarian, giving new meaning to the term 'puppy chow.' You laugh, but remember that furniture store you worked at that turned out to be a money-laundering operation? What tipped you off that something wasn't right about them, anyway?"

Simon shrugged. "I sensed the manager was metaphysically misaligned. And, I realized the window display hadn't changed in a year and the delivery truck tires were flat."

"You know, I could get you a job working with me at the

health spa," Kenny suggested. "You're a natural salesman. People believe everything you say."

"Then believe this, my friend," Simon said, laying his hand on Kenny's shoulder. "My path may be crooked, but my destination lies straight before me. I'm going to work for Going Platinum and I feel it will be a mutually insightful experience."

"You could end up arrested," Kenny said, "or dead."

Simon picked up the phone. "I've thought of that."

Chapter 2

Simon walked into the lobby of Going Platinum and breathed deeply, absorbing its clean, corporate atmosphere. He felt a tingle of excitement as he straightened his sport coat and tucked in the cleverly folded bed sheet he was using in place of a dress shirt. He wore a red velvet curtain rope for a belt on his newest Levi's. Simon caught a reflection of himself in a glass trophy case. He had to admit, he looked pretty sharp. He did momentarily wish he could have worn regular shoes instead of sandals and made a mental note to ask his parents for a pair for Christmas.

He was doing a simple yoga headstand to relax when the receptionist, a severe-looking woman in her late forties, invited Simon to sit down until the personnel manager was available. Simon balanced there on his head, smiling at her for a minute or so.

"Or maybe you'd like to levitate?" she sneered.

"I certainly would!" Simon enthused. "You can't imagine how hard I've tried."

"Can't I?" she muttered, pressing the intercom button. "Mr. Zhelev, your ten o'clock is here. Please come right away." She smiled tightly at Simon and drummed her artificial nails on the Formica.

"Call me 'Mr. Z,' " Mr. Zhelev said affably with a slight and undeterminable accent, steering Simon to a sumptuous leather chair across from a carved mahogany desk. "So

17

you're here about the job?" Mr. Z, a swarthy, powerfully built man of around forty, slid deftly behind the immaculate desk.

"That's right," Simon said. An antique clock on the wall ticked.

Mr. Z clapped his thick palms together with the appearance of eagerness. "Well," he said, "have you had any experience?"

Simon fingered his quartz crystal pendant and drew a breath.

"Never mind. I can see you have," said Mr. Z. He pointed at the crystal. "Is that supposed to have magical powers or something?"

"Darned if I know," Simon answered cheerfully. "Maybe it wards off evil spirits." He slipped it off and held it out to the man behind the desk. "Want to try it on?"

Mr. Z shrank back in his chair. "No, no. That's okay."

Simon noted the crystal's repellent effect on Mr. Z and tucked it inside his sheet.

Mr. Z leaned forward. "So you think you're a pretty good salesman, eh, Simon?"

Simon nodded. "I've sold things you wouldn't believe."

Mr. Z chuckled. "Me, too, Simon. Me, too. Okay, then." He looked around his office and snatched up a stapler from a nearly empty bookshelf. "If you're such a good salesman, sell me this stapler."

This was an old sales trainer's technique. Simon took Mr. Z's stapler and set it back down on the desk. "It wouldn't take much of a salesman to sell you something you clearly wanted enough to buy the first time." Simon glanced around the room for inspiration. There was a photograph of a younger, thinner Mr. Z in a soccer uniform with a group of other olive-skinned kids and another photo of Mr. Z shaking hands with a famous Italian-American actor. There was a plaque bearing what Simon assumed was the company logo: a gold-colored LP record, with the words, "Yakov Zhelev is GOING PLATINUM." On the wall behind Mr. Z's chair, a cheap replica of a Civil War saber hung from a nail. Crudely stenciled under it was, "Yakov, the Samurai salesman." Simon's ear twitched and he suddenly had second thoughts about working for the company.

"I'll tell you what," said Simon, "if I'm any kind of a salesman, I should be able to sell you something you don't want." Mr. Z tried to suppress a grin. Simon flipped the gold curtain tassel on his makeshift red velvet belt. "You want this?"

Mr. Z snorted. "Are you serious?"

"Not that I would want to give it up." Simon hoisted his loose-fitting jeans. "In a way, I'd be lost without it. But I can see you're a man of discriminating taste." Simon whipped off the curtain cord in one fluid motion. Mr. Z flinched. "I wouldn't be wasting your time if I didn't know you needed this more than I do."

Mr. Z scoffed. "What would I need that thing for?" He waved at his window. "I got mini blinds!" He laughed hard at his own joke.

Simon smiled indulgently. "Mr. Z, wouldn't you say a salesman's office is like a spider's web that attracts to him whatever he needs?"

Mr. Z looked perplexed.

"And wouldn't you say," Simon continued, "that if even one strand of that web were weak or out of place, it could leave an escape route for, shall we say, reluctant customers?"

Mr. Z's hand slid closer to the intercom button.

"Well, wouldn't you say so?" Simon demanded, stepping forward.

"Yes, yes. Okay," said Mr. Z.

"Then it is my duty to inform you that a strand of your professional web is dangerously weak. You have an empty, aching void in your office that cries out for this!" He shook the curtain cord like a vanquished cobra. "Your reputation—no, your honor as a salesman—depends on it." Simon stared at the wall behind Mr. Z and Mr. Z's eyes followed, as if magnetized, to the tin saber, dangling tentatively from a piece of twine.

"You son of a bitch!" he said. "You did it. I got to have that velvet rope for my sword."

"It wouldn't look right without it," Simon agreed.

Mr. Z took out his wallet. "How much?"

Simon looked him straight in the eye. "Fifty dollars," he said and smiled.

"You're hired," said Mr. Z. "I wasn't sure until you told me the price." They shook on the deal and when Simon withdrew his hand from Mr. Z's massive paw, he found in it a crisp new one-hundred-dollar bill. "Welcome to Going Platinum!"

Chapter 3

When he was free from his duties as personnel director, Mr. Z proved to be a personable guy. "I don't like hiring people," he confided to Simon as they made a quick tour of the building. "Going Platinum has always been a family business. We're a traditional company and our family traditions are our strength."

Simon noted that the plush white carpet was barely worn in the middle. "How long have you been in operation?" he asked.

"Three years," said Mr. Z. "When my father came to this country, he had no money, no friends. He couldn't even speak English—okay, he still doesn't speak so good English. But he had a dream. He wanted to . . ." Mr. Z struggled to find the right word.

"Make golf putters out of precious metal?" Simon prompted.

Mr. Z snorted. "Of course not! He wanted to get rich. My father wouldn't give a smelly goat's behind for golf. But as your Jesse James said, that's where the money is."

"Jesse James was a wise man."

Mr. Z nodded. "Thank you. As I was saying, I don't like hiring people outside of the family. But you can see, we are becoming very prosperous and we need somebody—you, Simon—to handle some of our growing retail business. It's that damned silly television ad. It's working me to death! Who would think anybody would be awake at two in the morning, wishing they had a platinum golf club with their company's name on it? It's an easy job. You go there. You show them a putter and you bring back their money."

"What about the pay?" asked Simon.

"Pay? Try to have them pay cash. We also take VISA and MasterCard."

A lanky, morose-looking man with a droopy mustache stepped out from an office, carrying a stack of manila envelopes. When he saw Simon, he closed the door quickly behind him and tried the knob to make sure it was locked.

"Ah, here is my brother, Pater," Mr. Z said. "Pater is our bookkeeper and office manager. Nothing goes on here that Pater doesn't know about. Say hello to the newest addition to our company, Pater."

Simon held out his hand. "Pleased to meet you."

Pater grunted and scuttled off down the hall.

"It's just as well Pater never went into sales," Mr. Z chuckled. "Behind those doors there, is our plating and engraving operation. It's run by my cousin, Josev. If you're lucky, you'll meet him when he hasn't been drinking. This last office on the left belongs to my dear brother, Rodion, our general manager and, more importantly, our paymaster." Mr. Z knocked on the door.

Rodion stuck only his fully-bearded head out of the door. "What is it?" Rodion demanded in a heavy Slavic accent.

"Rodion, how nice to see your smiling face. Where's the rest of you?"

Rodion growled something back in a foreign tongue. He suddenly noticed Simon standing next to his brother. "Who's this?"

"May I present Simon, our new salesman?"

"How do you do?" Rodion said formally, still mostly hidden behind the door.

Simon didn't even try to shake hands. "Very well, thank you. Actually, I'm glad we ran into you. I wanted to ask you what my position pays."

Rodion gave Mr. Z a dirty look. "I'm rather busy right now, Simon. Perhaps Yakov will be glad to explain it to you during the orientation. Goodbye," he said and closed the door.

Mr. Z cleared his throat. "Oh, look. Here is our display case."

There was a four-foot-high case built into the wall. It was glazed with the kind of thick Plexiglas used in bank windows and framed in dark walnut. Vibration and infrared sensors were conspicuously affixed to the acrylic. Inside, was a complete set of gleaming platinum golf clubs, arranged in a sort of teepee with the club heads fanning out at the bottom.

Simon suppressed a shudder at this shrine to leisure and excess. As he gazed into the case, he saw a momentary vision of a golden calf, cast from the accumulated trinkets of the poor. Did he really want to serve this idol? Was he willing to sacrifice his ideals on its altar to please Amy's parents? Simon felt a cold wave of dread sweep over him.

"Impressive, aren't they?"

Simon tried to hide his distaste. "Are they solid platinum?"

"Ha!" Mr. Z scoffed. "There isn't enough precious metal in there to fill your teeth. The platinum plating is so thin, you can practically read through it. We'd never make a nickel if we sold solid platinum putters. What we sell here is image. And we sell a lot of it."

Simon nodded, a dazed look in his eyes.

"Speaking of which, we need to get you some real clothes!" Mr. Z opened Simon's jacket. "What size shirt do you wear—twin or queen?" He roared with laughter and threw a meaty arm around Simon's shoulders. "I'm going to send you to my personal tailor. And for God's sake, don't tell him what kind of clothes you want. He'll know what to do. Just give him this."

Mr. Z handed Simon what looked like a dime. It was a penny.

"That's right," said Mr. Z. "It's platinum plated. Now it's worth about two cents." He laughed again. "Be back here Monday at eight a.m. sharp for your indoctrination."

Simon stared woodenly.

"Your training, Simon. Lighten up!"

Chapter 4

Amy had a stunning split-level duplex in Del Rey, next to a surgeon who never seemed to be home. It was enclosed by an adobe-looking wall with a masonry archway and a Spanish wrought iron gate. Amy and the surgeon shared a little courtyard made with hand-crafted terra cotta tiles. There was even a little fountain that ran night and day that was a regular stop for every bird in the neighborhood. A lush avocado tree with wide tropical leaves shaded a small round table, inlaid with a Pompeii mosaic, beside the fountain. Beside the table sat two empty redwood chairs.

Simon sulked on Amy's leather sofa. "I thought you'd be happy for me that I got a job."

"Of course, I'm happy for you." Amy checked her pulse rate on the Stairmaster and increased the tempo. "But don't you think it's odd that they hired you for a job, but won't tell you what it pays?"

Simon pondered the question a moment. "I guess I don't really care what it pays."

"That's so sweet!" she panted. "I'd have demanded to have an offer in writing. Then I would have run it by my attorney and my accountant. After that, I probably would have insisted on ten percent more. But you . . ." Amy stopped pumping. "You are so cute!" She dismounted the machine and threw her arms around Simon. "You're idealistic." She kissed him. "And you're trusting." She kissed him again. "And you have the loveliest blue eyes." Her green Spandex leotard slid over him, slick as snakeskin.

"I had a dream today," said Simon between kisses.

"Now that I've got you on the couch, why don't you tell Dr. Amy all about it?"

"Why do I get the impression you're not listening to me?"

Amy slithered against him. "Why do I get the impression you're not paying attention to me?"

"Want to take turns?"

"Ooo! I can see your momma raised you right," she said. "But you go first. My turn is going to take longer."

"All right," said Simon. "Well, it was more of a vision, really. You see, I was looking at this display case of a set of platinum-plated golf clubs, when the clubs turned into a cage made out of snakes. The snakes had human faces. After meeting a couple of Mr. Z's relatives, I was actually thinking about quitting."

"Look, Simon, you don't have to go to all this trouble on my account. I love you. I don't care if you never get another job the rest of your life. As for my parents—they don't have to understand. I don't live with them anymore. I want to live with you." Amy cleared her throat. "Well, actually— and this is nothing against your place—what I meant was, I want you to live with me."

"I love you too, Ames. But I'm not making this up. I haven't had a vision that clear since the night before my junior-senior prom."

"You mean this ranks up there with the first time you almost lost your virginity?"

"I knew there was something special about this job the minute I saw their ad. I tell you, it spoke to me."

"Yeah," said Amy. "It said, 'Sucker!' "

"It was more than that," Simon continued, unruffled.

"There is something spiritually out of synch in that company. If it is not set right, it could infect every employee in the place. It could spread throughout Los Angeles. I feel it is up to me to help restore metaphysical order to Going Platinum."

Amy rolled her eyes. "What you are probably sensing is that these guys are crooks. And, for what it's worth, I think you're right. But let it go. You can't reform the world. And you might even get hurt."

Simon put his arm around her. "You're a wise woman. But I need to do this. For myself. I won't be able to rest until I get to the bottom of it. Besides, I could use the money."

Amy extended her palms and looked heavenward. "I sense some pro bono work coming my way."

Simon snuggled closer. "That was all I wanted to talk about. Now, I believe it's your turn."

Chapter 5

Simon had left an hour early to beat the traffic on the Santa Monica Freeway and, when he entered the company conference room, he found himself alone and feeling a little uneasy. His new clothes seemed to chafe at his skin and the silk tie constricted around his uncharacteristically buttoned collar. He felt not so much dressed by his new clothes, as surrounded by them. He pictured himself as Hercules who, although he could not be defeated by men or monsters, died from wearing the wrong clothes.

Hercules killed the centaur, Nessus, who had tried to violate the hero's wife, Deianeira. As he lay dying, Nessus told Deianeira to soak a piece of cloth in his blood and if her husband ever fell out of love with her, to dress him in it. Then, after Hercules took Iole as his concubine, Deianeira gave him the cloth to wear as a tunic. Nessus's poison blood burned like fire and although Hercules tried to tear off the robe, it stuck to his skin and tormented him all the more. After she saw what she had done, Deianeira was sorry. But when Hercules could no longer stand the pain, he had himself cremated alive.

Simon adjusted his tie and was considering the advantages of a quick death by fire when Mr. Z burst through the door, carrying a display easel and followed closely by a determined-looking young man who had obviously been to the company tailor.

"Looking good, Simon!" said Mr. Z. "Simon, meet

Steve Merritt. He'll be training with you."

"Nice to meet you," Steve said, executing a well-practiced handshake. "I see they've got you in 'full Chicago' too."

"What?"

"Full Chicago. You know. Mafia clothes. Pinstripes, wide lapels, white tie. It's a nice look for you. Good luck this week," said Steve, doing a pantomime of a quick draw.

"Good luck?"

Zelda scurried in with two tiny, elegant porcelain cups on a silver tray. She set the tray down on the conference table without a word and left.

Mr. Z had set up the easel across from two folding chairs. At the top of the display board, he wrote in fluorescent green marker, the words FEAR and DESIRE. "Have a seat, gentlemen," he said. Mr. Z addressed the trainees as a general addresses his troops. "Over the next few days, you will hear things that may surprise you, or excite you, or shake your faith in human nature. After this week, you will walk out of here changed men. Your friends and family may not recognize you. 'What happened to Steve?' they'll say. 'He seems so focused, so alive.' 'Does Simon have a twin brother?' they'll say. 'Simon was never that sure of himself. And wasn't that a new car he was driving?' Yes, gentlemen, after this week, you may not even know yourselves anymore. This is the point of no return. So if you're going to back out, now is the time. But if you choose to stay, be prepared to have more confidence, more personal power, and yes, gentlemen, more goddamned money than you ever had before!"

"Amen!" exclaimed Steve. "I'm ready!"

Mr. Z seemed to swell with satisfaction. "But two things before we start." He pointed to the east wall. Over the doorway hung two platinum-plated golf putters, crossed like sabers in a Prussian officers' club. "First, gentlemen, let me draw your attention to the crossed putters. This is a symbol of our loyalty to Going Platinum and to our fellow salesmen in the company. You will notice a small plaque beneath the clubs that reads, 'Give us your poor, tired salesmen. Give us your hungry, greedy, envious, ambitious, fast-talking, desperate salesmen, yearning to make more. In this room there are no rejections.' What this means, gentlemen, is that you are now standing on sacred ground. No matter what lies you may need to use with customers, when you are in this room, you will tell no lies. No matter what differences you may have with each other or with me or with Going Platinum, when you are in The Room, you will have sanctuary. Think of this as your church where you can come to meditate on your spiritual development, on your financial goals, on your strategies for squeezing the most out of your next mooch. There is no better place than this room for you to practice your sales pitch because a good pitch in The Room means a good pitch in the field. We once had a salesman who used to come here every Friday night. He would practice his lines for picking up women and then he'd go hit the bars. He claimed it worked every time. Don't ask me how. It's just one of those mystical things about this place."

Simon rubbed the crystal pendant through his new starched shirt and marveled at his good fortune in getting a job with such a company. Steve surreptitiously checked his watch.

Mr. Z picked up the silver tray. "Now, I want to propose a toast." He handed each of them a cup.

Simon stared at the thick black fluid. "Is this some kind of coffee?"

Mr. Z looked at Simon with disdain. " 'Is this some kind

of coffee?' " he said mockingly. "Yes, it is a very special kind of coffee, to help you remember this momentous day. And to keep you positive and alert during your transition into the world of success."

"It smells delicious!" observed Steve.

"I don't drink stimulants," said Simon.

"And you don't eat lobster?" challenged Mr. Z.

"No," said Simon.

"And you don't drive brand new sports cars?"

"No."

"And you don't wear Armani suits?"

"No."

"And you don't go out with supermodels?"

"No."

"Well, don't you think it's time to start living a little, son?"

Steve snickered. Simon shrugged. "I just don't drink coffee. It interferes with my alpha waves."

Mr. Z looked thoughtful. "Oh, I see," he said. "Drink it!"

Simon took a tiny sip and shuddered. It was bitter as bile. But Mr. Z stood menacingly over him. Simon swallowed the rest of the special coffee in one gulp. His stomach nearly rejected it. He felt an instant jolt and the top of his spinal cord seemed to twist up in the back of his neck. His taste buds, accustomed to brown rice and whole wheat bread, went into sensory overload, and he wasn't sure if the taste was acrid or sweet or spicy. But he thought he detected a hint of nutmeg and vodka.

Simon felt suddenly alert, as if he'd been slapped in the face. His mind began racing randomly, indiscriminately, over the names of movies and fragments of Hindu scripture he'd read in college. He saw, in his mind, an exploded diagram of the garbage disposer he installed yesterday in apartment 4. He began to wonder if this was what it was like to be insane when that thought was swept from his mind and he realized he was staring into space with his mouth open.

"Good, isn't it?" prompted Steve with a knowing grin.

Mr. Z stepped back up to the easel and when he began to speak, Simon was grateful to have something to focus on.

"I'm sure you have noticed by now, the words I wrote on the board. FEAR and DESIRE. Before I get into the importance of these words to you as salesmen, I would like to hear what they mean to you." Mr. Z was becoming very animated and had started pacing. He walked in front of Steve's chair. "Fear and desire: what are they to you?" he demanded.

Steve's handsome, chiseled face showed no sign of intimidation. He said, "To me, fear and desire, well, they sum up who we are. They are what makes the world go round."

Mr. Z's black iris-less eyes shone, and it seemed to Simon that Mr. Z and Steve shared a moment of recognition. He turned his attention to Simon. "And you. What do the words fear and desire mean to you?"

For an instant, Simon imagined he was floating above the conference room, looking down on the scene, observing himself. It took a few seconds for him to get back into his body and answer. "I don't know. I suppose fear and desire are what keep humans from being gods. They are guardians at the gate of enlightenment. They are the root of confusion and evil."

Steve rolled his eyes and slumped in his chair. Mr. Z stepped up to the easel and rapped on the board. "Fear and desire are our best friends! They are the keys to understanding life as we know it. They are our most efficient tools for motivating ourselves and manipulating others. Without fear and desire, nothing would ever get sold. If nothing got sold, there would be no reason to produce anything. If nothing was produced, we would wander around like zombies until we died of starvation. Fear and desire are instincts that keep us sharp and alive. Even when we are not conscious of them, they protect and guide us."

Mr. Z's voice softened. "But we are not helpless little rabbits, driven from hole to hole by fear and desire. With the strength of our will, we can control our instincts and, more importantly, control these instincts in others. Regardless of how successful you are as a salesman, I'm sure you wouldn't want to live your life as a victim. WOULD YOU?" Mr. Z bellowed, kicking Steve's chair out from under him, sending it tumbling halfway across the room.

Steve landed on his feet in a fighting stance, focused and calm, waiting for Mr. Z's next move. Simon, now fully wired from the special coffee, had fallen out of his chair and was shivering with fright.

"Tai Kwan Do?" Mr. Z asked Steve.

"I take my brown belt test in two weeks."

The two slowly turned and regarded Simon with a combination of pity and amusement.

Mr. Z stood over him, offering a hand up. "Tell me the truth, Simon. Aren't you tired of being a victim?"

Simon fought to control his shaking. He tried a little yogic breathing, but his alpha waves were shot. He wanted to spring to his feet and say what a cheap trick Mr. Z had pulled and what a load of glib, manipulative, knee-jerk salesmanship he was dishing out and who did he think he was fooling, extolling the virtues of greed and dominance. But Simon couldn't get up off the floor. He felt he was looking up at his boss through the wrong end of a telescope.

He saw himself raise his hand up, pathetically short of Mr. Z's powerful hand. "Aren't you tired of being a victim?" The words still rang in Simon's head.

"Yes, I am tired of it," Simon heard himself say. "I'm tired of being a victim."

And with that, Mr. Z's hand extended lower and lower until it touched his own damp, trembling hand and lifted him up effortlessly, as if he weighed no more than a child, and sat him down in his chair. For a moment, Simon had the impression he had done something terrible. But this feeling quickly passed and he felt oddly excited.

"How do we start?" he asked.

Chapter 6

Mr. Z seemed gratified that his powers of enlightenment and persuasion had taken hold so quickly with such an apparently hopeless student as Simon. And, like a good shepherd, Mr. Z gloried more in Simon, the stray he saved from the wilderness, than in Steve, whose insights and instincts so closely matched his own.

For the next several days, Mr. Z pounded the virtues of fear and desire into their heads. He praised the vitality of greed, which can transform otherwise lifeless individuals into productive salespeople. Saying this, he looked significantly at Simon. But most of all, Mr. Z cautioned the trainees against the dangers of complacency. "Contentment is for cows!" he bellowed. "Do you want to spend the rest of your life giving milk?" Neither did.

Nevertheless, Mr. Z accused both of them of having weak goals. "Look at you," he sneered. "You are so comfortable in your failure. If you had any pride, you'd be ashamed of yourselves."

Mr. Z went on to explain that it is not until an ordinary mortal summons the courage to step out of his comfort zone that he can hope to become a salesman. "Comfort and happiness are a salesman's worst enemies," he cautioned. "Even if he is a millionaire, a salesman should feel cold and hungry. There must always be a gnawing in his belly for something more. I left Bulgaria because I wanted more from life than raising sheep and goats. I was like those guys in the movie *The Godfather* who believed America was the land of opportunity. Like the Al Pacino character, I worked and studied. But I was never happy. I wanted more."

Mr. Z pulled a thick wad of currency held together with a heavy silver money clip from his pants pocket and flipped through it like a cheap paperback. "Does this look like it belongs to a prosperous man?" he asked academically. Steve was clearly impressed and said that it certainly did. Simon, a speed-reader since the age of ten, counted one fifty-dollar bill, wrapped over twenty-three ones.

"Absolutely!" said Simon, equally impressed. "Seventy-three bucks is more than I make in a week."

Mr. Z glared at Simon and jammed the money back in his pocket. "The point is, I am never satisfied with the money I make, or the car I drive, or the clothes I wear. No matter what nice things I have, I always want something better."

"That's so sad," Simon sympathized.

"No, it's not sad at all, you mutton head!" shouted Mr. Z. "It's not sad because I know all I have to do is work harder and I can afford nicer things."

Simon frowned. "And if you didn't have that empty feeling, wouldn't you be happy with whatever you had?"

Mr. Z threw up his hands. "Steve. Are you happy with what you have?"

"Hell, no!" said Steve.

"Why not?" Mr. Z demanded.

"I've got a five-year-old car that needs a new transmission. I can't afford to go skiing every year in Colorado. The woman I've been dating wants to eat in classy restaurants. When I applied for a loan, the banker treated me like scum. Aside from that, I'm young, strong, and good-looking. I don't have any problems that money can't solve."

Mr. Z turned back to Simon. "And what could having more money do for you?"

Simon bowed his head in thought and said, "Maybe it would help put me in tune with the rest of the world."

"That would take a lot of money," Steve muttered.

Over the next two weeks, Mr. Z had Simon and Steve read Napoleon Hill's book, *Think and Grow Rich* over and over until they could practically recite it by heart. He taught them to think of money as elusive quarry that must be hunted with subtlety and persistence. He insisted they write down their goals, including the precise amount of money they intended to earn over the following month, quarter, and year. And twice every day during training and once right before they went to bed, he had them read their goals out loud.

When he was sure his trainees were thinking along the proper lines, Mr. Z began teaching them the art of selling platinum-plated golf putters. He taught them to handle their sample putter as if it were a rare art object and he taught them to wait until the customer asked the price before they tried to close the deal. In simulated sales presentations, Mr. Z showed them the value of leading the customer into questions to which he must answer, "yes," getting him into the habit of answering in the affirmative. And when it was time for the customer to buy, Mr. Z showed them the unassailable power of silence.

Simon was an attentive and enthusiastic student. But Steve had the talent. Simon could quote *Think and Grow Rich* like a Baptist quotes the Bible. But Steve absorbed the principles of what Napoleon Hill called "money consciousness" as if by direct revelation. To his credit, Mr. Z tried not to show favoritism. In fact, he made a considerable show of not showing favoritism. But it was no use. He and

Steve were like father and son. Although they had met only the day after Simon was hired, Mr. Z and Steve seemed to share a rich history of greed and envy, of minor indignities and the nagging belief that anybody with a dollar is hopelessly in their debt.

Mr. Z encouraged rivalry between the trainees to sharpen their competitive edge. He had them bet five dollars on who would be the first to get through their sales pitch without a mistake and even had them bet on who could sink a ten-foot putt into a plastic cup on the salesroom floor with a platinum putter.

Steve enjoyed the competition deliciously and doubled his efforts to beat Simon at every opportunity. Simon didn't mind the rivalry. But he was a little troubled when Mr. Z hinted there might be only one permanent position available and may the best man win.

Mr. Z stopped in the middle of a role-playing situation in which he was supposed to be the customer.

"What are you thinking of when you are trying to sell me a platinum golf club?" he asked Simon.

Simon looked down at his new, stiff wing tip shoes. "I'm, uh, thinking about how much you'd like one and how having your company logo on such a nice putter might be good for your business."

"Wrong!" exclaimed Mr. Z. "You should be thinking, 'This mooch has got my money. And I'm not leaving until he coughs it up!'"

"But, Mr. Z, how can you have respect for somebody if all you want him for is his money?"

Mr. Z pointed his finger at Simon like a gun. "Good question!" he said. "The answer is you don't need to respect him. You just need to get his money. The only reason you don't knock him over the head and take it is that selling him something pays better."

Steve snickered.

Mr. Z turned toward Steve. "What are you thinking about as you pitch a customer?"

Steve got a sly look in his steel gray eyes. "I think about all the things I want money for. I think about which of those things this customer is going to pay for. When I pitch him and he says no, I pretend he's just playing with me like a child plays with his parents when it's time to go to bed, delaying the inevitable. So I play along, knowing it's going to come out the way I want it to in the end."

Mr. Z tried to hide his admiration of Steve's precociousness. "You need money, Simon. Don't tell me you don't. Never, since I came to America, have I seen anybody who looks hungrier than you. If you pay attention, I can show you how to take what you want, not just wait for it to fall from the sky into your lap." Mr. Z shook his head. "I have to say, sometimes, training you to be a salesman has been like training a mushroom to be a wolf."

Steve looked over at Simon and sneered. "I hate to break this to you, old buddy. But tomorrow, when we start pitching real customers, I'm going to kick your ass." Mr. Z chuckled. "In fact, I bet you a hundred bucks I put more business on the board than you do."

Simon gulped. "A hundred dollars? Are you serious?"

"Simon's right," Mr. Z interjected. "That's sheep dip. Why not be a man and make it five hundred?"

"Okay, then," said Steve. "Five hundred it is!"

Mr. Z wrote the bet on the board. "Now let me sweeten the pot. Whichever of you brings in the most in sales tomorrow will get a one-hundred-dollar bonus from me." He paused for emphasis. "And a permanent position at Going Platinum."

"All right!" Steve cheered. "That job is mine!"

Mr. Z continued, "The one who comes in second will have my best wishes and a complimentary pass for nine holes at the country club."

Steve looked pityingly at Simon. "You don't even play golf, do you?"

Mr. Z drew himself up to his full height and clapped his heavy palms together. "You can pick up your leads tomorrow morning. Now, what do you boys have to say for yourselves?"

Spontaneously, Steve jumped to his feet, followed by Simon. "I WILL NOT BE DENIED!" they chanted their official cheer.

"I can't hear you!" mocked Mr. Z.

"I WILL NOT BE DENIED!" the trainees shouted, more or less in unison.

"Once more!" commanded Mr. Z.

"I WILL NOT BE DENIED!"

Mr. Z dismissed them and disappeared down the hall. Simon was two steps from the side door when he realized he'd forgotten his pencil back in The Room. When he turned to go back, Simon saw Steve with a set of lock picks, furiously working on the door to Pater's office. Simon's attention was drawn from Steve to Josev's engraving room. It was located one door up from bookkeeping, nearer to the side door where Simon was standing. A shadow moved across the glass on the door and this time, Simon could clearly make out the back of Pater's balding head. The bookkeeper silently watched Steve work the lock until there was a click. Steve slipped inside and Pater's head disappeared from the glass. Simon slid out the side door, closing it quietly behind him.

By the end of the training period, Simon was down fifty

dollars from the compulsory wagers. During this period of intensive training, he was obliged to perform his apartment maintenance duties in the evenings and some of the tenants were starting to grumble. Every day, Mr. Z talked about wealth and power, and every night, Simon went home to his humble one-bedroom apartment and his brown rice and bean curd soup. He would have been tempted to abandon this chance at undreamed-of wealth if it hadn't been for Amy. And, of course, Edgar Cayce.

Cayce was Simon's Siamese cat, who, like his namesake, the so-called "Sleeping Prophet," seemed to gather wisdom merely by sleeping next to books. Actually, Cayce the cat wasn't particular where he slept, but, because books covered most of the horizontal surfaces in Simon's apartment that were not already covered with dirty dishes or pipe wrenches, books were generally the most comfortable things on which to nap.

Simon hauled himself through his apartment door and closed it behind him by leaning heavily against it. He loosened his white gangster tie.

"I am a millionaire in the making," he recited. "I am the master of my fate." Simon careened towards his recliner and fell into it, knocking *Ideas and Integrities* by Buckminster Fuller off the armrest. "I am a force to be reckoned with." He closed his eyes.

On the end table next to the recliner, Cayce had been dozing on a tattered copy of Joseph Fletcher's *Situation Ethics*, until the book by the inventor of the geodesic dome hit the floor with a slap. Cayce stood up, stretched luxuriously, and leapt neatly into Simon's lap.

The cat nosed him under the chin and chewed vigorously on a tuft of hair sticking out from behind Simon's left ear. Simon stroked his back. "Cayce, you're good in social situations. Do you think I ought to call Amy and make some excuse? Or should I meet her and her parents for dinner tonight?"

"Berk!" said Cayce, as he hopped onto the floor and stood over his empty dish.

Simon smiled. "I might have known you'd go for the food."

Chapter 7

Ed Castor waved to his daughter and her date as they approached the table. Still smiling, he leaned over to his wife, Sabrina. "He looks like Bugsy Malone."

"I think he's very handsome," she said. "He's wearing his company's official outfit or something. Now don't cross-examine the poor boy."

Amy's father stood up, towering over Simon by a good six inches. He took Simon's hand and looked penetratingly into his eyes. "Ed Castor," he stated, as if it were a particularly envious accomplishment.

"I'm pleased to meet you," said Simon. "Amy's told me so much—"

"So you're in sales?" Ed interrupted.

Simon chuckled. "Well, the job market in comparative mythology is pretty weak right now, so—"

"There's money in sales, if you get in with the right firm. What's the name of your company?"

Simon sat next to Amy. "It's called Going Platinum."

Ed snorted. "The record business has always been flaky."

"It's not a record company, Daddy," Amy chided. "They do specialty advertising. Now, let's order. I'm starving."

"What kind of specialty advertising?" Ed inquired innocently.

Amy gave Simon an apologetic look. Simon cleared his

43

throat. "We sell platinum-plated golf clubs, engraved with the customer's company name."

"Golf clubs?" said Ed, genuinely surprised.

"Actually, golf putters mostly," said Simon. "I don't know anything about golf, but our putters are very nice looking and I'm sure customers like them—"

"And people really buy golf putters with their name on them? Amazing!"

Mrs. Castor picked up the menu. "I hear the veal is good here."

"What kind of company would sell personalized platinum-plated golf putters?" Ed asked Sabrina.

"Well, how should I know?" his wife whispered.

"Would you like to hear about the assault and battery case I defended today, Daddy?" Amy offered.

Ed suddenly rocked back in his chair. There was a queer smile on his face. "Oh, no," he said, shaking a well-manicured finger at Simon. "Going Platinum. Isn't that those Russian gangsters on late night TV?"

"Bulgarian," Simon corrected.

"I always thought that was some kind of joke." Ed turned to his wife. "Honey, you remember that big thug in the commercial with the white carnation and Slavic accent? What does he say? 'We're going platinum. Let us "putt" you into business.' " He laughed out loud.

"Daddy!" Amy scolded.

"They're not really gangsters," Simon explained to Amy's mother.

"Oh dear!" said Mrs. Castor, with a troubled expression. "I hope they aren't stealing."

Ed and his daughter exchanged glances.

"There's no stealing," Amy quickly assured her.

"No. No stealing," Ed said soberly.

Amy patted her mother's hand. Sabrina brightened and opened her menu. "I think I'll have the veal," she said.

An unctuous looking waiter sidled up to Amy's father as the one most likely to spring for the check. "My name is Thomas. I'll be your waiter. Tonight's special is brochettes of kidney and barbecued lamb chops with a delightful almond fruit flan—"

"I'll have whatever you've got with the most cholesterol," Ed broke in. "And another double Manhattan."

"That would be the prime rib with Caesar salad," said Thomas, not batting an eye.

Ed waved him away. "Yeah, whatever."

Amy ordered the special and Simon, finding nothing on the menu he could eat, was explaining to Thomas how to prepare the eggplant for Brinjal Sambal. Ed downed his Manhattan and signaled for another. He said to Simon, "That Indian stuff—that's not real food. If you were left out in the wilderness with nothing but a Bowie knife, you'd starve to death, looking for Brinjal Sambal."

Simon smiled weakly. "Red meat inhibits my alpha waves."

"I wouldn't doubt it," said Ed. "I've devoted a lot of time and energy to inhibiting my own alpha waves so that I'm the one eating red meat and not the one on the plate."

"Daddy's one of the toughest tort lawyers in the city," Amy said proudly.

"How about a nice green salad?" suggested Thomas.

"Fine," said Simon. "But no meat, no onions, or garlic. And no mushrooms."

"That would be the, uh, bowl of lettuce," Thomas muttered. "And what will the gentleman be having on his salad?"

"Have you got any fresh lime juice?"

Thomas inclined deferentially toward Simon. "How very tangy!" he said and shuffled off toward the kitchen.

Ed was already halfway through his third Manhattan. "I suppose this putter job is straight commission."

Simon looked up from his examination of a bread stick. "I don't know. The subject never came up."

Ed could not hide his disgust. "Did your new boss happen to mention medical benefits?"

"No," said Simon.

"Vacation pay?"

"No."

"Profit sharing?"

"Nope."

"Retirement?"

"No."

"Your own parking place, for Christ's sake?"

"Please Ed! People are staring," Sabrina whispered.

"Well, there was one thing," said Simon. "I do get a country club membership."

Ed's jaw dropped. "Country club? Just like that? I'd been a partner for two years before they gave me a country club membership." He suddenly slapped the table, sending the sesame seed bread sticks bouncing off the plate like a broken logjam. "You sly dog!" Ed pointed a prosecutorial finger at Simon. "You had me going for a while. 'The subject never came up'—my tuchas!"

"Ed!" said Sabrina, mortified.

"What are they really giving you?" Ed continued. "Stock options? A percentage of the gross?"

"I really can't give an exact figure," Simon said modestly. "Let's just say it's more than I made in my last position."

Ed reached across the table and gave Simon a good-natured swat. "I'll bet it is. You rascal!"

46

"Of course, there's a chance I might not get the job," Simon confessed.

"What do you mean?" This time Amy sounded like the interrogator.

Simon shrugged. "Well, I found out today that there will only be one position available and there are two candidates."

"Give us your assessment of your competition," said Ed.

"Steve has more experience than I do and he certainly looks the part. He has an uncanny knack for saying exactly the right thing at the right time. He's bright, intuitive, eager, and hard working."

"I guess we'll just have to have him killed!" Ed chortled and gulped the rest of his third Manhattan.

Amy giggled and pulled out her cell phone. "I'll make the call." Ed reached over and they exchanged a "high five."

Sabrina looked embarrassed. "You two! You're just alike." The conspirators looked very pleased with themselves.

"There is one thing that doesn't seem right about Steve," Simon continued soberly. "Today, as I was leaving the building, I saw him using lock picks to break into the bookkeeper's office."

Ed and Amy looked stunned.

"He was stealing," Mrs. Castor said simply. "He must be punished."

Chapter 8

It was one of those suspiciously perfect Southern California days. The Coppertone sun was burning off a light fog, making the immaculate landscape sparkle like a cinematic special effect. The Going Platinum country club basked in the warm glow of the sun's east lighting. A teasing breeze provoked slight flutters from the flags on the putting greens, casting long westward shadows and assuring Californians that they have more playtime hours than anybody else. Occasionally, automatic sprinklers popped up to nourish the Easter basket-green turf, stitched to the mummified desert landscape like plastic surgery.

Mr. Z centered himself over the ball and wiggled the driver in his murderous grip. Without looking up, he addressed Simon and Steve. "By this time tomorrow, we will know if either of you has any talent for this business. And we will know which of you has earned a permanent place with Going Platinum." He drew back his club and swung brutally at the small white ball. There was a harsh hiss as the club split the air. The ball was knocked crisply off the tee and sliced badly to the right, where it struck a palm tree and landed dead with a dull thunk. Steve looked slightly amused. "You'd never know it today," Mr. Z said, stabbing the turf with another tee and balancing another ball on it, "but only five years ago, this beautiful golf course you see before you—which was bought by our company very economically—was nothing but a landfill. That's right, just a dump, full of potato peelings and coffee grounds and dirty diapers. There's enough scrap metal under our feet to build a battleship. If these rich stiffs who shell out fifty bucks a round only knew, eh?" Mr. Z chortled and took a swipe at the ball, the topspin sending it skipping across the fairway into some weeds.

"And yet," Steve added philosophically, "there don't seem to be that many people using this course. The upkeep must be expensive—the taxes, the lawn service, the insurance, the equipment maintenance. How do you keep the doors open?"

Mr. Z regarded Steve malevolently. "There's a lot you don't know about the golf business," he said.

Steve was unfazed. "I guess there's a lot I don't know about the platinum-plated golf putter business, either. For example, you say we'll be selling putters for ninety-five dollars and get a fifty-dollar commission on each piece. The clubs and the plating have to cost something. Where's the profit for the company? You can't make up for it in volume because there has to be a limited market for this stuff."

Mr. Z kept his eye on the ball. "What do you think, Simon?" he asked.

Simon stared at the small white ball, balanced on its wooden spike, stuck into a veneer of well-tended sod, covering a mountain of rotting, rusting rubbish. He sighed. "This whole business is a miracle to me. And it doesn't do any good to analyze miracles. I have to accept its contradictions along with its bounty."

As Mr. Z prepared to take aim at the ball, Simon noticed a kind of blister the size of a cereal bowl under the sod about three feet from where his boss was standing. As he watched, the blister doubled in size. Simon glanced at Steve for confirmation that this wasn't another of his visions, but

Steve had his eye on the ball. At first, Simon thought it could be a gopher, but the grass seemed more puffed up than pushed up.

"You should think more like Simon," Mr. Z said to Steve, still watching the ball. "His mind will be on selling, while your mind is wandering unprofitably in areas that don't concern you."

Steve snorted. "If I don't outsell that space case two-to-one, I'll eat a platinum putter. And besides, there's no way I'd lose a five-hundred-dollar bet. The job is in the bag!"

Simon worried that he should say something about the pulsating sod. It might be dangerous. If it was an animal, it could be rabid. The turf blister was now about three feet in diameter and growing. He took a step back.

Mr. Z drew back on his club. "I wouldn't count my money yet if I were you." As he started his swing, a low, burbling, farting sound erupted from the bubble, quickly followed by a rancid smell that took Simon's breath away. Mr. Z hacked off a two-pound divot that flew several yards farther than the ball.

"What died?" exclaimed Steve, flailing his arms and staggering back.

"Curse this place!" Mr. Z growled and stomped the expended bubble flat. "It's methane gas rising from the decaying garbage. It was worse the first year we sodded over it. Somebody lit a cigarette and blew up the caddy shack. It was very dangerous. Now, it is merely an inconvenience."

"Now it is merely a giant elephant fart!" said Steve. "I guess this answers my question why more golfers don't play here."

Chapter 9

When Simon arrived at ABC Enterprises, the parking lot was empty and the blinds were drawn. Under the sign were two doors, both painted brown and made nearly invisible by the brown wall. Both doors were locked. Simon straightened his white tie and brushed the bean sprouts from his power breakfast off his wide lapels. He set his fedora at a angle, hoisted the custom-made violin case that held his platinum putters, and knocked on the door to the left.

There was a long silence. The morning fog was beginning to lift off the Long Beach coastline, and all along Ocean Boulevard loading docks gradually came into focus. In the alley, a homeless man of an indeterminate age laboriously pulled a homemade wagon full of crushed aluminum cans. One of the front wheels, taken from a shopping cart, wobbled and squeaked, sending the wagon skittering to one side and then the other. The man muttered and cursed a continuous stream, as if carrying on both sides of a heated argument. As he passed by ABC Enterprises, the man looked up briefly at Simon and gave him a knowing glance.

The door on the right suddenly opened a crack and was jerked to a stop by a heavy steel chain.

"Who are you?" demanded a gravelly Brooklyn voice from the darkness.

"Going Platinum," said Simon cheerfully.

The voice grunted and the chain rattled away out of view. The heavy metal door swung open, ponderously as a vault door, until it struck a packing crate. Now visible in the dim light, was a short man, less than five feet tall, but powerfully built. He had the face of a bulldog and chewed on the stub of an unlit cigar. He savagely kicked the crate out of the way.

"So much shit around here, it's not safe to walk!" He glared up at Simon. "A guy could get his neck broke."

Simon rolled the padded shoulders of his zoot suit the way he'd seen thugs do in 1940s gangster movies. "And a guy could lose a lot of ch'i in this place, too."

The bulldog man gaped at him. "What the hell did you just say to me? Did you say 'cheese'? A guy could lose a lot of cheese?"

Simon clapped the man on the shoulder. "Oh, you know—ch'i—the universal energy force. It's having a heck of a time getting into your building. Brown doors? Not a good color. When the door is partly blocked, that good energy can't get in. And look here." Simon strode to the end of the entrance hall that came to a T directly in front of the door. He tapped the wall. "Think of the energy as water. Even if it trickles through the door, it would hit this wall before it could get into where the people are."

Simon now had the man's full attention, although not yet his full understanding. "And why would I want my people to get wet?"

"Let me ask you this," Simon said. "After being cooped up in this building all day, do you ever feel crabby?" The bulldog man's eyes narrowed, as if determining whether or not he was being mocked. He emitted a kind of low growl. "Do you feel like you're in a fog until you step outside? Then does your head clear and you suddenly feel ten years younger?"

"The ventilation isn't too good in here." He gave into a

gurgling cough. "That's why I stopped smoking these." He plucked the wet, masticated tobacco plug from his mouth and held it up for Simon's inspection. A thin trickle of brown juice ran from the corner of his brutish mouth.

Simon swallowed and smiled. "That was probably a wise decision," he said.

The man shrugged. "So what's in the violin case, Bugsy?"

"I'm Simon." Simon chuckled and extended his hand. "Mr. Troller, we were having such a nice chat, I almost forgot why I came. Sometimes, I don't know where my head is at."

"Must be the ch'i." Troller almost grinned and Simon pointed a teasing finger at him, acknowledging his cleverness.

Troller led Simon through a maze of storerooms and stacked boxes until they arrived at a cramped little office, piled high with dented and rusting file cabinets. A gray metal government-surplus desk dominated the clearing in the center of the room. There was only one chair. Troller shoved aside some papers and clipboards and sat on the desk. He motioned for Simon to sit in the old swivel chair. "I believe you have something for me?" he asked, rubbing his stubby hands together.

"I certainly do!" said Simon. "I have an exciting new way for you to promote your business. Mr. Troller, did you know that more than half of the businesses in this country fail because of insufficient or inappropriate advertising?" Troller stared. Simon cleared his throat. "And Mr. Troller, I'm sure you'll agree that the type of upscale clientele your company serves probably spends a fair amount of time on the golf course. Am I right?" Troller gripped the edge of the desk until his knuckles turned white. "Would it surprise you, Mr. Troller, if I told you that as much as ten percent of all business conducted in the United States is concluded on the golf course?" Troller chewed up his cigar stub and swallowed it painfully. "Now, Mr. Troller, I'm going to ask you one more question and I want you to consider it carefully."

"Open the damned case!" Troller practically shouted.

"Mr. Troller, it's customers like you that make my job so easy. When my boss told me that our product could almost sell itself, I admit I didn't believe him. But now I see he was right. But before I show you the key to your new prosperity, I want you to show me something."

A sly smile of recognition spread over Troller's face. Perched on the edge of the desk, he looked like a grinning gargoyle. "Yeah, I get you," he said, hopping down. Troller pulled a thick envelope from his back pocket and dropped it heavily in Simon's lap. "It's all there," he said, still grinning. "Trust me."

"Mr. Troller, I trust you implicitly. And your faith in our product overwhelms me. Of course, I wouldn't expect you to pay me before you'd even seen the product. No, what I meant was, I wanted you to show me your product so that we can serve you better."

"You think I'm going to show you my operation?" Troller was incredulous.

Simon shrugged. "Well, Mr. Troller, you know I can't do my job until I know how you do your job."

"And if I don't, are you saying you'd just walk away from this deal?"

"You're testing me, Mr. Troller. And I appreciate that. But you can rest assured that with Going Platinum, customer service is our first priority." Simon chuckled. "If you know my boss, you know he'd kill me if I didn't give you the full treatment." Troller steadied himself against the wall. "So, yes, Mr. Troller, I'm prepared to walk out of here right now unless I can give you exactly what's coming to you."

Troller hesitated, as if sizing up the man relaxing in his chair. "You got some balls. I'll give you that." Simon crossed his legs as Troller extracted a cheap ceramic ginger jar from one of the file cabinets and handed it to him.

"This is very nice," said Simon.

"Yeah! Like it matters." Troller grunted.

Simon sniffed. "What's that smell?" He removed the lid of the ginger jar and sniffed again. "Coffee?"

Troller snorted. "It drives those dogs at the airport crazy. Now for the love of Christ, will you give me the stuff already?"

"Although I sympathize with the airport dogs, I can see you have a keen eye for marketing." Simon stood up and placed the violin case on the desk. He snapped open the cover and pulled out one of the putters. Troller flinched. Simon held out the gleaming golf club. "Now, Mr. Troller, don't you think your customers would love this?"

Troller snatched the club, held it up to his ear and shook it. "I can tell you right now, kid, my customers can't live without this." He looked at the putter as if he hadn't really seen it before. "What's this made out of?"

"Why, platinum, of course," said Simon.

"Platinum!" Troller was charmed with the idea. "That's class!"

Simon beamed. "Nothing but the best." While Troller was still dazzled, Simon scooped the putter out of his hands. "Do you want this engraved with ABC Enterprises or with your own name and address?"

"Yeah, right," Troller scoffed and reached for the club.

But Simon was already fitting it back into the case. "No, I mean, just leave it blank. I'll have it inscribed myself."

"No charge," Simon chirped, filling out the order blank. "Will it be just the one, or can I make you a deal on a half dozen?"

"Now wait just a minute! Those two are mine!"

"I love this job!" Simon chuckled. "Your enthusiasm warms my heart. But I couldn't possibly sell my samples."

Troller stood in front of the door. "You're not leaving here until I get those putters."

"Mr. Troller, your response is more than I could have hoped for. Wait until I tell Mr. Z."

Troller's bulldog face contorted with rage. "This is between you and me." He slipped his hand into his coat pocket.

Simon finished filling out the sales receipt and laid it on the desk. "Well, it would mean I'd have to drive all the way back to the office."

Troller drew out his hand slowly. It contained a wad of currency. "What'll it take, kid?"

"The deluxe platinum putters with the calfskin grip are ninety-five dollars each. Without the engraving, I guess I could let them go for one-hundred and eighty dollars for the pair," Simon said reluctantly.

Troller looked relieved and stuffed a handful of money in Simon's jacket. "Here's two hundred bucks. Keep the change, kid. You're a hell of a salesman." Simon handed over the glittering putters and Troller clutched them greedily in both hands.

"And don't forget that." Troller nodded to the envelope. "It's just a little something from me to Yakov."

As they headed for the door, Simon stopped. "You know, Mr. Troller, I feel kind of bad. I really shouldn't go until you hear about all the benefits of our product."

"Yes, you should." Troller had his hand on the middle of Simon's back, propelling him toward the door.

"Just remember what I said about the wall."

"The minute you leave, I'm going to take a sledge hammer and knock it down," said Troller.

"I think you'll feel better when you do," said Simon.

Troller nodded. "I know I will."

Chapter 10

It was only four o'clock and Simon had already sold three sets of putters and was coming back to the office for a fourth set. He danced through the front door of Going Platinum, doing his best imitation of Gene Kelly.

"I'm si—i—i—i—nging in the rain!" Simon warbled. The receptionist tried her best to shush him but that only focused Simon's attention on her. "Zelda!" he sang. "Isn't this a beautiful day?" He capered to one side and made a picture frame around her stern face with his hands. "And don't you look lovely today!"

Zelda successfully fought off a smile. "Are you out of your mind? No, don't bother to answer that. Mr. Z and the others are having a conference and they don't wish to be disturbed."

"I'll be as quiet as a mouse," Simon whispered, doing an exaggerated (and loud) pantomime of somebody tiptoeing. "I'm sure they wouldn't want to be disturbed by hearing about my five hundred seventy dollars IN SALES!" Simon practically shouted down the hall.

Zelda raked her red artificial fingernails across her computer mouse pad. "Simon, I'm sure if you can wait patiently for ten minutes until the end of the meeting, you will be able to speak to whomever you want, as loudly as you want. There are magazines on the table. You could read for ten minutes. Or you could astrally project yourself someplace far away. If you can do it quietly."

"Thanks for the suggestion, Zelda. But I gave up astral projection because I was afraid sometime I wouldn't be able to get back into my body. I'd be a zombie the rest of my life."

"Zombies are basically quiet, aren't they?" Zelda asked wistfully.

Ignoring Zelda's protestations, Simon tap-danced down the hall to the conference room. He adjusted his wide white tie and was about to knock on the door, when he heard Mr. Z talking with somebody whose voice he failed to recognize.

"What do you think you're doing, you goat's pizzle?" said Mr. Z. "Don't mix up the regular putters with Simon's. What's the matter with you? Do you want someone to get killed?"

"I don't know why you bothered to spend so much time training that lunatic to be a salesman," the other voice grumbled.

Mr. Z snorted. "You lived in Bulgaria forty years and you never heard of brainwashing? Besides, I had to find out which of those two was the most gullible." The other emitted a laugh that sounded like a groan.

Simon took a step back and was about to leave when the door opened and Mr. Z's cousin Josev, the engraver, stepped out. Josev was a slight, intense middle-aged man with thick, wire-framed glasses that magnified his iris-less black eyes. "What do you want?" he demanded in a heavy Slavic accent, glaring up at Simon.

"I was here to see Mr. Z, I'm, uh, Simon," Simon stammered.

"Then why don't you knock instead of standing at the door like an idiot?" Josev said and stalked off without waiting for a reply.

Mr. Z glanced up through the open doorway at the

sound of the conversation. He seemed momentarily startled, but quickly recovered.

"Simon, my star salesman!" he called. "Come in, come
in. I suppose you've come for more putters, you animal!"
He picked up a pair of gleaming golf putters from the stack
of clubs on the left. "The next thing I know, you'll be eating
red meat and chasing strippers." Mr. Z laughed a little too
loudly.

Simon's eyes drifted involuntarily to the stack of putters
on the right. "Maybe I'd better take another set just in case
I get lucky." He reached out his hand, but as he did, Mr. Z
grabbed him by the elbow.

"You don't want one of those." There was a sudden
menacing look in Mr. Z's eyes.

"Why not?"

"Well," said Mr. Z, softening, "because those are for
Steve."

"Steve has his own clubs?" Simon asked.

"Sure. And you have your clubs. These clubs are to be
engraved for Steve's customers, so I'm keeping them separate.
Did I tell you, Steve sold four putters today? You better
watch out, he could catch you."

"So these are being engraved," Simon said. "Two piles."

"Two piles," confirmed Mr. Z.

Simon chuckled. "Well, I wouldn't want a putter from
Steve's pile, would I?"

Mr. Z chuckled back. "Hell no. It might be bad luck."
He laughed again. "Here, take these," he said, twisting the
head of one of the putters on tighter.

"Luck is a strange thing." The voice came from the
doorway.

"Steve! How's it going?" said Simon awkwardly.

Steve looked haggard and sinister in his gangster suit.

60

He leaned against the doorway for support. "I'm a professional salesman. I've sold water conditioners, real estate, magazine subscriptions, storm windows—you name it. I hit the streets this morning at eight a.m., knowing there wasn't a salesman alive who could beat me. But you know what's funny?" Steve's dark eyes fastened on Mr. Z. "Mr. New-Age, sunshine-up-his-ass Simon here sells six platinum-plated golf putters and I could only sell four." Steve started pacing across the room. "We were both given four leads apiece. We were both given the same kind of putters, right?" he pointedly asked Mr. Z. "I sold one of my four leads. The other three didn't even know I was coming and had never heard of Going Platinum. My only other sale was a cold call. The receptionist says Simon here is three for three so far today. Would you call that 'beginner's luck'?" Steve was now almost toe-to-toe with Mr. Z.

"Simon has natural talent," Mr. Z said steadily.

Steve glared back at his boss. "I had a friend run a check on Simon's leads. One thing I agree with you on, Simon's success has nothing to do with luck." With that, Steve stuck his hand into his inside coat pocket, whirled around toward Simon. "This is for you!" he said.

Simon staggered back a step and stared at Steve's hand, which held five crisp hundred-dollar bills. "What's this?"

"I never welsh on a bet," said Steve.

"The day's not over yet," Simon said as cheerfully as he could.

"Yes it is. Take it." Steve jammed the money into Simon's coat pocket and headed for the door.

"Aren't you forgetting something?" Mr. Z called after him.

Steve stopped but did not turn around.

"You swore if Simon beat you, you'd eat a platinum

61

putter." If Mr. Z was angry, he was not letting it show. His voice was patient, parental. "Well," he said, "we're waiting."

Steve snorted in disgust and stalked out the door.

Simon watched the empty doorway. He distractedly stuck his hands in his coat pockets and appeared surprised to find one of them stuffed with Steve's one-hundred-dollar bills.

"It looks like I owe you a hundred dollars," said Mr. Z cheerfully.

Simon turned toward his boss. "I don't understand," he said.

"Don't you remember? I promised to kick in another hundred bucks to the winner of the bet."

"I thought this was what Steve wanted. He's a great salesman and he loves the competition."

Mr. Z shrugged. "All I know is, he lost and you won. He gave up and you didn't. It's that simple."

Simon studied the two stacks of platinum-plated golf putters. "But how could I have won?"

Mr. Z put his arm around Simon and joined him in staring at the putters. "Simon, I didn't want to say anything before, because it wouldn't have been fair to Steve. But the day I met you, I knew you had a future at Going Platinum. We are very selective. You can't imagine how many applicants we had for this job. I can tell you now that every single one of them had better qualifications than you. Every one of them was dressed better than you. Every one of them had more polish and professionalism than you. And yet I knew as soon as you hit the streets, you were going to leave Steve in the dirt." Mr. Z looked at Simon with genuine admiration. "You had a quality our friend Steve probably never had. Sincerity. When you listened, you listened with your heart." Mr. Z thumped his barrel chest. "And you had innocence," he said with enthusiasm. "Customers love that shit!"

Simon looked wistfully at his boss. "Thanks," he said.

Mr. Z firmly grasped Simon's right hand. "No, thank you, Simon. It's an honor to have you with us at Going Platinum." He pulled out a fat roll of hundreds, peeled one off, and stuck it in Simon's palm. "It's official. You're one of us. Now go out there and make your last sale of the day!" Mr. Z scooped up the two putters on the left. "And don't forget these."

Chapter 11

The door to Simon's ground-floor apartment opened to within three steps of the pool. Once as he headed to get his mail, deep in thought, trying to recall the Sanskrit name for Krishna's consort, Simon was surprised to find himself dog-paddling in the deep end. But, since he was already wet, he took a moment to enjoy the warm water and have a little swim. Although Simon spent nearly two hours a week cleaning and chlorinating it, almost nobody ever actually swam in the pool. Most of the residents, coming home from a stressful workday through bumper-to-bumper traffic or rushing out to their cars in the morning, coffee cups in hand, walked around the familiar obstacle of the pool, not really seeing it.

The apartments in the two-story complex surrounded the pool so everybody could look out and admire it. Besides collecting bugs and leathery fibers from the husks of nearby palm trees, the pool collected money. Generally not more than five dollars or so a week, mostly pennies, and never quarters, because they worked in the laundry machines. From time to time, Simon would hear the characteristic blip of a coin, tossed over the upper railing and into the pool or the ping and blip of a coin flipped off a thumb and sent to the bottom of the pool where it winked in the sun and waited for Simon to retrieve it.

It turned out to be a regular part of Simon's job to collect the change that accumulated in the swimming pool the residents used primarily as a wishing well. As custodian of the tenants' collective wishes, Simon treated the coins almost with reverence, as if they had been imbued with special prayers. He kept the change in a brass urn and once every three months, he would cash it in and organize a little celebration for the tenants. There were cookouts and ice cream parties. Once there was free laundry for everyone. Although the free laundry party was remarkably well received, the apartment owners put a stop to it because they claimed it was hard on the machines and the tenant who lived above the laundry complained that the drain gurgled all night and kept her awake.

Simon had treaded water, fully clothed, in the pool following his absentminded dive. It occurred to him that the coins he collected from the bottom of the pool no longer contained the wishes of their owners. He hypothesized that the act of hitting the water released the wish from each coin to do what the wisher wanted. But, because many wishes don't come true, maybe some of that unrealized spiritual energy remained in the pool. And as the only person who ever really got in the pool, Simon speculated that he might be soaking up that unused portion of their wishes. Did that mean, he wondered, that his own wishes were now more likely to come true? Or perhaps, having absorbed the essence of his fellow residents' wishes, was it his responsibility, in some general way, to see that they were carried out?

As he attempted to float these ponderous questions, Simon looked down and saw something glittering at the bottom of the pool. It turned out to be a two-carat diamond engagement ring. In spite of numerous announcements, no one ever came to claim it and the ring remained in the lost-and-found shoe box, a broken promise with the wish washed off.

★ ★ ★ ★ ★

Now, Simon sat in the huge gold overstuffed chair that had been left by the previous tenant. It served as his reading chair, his dining room table, and, too often, after a long evening of contemplating the manifold complexities of some obscure cosmology, his bed. It was made of heavy, tightly woven fabric, densely embroidered with fanciful renderings of flowers and trees. The upholstery was riddled with holes and tears; the wooden ornamentation was scarred and stained. It was the only piece of comfortable furniture he owned—which was why, most of the time, the chair was occupied by his cat, Edgar Cayce.

But when Simon was home, Cayce was delighted to share the chair. Having scaled its arched back, the Siamese leaned luxuriously against Simon's collar, marking the territory with short strands of his fur. Simon didn't seem to mind. At the end of the day, when he found both Cayce's tawny fur and strands of Amy's blonde hair on his collar, he regarded it as proof of the existence of God and as a sign that he was loved.

Still in his gangster suit, Simon reached back to stroke Cayce's ear.

"Didn't I tell you it was destiny for me to end up at Going Platinum?"

Cayce gave Simon a head butt, a special show of affection.

"I mean, look how it's all falling into place. I needed a good paying job and like magic, I have one. I needed respectability and suddenly, I have a country club membership. I think Amy's dad was impressed. My boss really likes me. He says I've got natural talent for this job. He says I have a future at Going Platinum." Cayce dug his claws into Simon's jacket and chewed on a stray curl on the back of his head. "Okay, so maybe it feels like there is some strange energy around the place. That could be because this kind of company is unfamiliar to me." He pulled the six one-hundred-dollar bills out of his pocket and closed them in a book on karmic astrology to hold his place. "And all this money!" Simon giggled. "This is so weird! Of course, I'll have to quit the apartment maintenance job. And I won't be around here during the day any more." Simon scooped Cayce off his neck and cradled him in his arms. "But you'll be all right, won't you?"

A knock at the door startled Cayce out of his reverie and he looked to Simon for reassurance. Simon glanced at his watch. It was after ten p.m. Who could that be? Kenny was working late at the spa tonight and Amy was out of town taking depositions for her upcoming telemarketing fraud case. He set Cayce gently on the seat of the chair and was on his way to the door when the knock came again, but louder this time.

Annoyed, Simon pulled the door open a little too quickly, to reveal the silhouette of a very large man with a squarish head.

"Are you Simon?" the man asked, taking a step forward, forcing Simon to retreat a step back into his apartment. A dim fluorescent light from the kitchen reflected off the policeman's badge.

"Yes, I am," Simon said. "Is there a problem?"

The towering officer looked Simon up and down. For a burly man, he had an incongruously soft-looking face. He seemed to be suppressing a grin. "You making a gangster movie?" he asked.

Simon frowned, perplexed. "No, I . . ." He glanced down at his suit. "Oh, this is kind of our uniform at work." He noticed his white carnation had wilted.

"I'm Detective Bob Bentley," the big man said, still fighting off a smile. "May I come in?"

Simon motioned for him to sit in the chair, but Cayce, glaring at him, refused to abdicate. Detective Bentley chose to remain standing.

"Can you tell me where you were this evening between the hours of six and eight p.m.?" Bentley asked, assuming a stony expression.

Simon loosened his white tie. "Well, yes. About five-thirty I got on the Santa Monica Freeway and headed north from Long Beach. I arrived here an hour later and I've been here ever since."

"Was anybody with you during that time?"

"No, nobody was with me. Why should anybody be with—"

"Did you make a cell phone call during that time?"

"No."

"Did anybody see you?"

Simon shrugged. "I was alone. I wasn't invisible."

Detective Bentley burst out laughing. "No, you sure as hell aren't invisible!" He quickly regained his composure. "Well, sir, it is my sad duty to inform you that your co-worker, Steven J. Merritt, was killed earlier this evening."

"Killed?" Simon asked, astounded.

"Murdered."

Simon stumbled backwards and sat heavily on the arm of the chair. "Are you sure it wasn't an accident?"

"Pretty sure."

"How did it happen?" Simon asked.

Bentley stared evasively at his shiny, size fourteen shoes. "I'm not at liberty to divulge the details of Mr. Merritt's murder. But I can say that the cause of death had some-thing to do with getting whacked on the back of the head,

68

then having a platinum-plated golf club shoved down his throat."

"But who would do such a thing?" Cayce was ignoring the large intruder and began comforting his distraught friend by nuzzling his hand.

"I thought maybe you could tell me that," said Bentley. "It was widely known at Going Platinum that you two didn't get along."

"I certainly never had anything against him—"

"And that you were both competing for the same job."

"It was pure luck that I won," said Simon. "I assumed Steve had it in the bag."

"And that he owed you a lot of money."

"It was just a silly bet. I would never have held him to it."

Detective Bentley looked Simon right in the eye. "And after the fight you two had over this bet, you were the last person to see Mr. Merritt alive."

Absentmindedly, Simon picked up the book on karmic astrology and started flipping through it. "Well, that's ridiculous, Detective Bentley. I had no reason to kill Steve. Maybe he didn't think very much of me as a salesman. But there were no hard feelings between us. Our differences were purely professional. And I certainly wasn't trying to get money out of him." Simon stood up indignantly and, as he did, six one-hundred-dollar bills fluttered to the ground.

"Good book?" asked Bentley, amused.

"If you accept the premise of reincarnation," said Simon.

Bentley pointed to the pile of money at Simon's feet. "You wouldn't happen to be the reincarnation of Ben Franklin?"

Simon swallowed hard. "Would you believe I had a good day today?"

Detective Bentley looked around Simon's apartment. There were piles of books on the floor; a couple of mismatched dishes lay in the sink. An inexpensive William Blake print was stuck to the wall with thumbtacks. "I'd believe you don't have good days very often," he said.

"What do you mean by that?" Simon said defensively.

"Look," said Bentley, "I don't know if you killed Merritt or not. From what I hear so far, the guy was a jerk and a lot of people had it in for him. But don't try to leave town, okay? And if you're not a criminal, you might want to look for a new job."

"I happen to think Going Platinum is a very nice company and they've all been good to me," said Simon. "They're running a legitimate business selling golf clubs and I've got a good future there."

Bentley shrugged. "All I'm saying is, keep your eyes open. Things aren't always what they seem." He backed out the door. "We'll be in touch. And remember, don't leave town."

Chapter 12

Kenny leaned heavily on the abdominal crunch machine. "You've done it this time, old buddy."

The clatter from the nearby weight machines nearly drowned out Kenny's words. A short, over-developed man wearing a wide leather belt stood under the squat press machine, trying to psych himself up to lift what looked like enough iron to build a bridge and making sounds as if he had a painful case of the dry heaves. Elsewhere in the spa, several rows of mostly young women in colored leotards pranced to the throbbing music of their aerobics class.

"But I didn't do anything," Simon protested.

Kenny regarded him sympathetically. "You don't have to do anything. Trouble has a way of finding you. It's amazing. I mean, sometimes I'm almost envious of all the attention you get."

"I'm under suspicion for murder," Simon reminded him.

"I know, I know. But it's like Fate has a special plan for you. No matter what you try to do, you always end up cleaning up some corrupt company from the inside. It must be nice to be needed."

"Oh, come on, Kenny. The spa needs you."

Kenny struck a bodybuilder pose. The effort distorted the lettering on his power lifter's T-shirt, which read, 'Go Heavy—or Go Home!' "Yeah." Kenny grinned, looking at his shapeless bulk in the aerobics mirror. "They need me for inspiration."

The man with the leather belt now had a one-hundred-pound dumbbell in each hand and was trying to perform alternating curls. He was being spotted by a young man who looked like one of those anatomical models in the encyclopedia that, depending on which plastic overlay is used, shows bones, internal organs, muscles, or the complete body. He was the one with muscles and no skin.

"Hit me!" demanded the man with the belt. With blinding speed, the skinless man slapped him hard across the face. "Ugggh!" grunted the belted man, simulating an attack of dry heaves as he hoisted the right dumbbell and let it back down with a jerk.

"You're looking huge!" the skinless man bellowed in his face. "You're a freak of nature!"

"Again!" commanded the belted man. And again his partner whacked him across the face, spurring him to heroically raise his heavy left hand.

Simon frowned. "Bentley hinted that Going Platinum is a crooked business. But it can't be. Sure the company is making a lot of money. We have a good product and customers like it. Is that a crime?"

"You're working there," Kenny offered. "So how legitimate can it be?"

"And they like me. Did I tell you, Mr. Z said I had natural talent for this job? Do you know how many jobs I've had?"

Kenny thought a moment. "Let's see. We were dead even until last September when you got three jobs in two weeks. After that, I threw in the towel. You're the champ." Kenny made a quick calculation, scribbling in the chalk dust under the parallel bars. "I'll say forty-one."

"And of those forty-one jobs, how many did I show natural talent for?"

"Well, I thought you were pretty good at selling oil wells for that investment firm."

Simon looked disgusted. "But it turned out there weren't any oil wells."

Kenny nodded. "There, you see? You have natural talent for abstract concepts."

"That's just it, Kenny. I'm spending my life pursuing abstractions. And there's no market for abstraction."

"Like you care," Kenny interjected.

"But I never thought a normal life was an option for me. I never thought I'd ever have a new car or a house. Even to get married, you need a regular job."

"Amy makes six figures. Marry her and the concept of work can remain an unattainable ideal. You'll both live happily ever after."

"What I mean is, I feel this is my shot at a normal life."

Kenny choked. "Selling platinum-plated golf putters?"

"Going to work every day, making money, learning a business, and having a company depend on me. Of all the bosses I've worked for, do you think any of them really miss me?"

"Not any more," said Kenny. "Now they have their parole officers to look after them."

Simon looked around the room. "Maybe I just want to see some tangible results for my efforts."

The aerobics class was nearing the end. All of the women were sweating. Their hair clung to their flushed faces and their Spandex clung damply to their bodies. Their makeup was streaked and their eyes shone with a look of weary desperation. A couple of them seemed ready to pass out.

"One and two," panted the springy instructor, calling out the cadence the way the galley slave captain in *Ben Hur* pounded out the rowing rhythm with his huge wooden mallets. "One and two!"

"I've thought about getting an office job," said Kenny. He waved his arm loftily across the room. "But, honest to God, I'd miss this place."

On the opposite side of the room, a slender teenager lay on his back on the bench press, hands clutching the barbell, struggling to get lift-off.

"Come on," said Kenny. "One of my flock needs tending. Yo, Arnold Schwarzenegger!" Kenny smiled down on the struggling youngster. "What do you say I take off some of those weights and give you something to work up to?"

The young man scowled. "I can do it. And my name is Rick."

"Oh, I know you can do it, Rick," said Kenny. "But not just yet. You've got to start out light and work your way up."

"I came here to get results. I came here to get big."

Kenny leaned over the barbell and gently lifted it off the boy who was pinned under it. His belly hung over the bar as he raised the weight easily onto the stand. "I said the same thing when I was your age." He patted his stomach. "And look what happened to me?" Rick cracked a smile. "Let me ask you something, Rick. Do you like working out?"

"Yeah, sure."

"What do you like about it?"

Rick lay on his back, squinting into the overhead lights. "Well, it makes me feel strong and loose. I like pushing myself to get better and I like to sweat. And it's so cool. It makes me feel—"

"Big?" suggested Kenny.

Rick squinted at him. "Yeah. It makes me feel big."

Kenny nodded thoughtfully. "So it sounds to me like you get results every time you work out, no matter how much weight you use."

Rick shrugged. "I guess so. But I've only got a free one-month membership to the spa. I can't afford a regular membership so I have to make progress fast."

"Oh!" Kenny exclaimed as if discovering a great revelation. He pulled out a slip of colored paper and scribbled something on it and handed it to Rick. "Here. Sign this. I just extended your free membership to six months. Now you can take your time and enjoy yourself. Getting big will take care of itself. You can trust me on that." Kenny slid several of the iron plates off Rick's barbell and lowered it gently into his hands.

"Thanks, mister," Rick said.

Simon and Kenny walked off, leaving Rick pumping the lighter weight a little too rapidly.

"Mister," Kenny muttered. "I feel like a dinosaur."

Simon clapped Kenny on the back. "You're all right, Kenny," he said. "For an old Stegosaurus."

Chapter 13

Simon spooned down the last of his whey and bean sprouts breakfast cereal and was adjusting his white tie when the telephone rang. It was Amy.

"Simon, I heard about Steve on the news last night. I've got to be in court in fifteen minutes so I'm going to make this quick. As your attorney, my advice is to seek other employment as soon as possible. As the love of your life, my advice is to quit that company now. Don't give thirty days notice. Don't even pick up your paycheck."

"But Ames, Sweetheart, I can't quit. I have a career at Going Platinum. I have a responsibility."

Simon could hear Amy taking a deep breath. "I know, Angel Face. You also have a responsibility to stay alive. You'll have to decide for yourself which one you think is more important. I've been doing a little checking on Going Platinum. I haven't heard back from Interpol yet, but I expect the news won't be good."

"What makes you think they're crooked?" asked Simon indignantly.

"Well you're working for them, aren't you? Just kidding. I don't know if they *are* crooked, but if they cheat you out of a nickel or harm one lovely brown hair on your head, I'm going to slice open their financial arteries and bleed them white. Then when I send them to prison, I'll make sure they get the meanest, hairiest cell mates—"

"Thanks, Honey," Simon chuckled nervously. "I know it

seems like it's my fate to work for criminals. But in *Think and Grow Rich*, the great Napoleon Hill says that nobody is doomed to failure. Although Steve was brutally murdered and all the evidence so far points to me, I must not dwell on the negative. I must not doubt my employers and the path I have chosen. Napoleon Hill says, 'Every man is what he is because of the dominating thoughts which he permits to occupy his mind.' "

"In your case, I guess that explains a lot," said Amy. "Listen, I've got to go. One more thing. Quit that evil job! Bye, bye, Baby."

After he hung up the phone, Simon took a deep breath and clapped his hands together three times. He had read once that a famous motivational speaker used this technique to bolster his confidence when uncertainty began to creep up on him. He said it was like giving himself applause. "I have to control the 'inner audience' of my subconscious mind," he said. Simon picked up *Think and Grow Rich* and opened it to the section on the six basic fears. "What do I have to be afraid of?" Simon addressed Cayce, who lay at his daytime post on the windowsill by the door. "Napoleon Hill says the most destructive fear is the fear of poverty. But I've never been afraid of poverty." He stroked his cat's ear. "Money doesn't interest me much. The second fear he describes is the fear of criticism. Nobody criticizes me," he said to Cayce, "do they?" Cayce purred uncritically. "Ill health? Old age? Death? These are all natural processes in the continuum of life. Why would I be afraid of them? Fear of losing the love of someone?" Simon closed the book. "That is frightening." He grabbed the violin case that held his platinum putters, patted Cayce on the head, and walked quickly out the door.

Simon maneuvered his Honda 600 into the main corridor of Century City. As he drew closer to the high-rises that rose up on both sides of the road, menacing the tiny car, Simon thought of Scylla and Charybdis, the clashing cliffs that nearly ended the famous voyage of Jason and his Argonauts. He was trying to think positive thoughts, but he was sure there would be little hope of finding a parking place in the same time zone as Mr. Harriman's office.

Then, as if by a miracle, a parking place appeared. Actually, it wasn't a whole parking place. The space was less than a full car length long. It was really little more than a gap between the two limousines on either end of it. It would not be humanly possible to parallel park in such a space, even for a car as small as his. Simon slid next to the space, turned on his blinkers, and, with the vicious morning traffic darting around him, got out and stood behind his rear bumper.

"Yo, Don Corleone!" yelled a motorist who found himself at the head of a line of traffic, stuck behind the Honda. "Get the hell out of the road!"

Simon smiled and flipped him the "peace" sign, which only infuriated him more. Then Simon took a firm grip on the back bumper, hoisted it upwards with all his strength and let it drop, and up again, bouncing it three times. On the third bounce, Simon scooted the rear of the car neatly into the parking space. As the amazed commuters looked on, he repeated the process with the front end of the Honda, slugged the parking meter, scooped up his violin case, and started on his way.

In spite of Napoleon Hill's advice that anyone wishing to become successful should associate with the rich and powerful, Simon felt uneasy around such people. He thought they had a way of sifting through humbler folk for what they could use and then casting them loose. Outside the office building, Simon tried to steady his nerves. He found himself silently repeating the chant Mr. Z drummed into him in training. "I will not be denied! I will not be denied! I will not . . ." Simon caught himself. He had made four sales pitches since he started this job and every customer bought without so much as a single objection. Even allowing for the excellence of Mr. Z's training and his own native abilities and charm, that kind of luck was still practically unheard of. "I never am denied," he muttered at the revelation.

"Excuse me." A distinguished looking man in his fifties stood behind Simon, whose hand rested on the door handle. "Are you going in?"

Startled out of his reverie, Simon opened the heavy glass door for the man with a flourish. He looked over the man's shoulder and saw a stooped figure shuffling down the sidewalk, pushing a homemade shopping cart. He was shaking his head and appeared to be having a conversation with himself. Suddenly, he stopped and looked straight at Simon.

Simon turned and entered the glass and steel cathedral to capitalism, catching up with the distinguished gentleman at one of the many elevators.

"Going up?" the man asked him.

Simon thought this over briefly. Yes, he seemed to be going up. He was trained to go up. All the smart and rich people agreed that going up was a good thing. Why shouldn't he be going up? "Yes," he said out loud. "I believe I am."

The man pushed the "up" arrow and the stainless steel door slid open. He invited Simon to go in first and followed behind him, quickly hitting the penthouse button and closing the door before anyone else could enter. The man turned to Simon and smiled a handsome, well-practiced smile.

"I'm J. D. Harriman," he said, with a hint of irony in his rich, resonant voice. "Welcome to my office."

"But I was supposed to meet you on the thirteenth floor," Simon stammered.

"There is no thirteenth floor," Mr. Harriman said as if explaining that there was no Tooth Fairy. "Now, Simon, time is money. I believe you have something for me." Without changing his cheerful expression, he said, "And if you think you're going to shake me down like the last guy did, you are sadly mistaken."

"I, uh, understand that not every salesman has your best interests at heart. But I assure you, Mr. Harriman, that we at Going Platinum only succeed if you do." There was something about Harriman that troubled him. He wished he could see auras the way his Grandma Louise could. "I have a great new way for you to advertise your business." Simon's sales pitch was on autopilot. He felt his spirit rising to the top of the elevator, looking down at himself and his client. He heard himself ask Mr. Harriman if he was aware that more than ten percent of the country's business was concluded on the golf course. He suddenly wondered if this statistic was true.

"Don't mess with me, kid," Harriman growled, his handsome face twisting with cruelty. Simon found himself back in his body. Harriman reached into his coat pocket. "What's it going to be, kid? Are we going to do business? Or do I leave you and your empty violin case here on the floor?"

Mechanically, Simon snapped open his case, containing two immaculate platinum-plated golf putters. He held it out to his customer.

"Good decision," Harriman said. He scooped up the putters with his free hand. His right hand shifted slightly and drew out a bundle of cash, held together by two rubber bands. He dropped the money in the case and closed it. The elevator jerked to a stop and the bell announced they had arrived at the penthouse. Harriman's Hollywood smile had returned. "Here's where you get off," he said.

Chapter 14

Simon knocked on Mr. Z's office door.

"Come in, Simon," he muttered, shuffling a pile of papers on his desk.

"I made three sales today, Boss. Here's the paperwork." Simon dropped the forms on the desk.

"Good work, Simon. You're doing very well." He did not make eye contact.

"If I keep this up, I'll break seven hundred dollars in commissions this week."

Mr. Z looked up. "That's great. I'm sure you've heard about Steve by now—"

"Yeah, that was awful," Simon interrupted. "The crime rate around here is getting terrible, isn't it? It was probably a robbery gone bad. Did they say it was a robbery?"

Mr. Z studied Simon's face a moment for cracks in the armor of his sincerity. "They didn't say." He motioned for Simon to sit down. "You know, Simon, the police will be asking a lot of questions around here until this thing is settled."

Simon nodded. "I know. They already talked to me."

Mr. Z's eyes flashed. "What did they say?"

"They think I did it." Simon grinned.

"And did you?" Mr. Z did not smile back.

"Oh, come on," said Simon. "Steve thought I was a lousy salesman and he was upset that I won the bet—"

"He was furious," Mr. Z interjected.

"Okay, he was furious. But I had nothing against him. I thought he was totally neglecting his top three chakras, but I wouldn't kill him over it."

"His top three what? Never mind. You're a good boy, Simon. You remind me of a shepherd in our village. He had a kind face like you. Not very attentive and the wolves did eat most of his sheep. But we all liked him and we looked after him." Mr. Z reached across the desk and patted Simon's arm with one of his meaty paws. "You have a positive outlook. That means more in this business than shrewdness. I know you're still new here, but I am going to offer you a rare opportunity to prove yourself. I am going to turn over one of our best accounts to you. No, don't say anything. There's no need to thank me. By accepting this account, you will either sink or swim. If you swim, it will be worth an extra two hundred dollars a week to you guaranteed."

Simon stirred in his chair. "Wow! Two hundred bucks! I won't let you down, Mr. Z."

"And if you sink . . ." Mr. Z fixed his wolfish eyes on Simon. "You sink to the bottom. You'll be out. This is a tough business and I need to know that you are tough enough to handle it." Mr. Z leaned back in his opulent office chair. "Your contact—uh, client—is a Mr. Chen. You will meet Mr. Chen tomorrow at ten o'clock on the six hole. You will be his caddy."

"But I don't even know how to play golf," Simon objected.

Mr. Z seemed surprised. "You can't play golf? Well, no matter. Neither can Mr. Chen. Your caddy outfit will be waiting for you outside the caddy shack. There will be a full set of clubs in a golf cart. Mr. Chen will be wearing an orange and green plaid jacket. He will play three holes. He

Daniel B. Brawner

will then tell you he has an urgent meeting and will drive off with the cart and the clubs. But before he goes, be certain that he gives you his jacket. The payment is in one of the pockets. It is not necessary to count it, just feel it to know that it is there. Can you remember all this?"

"No problem," said Simon. "But isn't this kind of an unusual sales presentation?"

Mr. Z nodded thoughtfully. "Going Platinum is, as you know, an unusual business. Our customers are sometimes eccentric. I'm sure you of all people can appreciate that. Mr. Chen is a deadly serious businessman. He works fifteen hours a day and has an annual income bigger than some small countries. Maybe he feels, as a rich man, he should play more. But any activity that doesn't make him money bores him and he cannot endure it for long. So he plays two or three holes and buys an expensive set of clubs. If it makes him feel better and puts money in our pockets, who are we to question him?"

"Who indeed!" said Simon.

Chapter 15

Amy blinked to clear the water from her eyes and fumbled through the shower door for the thick royal blue towel that hung near the plate glass mirror. If Amy had not been thinking about the identity theft case she was defending that morning, she might have noticed the sound of her front door opening or at least the footsteps in her hall. She certainly would have heard the bathroom door open.

But Amy was already mentally in the courtroom, delivering her opening remarks and filling impressionable jurors with her own certainty of the defendant's innocence. She liked getting up early in the morning while most of the rest of the city slept. It increased her sense of supremacy and gave her the leisure to visualize how her current legal battle would unfold. Like a grandmaster chess player, Amy could see several moves ahead of her opponent. Instead of singing in the shower, Amy argued her cases out in the shower, shouting objections and citing precedents, all muffled by the running water. She tried out different vocal intonations until she found one that worked best. She practiced her timing and worked out effective gestures. Like an Olympic high diver who visualizes every twist and tuck before mounting the platform, before Amy entered a courtroom, she had already won her case in the shower.

So that morning, having dispatched a smug prosecutor and shredding the credibility of his star witness somewhere between the second application of shampoo and the herbal conditioner, Amy had to stare for several seconds at the reflection in the mirror as it cleared from the heavy steam. For just a moment, Amy felt she had lost control, that she didn't know what to say that would invoke Justice and lead the offender away in handcuffs. The face that stared back at her through the fog appeared calm and resolute. She knew that face.

"Mom!" she gasped. "You scared the dickens out of me!"

"Good morning, dear," Sabrina said solemnly. "Is there someone in there with you?"

Amy wrapped her hair in the towel and threw on her terrycloth robe. "What's going on, Mom? It's not even daylight."

"I made some coffee. Do you want some? How about a nice Belgian waffle?"

Amy stepped into her slippers. "Some coffee would be great. But what's the matter, Mom? You never get up before eight."

Sabrina looked troubled. "I couldn't sleep," she said. "Let's talk downstairs. How can you breathe with all this humidity?"

Amy sat across the kitchen table from her mother and patiently sipped her espresso. She knew it didn't do any good to rush her mother, who had always been a methodical woman. She had worked her way through college as an illustrator of medical books and still occasionally took on freelance jobs. Her work was clear and precise. Her art tools and materials were always laid out neatly and once she began a project, she proceeded straight through without stopping, even for corrections. She thought about things for a long time before she expressed her opinion or took action.

But once she made up her mind to do something, there was no distracting her. One time, Amy's father had been slow to take their Mercedes in for repairs. Six months pregnant with Amy, Sabrina bought a thick automotive shop manual and rebuilt the car's three Holly downdraft carburetors herself, carefully laying out the springs and screws and rubber diaphragms on the kitchen table, cataloging each intricate piece with detailed illustrations. It took her two weeks. And when she was through, the old Mercedes purred like a cat. She never said a word of recrimination about it to her husband. It was just a job that needed to be done, so she did it.

Sabrina stirred three tablespoons of sugar into her coffee and stared at it, frowning. "It's about your boyfriend, Simon," she said finally.

"Look, Mom," Amy jumped in. "Simon and I have been going together for quite a while now. I know I should have introduced you sooner. Okay, he's kind of different, but I was hoping you and Daddy would see past—"

Sabrina looked up from her coffee. "There's something about Simon's job that isn't right."

Amy was momentarily startled. "I've been thinking the same thing, Mom."

"All those big smiling men with gangster suits and Russian accents, selling gold golf clubs—"

"Platinum, Mom."

"Well, I don't think they're selling platinum golf clubs at all." She took a gulp of her coffee and made a face. "I can't put my finger on it, but there's something about that whole business that is not quite . . ." she struggled for the right word, ". . . not quite symmetrical."

"Simon mentioned he thought there was something out of balance there, too," Amy said, half to herself.

"Well, it bothers me," said Sabrina. "Like a picture

hanging crooked. I have to tell you I won't be able to rest until it gets straightened." She looked up at Amy and breathed a sigh of relief. "There! I've said it. I just wanted you to know."

Amy scanned her mother's face for clues. "Now Mom, you aren't thinking about, you know, doing something yourself, are you?"

Sabrina stared at her coffee and nervously stirred in another spoonful of sugar. "Well, if you really do like this boy," she said evasively, "I wouldn't want him to get into trouble. I mean, if it turns out there really is, well," she whispered, "stealing. It must be stopped—you, of all people, can appreciate that, and Simon seems like such a sweet boy to get mixed up with that sort of element—not that I am an officer of the court like Ed or you but . . ." Sabrina held her breath and waited.

Amy Castor, attorney at law, said with a tone of finality that was perfected in the shower and proven unassailably in the courtroom, "I'll take care of it."

"I know, I know." Sabrina's long sensitive hands danced on either side of her coffee cup like courting robins. "I only want you to be happy, dear."

"I *am* happy, Mother," Amy said through clenched teeth.

Chapter 16

That evening, still wearing the Anne Klein power suit she had worn to work, Amy stirred the leftover curried rice and cauliflower and popped it into the microwave. Several thick law books were open on the dining table, along with her laptop computer and a draft of a brief she was writing. Through her kitchen window, she heard two car doors slam. She set the timer to fifty-six seconds and was about to push the start button when she heard raucous singing and what sounded like the instrumental lead-in for a well-known song by Pink Floyd.

"Dum—de—dum, dum, dum, dum. Dum, dum, dum. Dum—de—dum, dum, dum, dum, dum, dum, dum—"

"Mon—ey! Get away. Get a good job with more pay and you'r—r—r—r—re okay."

There was a brief percussive clatter as somebody tripped over the cans in the recycling bin she had left by the curb.

"Mon—ey!"

"Dum—de—dum—dum—dum. Dum, dum, dum—"

"It's a gas."

Amy peeked out of the window to find Simon and Kenny dancing their way in a circuitous path over her lawn, apparently heading for her front door. Simon was carrying a twelve-pack of beer and Kenny was hoisting a large pizza box behind his head. Pointing his other hand, palm down at eye level, and thrusting out his chin in time with the music, Kenny, remarkably agile despite his bulk, was attempting a dance step once known as "Walk Like an Egyptian."

"Grab that cash with both hands and ma—a—a—a—ke a stash," wailed Simon.

Amy sighed and shook her head. She quickly began shutting down her laptop.

"Mon—ey!"

By now, the source of the neighborhood disturbance was at her door.

"So they say. Money is the root of all—" Simon sang. She opened the door.

"—evil to—o—o—o—o—day. Hi Ames." Simon grinned.

"You eaten yet?" Kenny called over Simon's shoulder.

"This is too strange," said Amy. "I was just sitting here, working on a brief, thinking I do not have enough entertainment in my life. And wouldn't it be nice to have a big greasy pizza?"

"Whoa!" Kenny shook his head in wonderment. "Then I guess it was lucky for you we came around when we did." He flipped open the pizza box and thrust it toward her. "I saved the cheese part for you and Simon and I've eaten most of the anchovies off the other half. So knock yourself out."

Amy waved away the fishy smell from Kenny's breath. "Yes, that might help." She turned to Simon. "I never thought I'd see you eat pizza."

Simon looked a little flushed. He took a deep breath, like a four-year-old screwing up his courage to confess to his mother. "This is kind of a special occasion."

"That's a relief," Amy said. She studied him closely. "Have you been drinking beer?"

Simon shook his head. "No," he said emphatically. "No. No. No." He paused. "Yes." Kenny started to giggle and Simon joined in. "This is all Kenny's fault. I'm sure I don't have to explain. You know how he is.”

“And if Kenny told you to jump off a bridge, I suppose you’d do it?”

“Yes, I’m afraid I wouldn’t be able to help myself,” said Simon, shaking Kenny roughly by the collar. “He’s just too persuasive!” Simon and Kenny cackled at their bad behavior.

Amy rolled her eyes and smiled. “Well, I suppose you might as well sit down before you fall down.”

“You are such a gracious hostess.” Kenny gallantly kissed her hand.

“Amy’s been to charm school,” Simon confided to Kenny. Amy kicked him not too gently in the shin.

Kenny straightened up and sniffed the air. “What do I smell?”

“Do you really want me to guess?” Amy said.

Amy was standing in front of the microwave with her arms folded. Kenny gently picked her up off the floor and set her to one side. “It smells like your special curried rice!” He opened the microwave and looked as happy as a grizzly bear with a honeycomb, scooping the cold rice from the bowl with his hand and making little orgasmic moans of pleasure.

By this time Amy could no longer keep a straight face. “Would you like a spoon?” Kenny licked his sticky paw with abandon. “Or would you like us to leave you alone for a while?” She was laughing so hard, Simon had to hold her up to keep her from falling into the spice rack.

Kenny set the empty bowl on the table and a trickle of sweat ran down the side of his face from the hot curry. Languidly, he fanned himself with a photocopy of a Supreme Court decision that had been lying nearby. “If you decide not to marry Simon, would you marry me? I promise I won't be any trouble. I'll mow the lawn. I'll pick up my socks. I'll be your slave. All I ask is that you leave me a bowl of something you made and I'll be happy. I really will."

Amy put her arms around Kenny—not all the way around him—but as far as they would go. "Kenny," she said. "One day, you are going to make some lucky woman's dream come true. Besides, it doesn't make any difference to me which one of you I marry. I should know by now you two are a package deal."

"You got that right!" Simon said, doing his best to hug them both.

When they broke from their huddle, Amy asked, "So what's the occasion anyway?"

Simon and Kenny looked at each other together, counted, "One, two, three . . . Dum—de—dum—dum—dum. Dum, dum, dum. Mon—ey!"

Simon then proceeded to describe his frightening and profitable encounter with J. D. Harriman and his new bonus account with the shadowy Mr. Chen.

"So let me get this straight." Amy sat across her butcher-block kitchen table from Simon. "One of Mr. Z's thug clients threatens to kill you if you don't turn over the putters which contain heaven knows what. You're a suspect in Steve's murder. And now you're taking up with the Chinese Mafia. You are risking five to ten years in prison on a half dozen charges ranging from criminal facilitation to conspiracy to murder. If you had any sense, you'd quit." Amy had been making notes on a yellow legal pad and threw her pencil down in exasperation.

"I thought you'd be happy for me." Simon looked sheepish. "I can't quit now, Ames. I have to get to the bottom of Steve's death. I have to clear myself. I have to set things right." He managed a grin. "Besides, I'm making money."

"What the hell's the matter with you, Baby? Whatever happened to that sweet, idealistic, gentle boy I fell in love with? A couple of weeks on this job and suddenly you're drinking beer and rhapsodizing about goddamned money! What did they do to you?"

Simon seemed to suddenly regain his sobriety. "I can take or leave the money. But I have to find Steve's killer."

Amy rapped on the table. "Earth to Simon! Earth to Simon! Come in, Simon. You are not a cop. You are not even a private investigator. You don't have the training to do what you are proposing to do and you don't have the authority. What's-his-name Detective Friendly already thinks you're the killer. He's just waiting until he has proof you're involved so he can arrest you. And, guess what? You're guilty. Maybe you didn't kill anybody. But you're Mr. Z's mule. You're selling drugs, or military secrets, or something illegal. Just quit the job and tell the cops what you know. They'll take care of it."

Simon took Amy's hand. "You're wrong, Sweetheart. I am trained to do this. I've read *Mort d'Arthur* and the *Upanishads* and everything Joseph Campbell ever wrote. I've worked for dozens of career criminals and I believe I'm getting a feel for identifying the criminal spirit. Sure the police could arrest Mr. Z and his pseudo-Sicilian, sheep-herding outlaws. But would that restore their mythic authenticity? Would that improve their spiritual equilibrium? Would it prevent a cosmological short-circuit from happening again?"

"Honey," Amy sighed, "I don't know what in the world you're talking about. But if you don't quit that job, two things are going to happen. First, the police are going to haul your narrow ass to jail. And second, you and I will be through."

Simon looked stricken. "You can't mean that, Ames. Remember all we've been through."

"Exactly what I was thinking," she said. "I think of all the times I put my caseload on hold while I pleaded with cops and judges and made deals with prosecutors to keep you out of jail because you just couldn't leave some criminal employer until you'd restored his mythic imbalance. And, may I add, for free."

"You were great," said Simon.

"It was valuable experience," Amy admitted. "But now I'm through!" She sniffed. "I can't take it emotionally. You can only go to the well so many times, Simon. I don't want to be there when you finally fall in."

"You're my strength, Amy. You're my knight in shining armor. I pick fights with dragons. I can't help it. Everywhere I go, I'm tripping over dragons. But without you to deflect their fire, I'd be toast."

"Then butter up, buddy. Because I'm out." Amy walked to the front door and held it open for him. "If you change your mind, call me. And, for the last time, quit your job with Going Platinum before it's too late."

Simon thanked her for all her help and, with Kenny in tow, stumbled out the door.

Chapter 17

Simon spent a sleepless night talking with Cayce about Amy, the future, and his place in the world economy. Cayce clearly sided with Amy. She brought him fresh salmon and quickly caught on to his game of fetch with crumpled-up paper. Simon tried to argue that Amy could try to be more understanding about his forays into employment.

"Everybody needs a job," Simon postulated.

Cayce lay straddled on the arm of the chair, limp as a rag doll, and purred.

"Well, maybe not everybody," Simon conceded.

In the end, Simon had to admit, after he had been threatened by a customer and after Steve had been brutally murdered, that Going Platinum had some suspicious elements. And as reluctant as he was to give up on the place, he could not bear to lose Amy.

"Okay, I'll quit," he assured Cayce. "But I did promise Mr. Z I would meet with his big shot Asian client. I owe him that much at least."

Simon was surprised to find that after having dressed like a Depression-era Chicago gangster, it did not feel odd to now dress up as a golf caddy. After all, he told himself as he checked over the complete set of platinum clubs in the cart, salesmen, like actors, are always assuming different identities.

Mr. Chen was a small, scholarly-looking man with bright

black eyes that shone as lifeless as a doll's eyes. Instead of the usual garish outfit worn by other golfers, Chen wore a well-tailored, lightweight wool suit with supple dark shoes that looked like slippers. He was accompanied by two squarish Asian men also wearing dark suits. Nearly identical in their features, they stood on either side of Chen like bookends. One of them held a green and orange plaid jacket, which he helped Chen put on. Although he was probably in his late seventies, Chen's movements were crisp and decisive. He shook Simon's hand firmly but without warmth.

"You have the clubs?" Chen inquired, his speech betraying no hint of accent or emotion.

"I sure do," said Simon. He extracted a gleaming driver from the calfskin bag. "As you can see, they are the most elegant—"

"Take me to the four hole," Chen commanded, hopping lightly into the golf cart and followed by his two assistants. After Simon climbed in and began driving, Chen added, "I only play the four hole. When I eventually make par on the four hole, I will play the five hole until I learn it and so on." Simon thought he sounded rather grim about it.

"I see you have little interest in golf," Simon said brightly. One of the bodyguards glared at him. "Only in mastery."

Chen seemed momentarily puzzled that a person of such low station would address him in this familiar way. But he quickly recovered and a hint of a smile crossed his otherwise blank face. "A man who can make par on the four hole might also be capable of many other great things," he said.

Simon nodded in agreement. "Indeed any man who has made par on the four hole has already done many other great things."

"Such a person," continued Chen, getting into the spirit, "is to be feared by men."

"And admired by women," Simon added.

Chen actually chuckled, eliciting expressions of confusion from his identical bodyguards. When they arrived at the four hole, Mr. Chen's associates hopped out and began looking fiercely in all directions for potential enemies. Chen himself paid little attention to them. He had brought along his own set of graphite clubs, selected one, and took a practice swing to limber up. He handed the driver to Simon. "Would you do me the honor of playing this hole with me?" Chen asked.

" 'If you try to cut wood like a master carpenter, you will only hurt your hand,' " Simon said.

Chen smiled. "Lau Tsu also said, 'Practice non-action. Work without doing. Taste the tasteless. Magnify the small, increase the few. Reward bitterness with care.' Beware the Tao, my friend, or you could end up contemplating much and doing little." He removed his plaid jacket and handed it to Simon. "There is a chill in the air; please put this on."

Simon slipped on the gaudy and diminutive coat with some difficulty. The cuffs rode halfway up to his elbows and the back stretched tightly between his shoulders. He could feel the heavy envelope in the breast pocket and resisted the temptation to touch it. He returned the club to its owner and when Chen produced a tee, Simon said, "Please, allow me," and thrust his hand into his back pocket.

Immediately, the bodyguards each drew out a small machine pistol and aimed it at Simon's chest. His eye was drawn to the dancing orange dots from the weapons' laser sights. Slowly, Simon raised his hand up for them to see that, instead of a gun, all he had was a golf tee. The bodyguards put away their weapons but left their murderous expressions leveled at him. A bit shaky, Simon walked over to where Mr. Chen was going to tee off, holding the little wooden spike in full view as a magician holds his top hat to show that it does not yet contain a rabbit. He was about to poke the tee into the turf when Chen instructed him to move eighteen inches to the left. Simon looked up to get Chen's final approval, then down at the grass and stabbed the tee into the earth.

But, instead of remaining impaled in the turf, the tee popped up and lay on top of the ground. There was a slight hissing sound. Once again, Simon stuck the tee into the grass, only this time he used a bit more force. Just then, the sod below him heaved and burst violently into his face with a gagging reek of rotten eggs. Simon reeled backwards and felt himself slipping into unconsciousness.

He was dizzy and a little nauseous. The horizon seemed to tilt and, in his delirium, he saw Cayce sitting in his chair, not as a cat would sit, but as a person. "You should have stayed home with me today," Cayce chided. "Now look what happened. You're dead. What am I supposed to do now?" Cayce shook his head. "And another thing, that canned food you feed me that you think stinks so much? Well, I think it stinks too. Cats are more sensitive than people in every way. When you don't come home on time, it hurts my feelings. And that dumb thing you do when you clap your hands in the morning—it scares the wits out of me. Look, I don't mean to pick on you—especially in your deceased condition. I just thought you should know. Also, I love you more than sunshine or raw salmon. By making me your cat, you have made me special forever." Cayce gave him a love wink that cats give people only if they trust them completely. "But if you do come back to life, get me some different food."

"His eyes are open," observed Mr. Chen.

"That's normal," said one of the bodyguards, "for a dead person."

Chen cradled Simon's head in his arms. "That poison gas was meant for me," he said matter-of-factly.

The other bodyguard pulled a small mirror from his coat pocket and held it up to Simon's nose to see if he was still breathing. He looked over at Mr. Chen and shook his head. Simon could see a faint residue of white powder in the corners of the twenty-four-carat gold frame. He imagined he was getting some kind of contact high from it.

As he stared into the mirror, the clouds reflected in the glass from behind him began moving very fast. The alternating shadows and sun took on a strobe effect he found dazzling. The clouds cleared to reveal the head and upper torso of Steve Merritt, which appeared to be floating in space. Steve was looking right at him.

"You thought you won, didn't you?" Steve laughed. His mouth didn't move. "If the contest hadn't been rigged, you know I would have kicked your ass."

"You're dead," said Simon.

"Look who's talking." Steve did not even change expression. "But first, you have to do something for me. You have to find my killer."

"Didn't you see who it was? Besides, what difference does it make now who killed you?"

"I was hit from behind and I don't have time to explain the fine points of getting around in the next world to you. Let's just say I can't move on until I find out who killed me and why."

Simon said, "If you can visit me, why don't you haunt the police station? This is a matter for the authorities. Besides, I'm quitting the company today."

"You're going to quit a lot more than that," Steve replied, "if you don't start breathing real soon."

"I'm prepared for the hereafter," said Simon.

"I don't think you realize what a bad idea it is to argue with a ghost. Did they tell you where I died?"

"No, I . . ." Simon noticed that his mouth also did not move as he spoke. This made him so self-conscious, he suddenly found himself unable to speak.

Steve nodded and almost smiled as if he understood the problem Simon was experiencing. Steve didn't look so good. There seemed to be something wrong with his mouth. "My killer knocked out six teeth when he jammed the golf club down my throat after I was unconscious," he said, reading Simon's thoughts. "Simon, I died in The Room."

He felt Steve's words in his solar plexus. "But that was sacred space," he thought. "The Room was supposed to be our sanctuary."

Steve answered, "So you'll help me." But Simon felt a searing light boring into his forehead and could no longer think at all. "I'll bring you back to life and you'll help me," Steve stated.

"We cannot be here when the police arrive," Chen said. "And look, you idiot! You got cocaine from your infernal mirror on his face." Chen leaned over and gently blew the trace of white powder from under Simon's nose.

Simon felt as if he had been under water a very long time and had just broken the surface. His eyes opened wide and he gasped deeply with a desperate shriek of inhalation. One of the bodyguards cried out and fell as he tried to run backwards. His colleague remained frozen in his tracks. Mr. Chen stared at Simon with a beatific expression. He bowed his head and said something softly in Chinese.

Simon looked around and noticed he was lying on the ground in Mr. Chen's arms. He grinned tentatively. "What's going on?"

"You're alive," pronounced Chen.

"I am," said Simon, feeling refreshed and oddly comfortable, cradled in the arms of the Chinese mobster. "Did I miss something?"

Chapter 18

Mr. Z, who had been called to deal with Simon's supposed death, tried to explain that the explosion of "poison gas" that knocked Simon out was nothing more than a large pocket of methane, produced by layers of decaying subsurface garbage. But the paranoid Mr. Chen insisted that it had been a booby trap set by one of his many enemies and that Simon had heroically laid down his life for him. Always fast on his feet, Mr. Z quickly confided that Simon was his right arm at Going Platinum and that he had trained him from a young age to throw himself between his customers and certain death.

"Simon is like a son to me," said Mr. Z, looking teary-eyed.

Chen clenched his jaw and bowed to Mr. Z. "You have done well," he said. "As of this day, I am moving my entire industrial information acquisition pipeline through your office, as well as thirty percent of the uncut Brazilian diamonds."

Mr. Z practically quivered with glee. "We will not let you down, sir!" he said.

"I am sure of that," said Chen. "Also, ten percent of all net profits arising from our increased business will be deposited into Simon's bank account. Your books will be audited once a month to be sure that this is done. I trust there will be no accounting irregularities."

Mr. Z swallowed hard. "Oh, none, sir, I assure you."

★ ★ ★ ★ ★

While Mr. Z was busy with Chen, Simon relaxed comfortably in Mr. Z's office. He declined to be examined by a doctor but agreed to recuperate on his boss's big leather couch. But Simon felt such close proximity to that much dead animal skin was disrupting his karmic balance, so he sat on the Oriental carpet which he observed was made from natural fibers and vegetable dyes.

"A—a—o—o—oom—m—m! A—a—o—o—oom—m!" Simon chanted. He was in remarkably good spirits. He smiled to himself, thinking how refreshing it was to die. He had read Dr. Moody's book, *Life After Life*, about near-death experiences, none of which corresponded to his own. There had been no tunnel of light, no warm, comfortable feeling, no beckoning by dead relatives. Visions were something he had occasionally anyway. Mr. Chen told him he had stopped breathing for about five minutes, but it seemed much longer to him. Although it was true he was disturbed by Steve's death, he did not see what symbolic value a vision about Steve would have for him. What lesson was he supposed to derive from it? And what was he to make of the promise he'd made to find Steve's killer? Of course, it would not occur to him to take such a vision literally. Joseph Campbell said that confusing symbolic spiritual messages with historic facts had deprived followers of Judaic-Christian religions of their mythic roots. There was no actual serpent that had tricked the first human female into eating an apple. That story was borrowed from an ancient fertility ritual. And so on. Still, when Steve spoke to him, it seemed so real. Had his near-death experience allowed him to bypass the rational barriers to his unconscious? Or was it possible that he had somehow truly made contact with Steve's tormented spirit?

Simon tried to banish these half-formed ideas chasing their tails in his head. He tried to calm the ripples on his mental pond, breathing in through his left nostril and out through his right. In through his left and out his right. But it was no use. Sometimes, he thought, you've got to let your mental fish splash around the pond.

Simon opened his eyes and experienced a brief moment of panic. For an instant, Mr. Z's office seemed completely unfamiliar to him. The massive walnut desk held no associations of his boss sitting behind it with his feet up. The photos on the walls bore no resemblance to anyone he knew. The plaques appeared to be engraved in some strange language he had never seen before. He could be anywhere, in any city in the world, in any period in history. And then, just as suddenly, Simon was again oriented in the here and now.

To reassure himself, he stood up and walked over to a certificate hanging on the wall. It read, "Our deepest appreciation to Yakov Zhelev for your generous contribution to the Boys' Athletic Association. Without you, dozens of underprivileged boys in the greater Los Angeles area might never have learned to play golf. Please accept our highest honor, the BAA Certificate of Merritt."

Merritt? Simon blinked hard. The letters danced on the certificate, mocking him. A fly buzzed by his ear. Automatically, he waved it away. The letters fluttered back to their original places on the page like startled swallows returning to a telephone wire. The fly strafed his ear once more. "E—e—e—e—e!" it Dopplered past. "Ste—e—e—e—ve," it whined by again. Simon steadied himself against the wall. Oxygen deprivation must be making him hallucinate. "Z—e—e—e—e—e!" the fly's wings cried plaintively.

"Look here," said Simon to the circling fly. "Are you

saying that Mr. Z killed Steve?" The housefly was now batting its head against the textured glass door. It bounced off the glass and aimed straight for him. "Or could it be Zelda? I always thought there was something unbalanced about her. But murder? Anyway, I think she actually liked Steve. If she was going to murder anybody, it would probably be me."

Just then, Mr. Z burst into the room. "Simon, you are looking a little pale. Are you feeling all right? I thought I heard voices. Was there someone here with you?" He looked around the room. "That's okay. I don't really need to know. I only wanted to say how proud I am of you for your bravery today with Mr. Chen. To tell you the truth, he never liked me. That's why I asked you to handle the transaction this morning. But because you saved his life—"

"But I didn't save his life," interrupted Simon. "That is, I hadn't intended to."

"The point is," said Mr. Z, "Chen thinks you did and he is throwing more business our way, which means more commissions for you, my boy."

Simon looked uncomfortable. "Actually, Mr. Z, I'm afraid I'm going to have to resign."

Mr. Z looked stricken. "That's ridiculous! Absurd! I won't hear of it. I trained you. The customers love you. You're going to be a wealthy man. Your home is with us."

"Because I'm working here, my girlfriend left me and—" Simon began.

Mr. Z held up his huge paw as if stopping traffic. "Say no more," he said. "Your Uncle Yakov will take care of you. Everything is under control. Like you young people say, 'no problem.' Now go home and get some rest. Tomorrow is the first day of your wealthy life." He slapped Simon affectionately on the back. "You rich son of a bitch!"

Simon would have protested, but he thought he detected a hint of fear in Mr. Z's outwardly jovial countenance. He edged his Honda onto the perpetually overcrowded Santa Monica Freeway and jammed the accelerator to the floor. Before long, he reached his top-end speed of forty-five miles an hour, which allowed him to keep up with the Ferrari and BMWs. The fact was, he didn't really want to quit Going Platinum. And the way the signs were beginning to stack up, it might be fighting against the cosmic order to try. Amy would understand, he thought. He would explain about the way Steve came back from the dead and appeared to him through the bodyguard's cocaine mirror, imploring him not to quit the company until he found the killer. And then there was Mr. Z's certificate of "Merritt." As an officer of the court, Amy could appreciate a case built on a preponderance of evidence. For his closing argument, he would tell her how a fly was dropping hints as to the killer's identity. That should convince her. He downshifted into the driveway at his apartment complex and slipped deftly into his parking space. That should convince her, Simon thought glumly, that I am incompetent to marry her by reason of mental defect.

Simon started to get out of the car when he noticed a man towering over the tiny vehicle. The man leaned casually against the driver's door, resting his elbows on the hood. Since he could not open the door, Simon rolled down his window and spoke to the small of the large man's back.

"Detective Bentley, what a pleasant surprise."

The bulky policeman sighed heavily. "Simon, Simon, Simon. What are we going to do with you? Not only have you ignored my friendly advice and kept working for that disreputable company, but now you've graduated to consorting with the Chinese Mafia."

"You've been following me?" Simon was incredulous.

Bentley chuckled. "If you've chosen a life of crime, Simon, you really ought to practice lying your way out of leading questions. You're supposed to say, 'Gee, Detective Bentley, I thought that nice Oriental gentleman was just there to play golf. I didn't know he was a bad man.' "

"First of all," said Simon, "I don't know that Mr. Chen is a bad man. Second, as far as I know, he *was* just there to play golf and to buy a set of platinum clubs from me. And third, if I am being charged with something—"

"Take it easy." Bentley turned around and sat on his heels facing the window. "Nobody's charging you with anything." He winked. "Yet. You may not personally be a criminal. But you have to admit, Simon, crime follows you around like a puppy." Bentley giggled at his analogy, sticking his tongue between his teeth like a geeky fourth grader.

The sight of this big, goofy cop giggling and snorting cracked Simon up in spite of his efforts to the contrary and this only made Bentley laugh even harder. "Okay, okay," said Simon trying to bring the conversation back to earth. "What is it you want from me?"

Bentley suddenly looked like a big sad puppy himself, scolded for having had too much fun. "Well, if you didn't kill Steve Merritt, you could tell me who did."

"But I don't know who did. I suppose you checked the murder weapon for fingerprints."

Bentley looked perplexed. "You know? We did. But the really disturbing thing is that the only prints we found belonged to you." He shook his head. "And you say you didn't do it. Also, the only person we could find who had a motive to kill Steve Merritt was you. And, according to our source, the last person to see him alive was also you. But you say you didn't do it, so there goes all our evidence up in smoke." Bentley's big pumpkin head was bobbing up and down and he was grinning like a jack-o-lantern.

"It's circumstantial evidence and pretty thin at that." Simon scooted to the other side of the car and grabbed the passenger side door handle. "So, as nice as it has been talking with you, Detective Bentley, I must be going now."

As if an invisible center had just snapped the ball, Bentley rocked onto the balls of his feet, let out a terrifying roar, and slammed into the side of the small car like a lineman for the L.A. Rams laying into a 300-pound defensive tackle. The ten-inch tires on the Honda 600 squealed as the car slid sideways over the cement, scraping trails of black rubber until the vehicle came to rest against the steel support pole of the open carport, pinning the door closed. Simon gasped in horror and flattened himself against the door.

Detective Bentley grinned, panting just a little. "I had one more question before you go."

All Simon could do was stare.

Bentley aimed a deadly serious look at Simon. "Did you kill Steven Merritt?"

Simon was still shaking, but answered as steadily as he could. "No," he said. "I did not."

Bentley rose quickly to his feet. "Okay," he said cheerfully and sauntered down the driveway and out of sight.

Chapter 19

Cayce sat in Simon's lap with his eyes half closed, purring steadily, apparently oblivious to Simon's state of agitation.

"You remember when I told you what Mr. Z said, that we are all masters of our own fate—I know 'fate' implies predestination. But his point was that each of us decides the direction of our particular quest. Ultimately, nobody else makes us do what we don't want to do. You with me so far?"

Cayce was. Clearly nobody, not even Simon, was going to disturb his moment of bliss with a lot of talking.

"But I'm not so sure. First, Fate told me that I should work for Going Platinum. I felt it was more someone or something else's decision. But I did it. Then, Amy, who has remarkably good judgment, told me to quit and I was planning to do just that. Later, Steve's ghost tells me to stay with the company and find his killer, and then a fly starts whispering cryptic hints in my ear. Now Detective Bentley wants to arrest me for killing Steve. So I can't quit. I know what I have to do. I have to set things right. I have to help restore the cosmic harmony surrounding Going Platinum and I wouldn't be surprised if, somewhere along the line, I solve Steve's murder."

"I'm very happy with my new food," said Cayce.

Simon regarded Cayce with curiosity. "If this were a hallucination or a waking dream," he said, trying to keep rational, "you might have spoken like a figment of my imagination, responding to my fears or reminding me of my obligations." He petted Cayce's head gingerly. "But you talked like a cat, if a cat could talk."

Cayce purred. "I appreciate it," he said. "It's really good food. You're awfully nice to me."

"You're welcome," said Simon. "So I guess this means I have at least partially crossed over. I've met mystics and psychics who could read minds, foretell the future, talk with animals. But I never could. I knew there were spiritual signs hidden in plain sight, like the 'Where's Waldo' puzzles, but I couldn't see them. Sure, I had visions. But, by themselves, they didn't usually make sense. I wonder, when this is all over—if I do what I'm supposed to do—if I'll ever get to go back to normal."

"Why don't you rub my tummy?" Cayce suggested, assuming the position.

"Okay," said Simon, still preoccupied with his new role in restoring the cosmic order.

A short time later, Cayce scrambled to his feet. "That's enough. I'm going to sleep now. I love to sleep. Where's my friend Amy? She has the best food. That man with the big feet likes you. I'm sleepy."

Simon wondered, was this what he had been working toward all his life—what he had been dreaming about? Was this the kind of transformation that the great Hindu mystics and Aborigine shamans went through? He had studied mystical literature and spent countless hours in meditation. He had faithfully done Tai Chi and yoga. It had been refreshing, not life-altering. But now Simon felt his body resonate with some unearthly inspiration. He was now literally a new man. And it had happened so easily. But why?

It was nearly dark outside by now. Simon was feeling a little giddy over his newly-acquired mystical powers and decided to go for a walk and think things through. He said goodbye to his chatty cat and stepped into the rich evening air. An ocean breeze washed overland through the palm trees and stucco apartment buildings. It was a fishy, almost spicy smell. Simon took it deeply into his lungs and closed his eyes. He could see the foaming breakers prostrating themselves onto the beach, endlessly worshiping the land, so hard, so foreign, so other. Its prayer went on forever, asking nothing.

Simon opened his eyes and shivered at the clarity of the image. A dim gray cloud, barely distinguishable in the fading light, scudded across the steel-gray sky. A cluster of tall palms rustled and swayed and Simon swayed too. He started walking down the sidewalk, stopped, and took off his sandals, leaving them where they lay. He walked on the lawns, his toes relishing the cool, springy, closely clipped grass. The earth underneath gave off a fertile, loamy scent like mushrooms. It made his mouth water.

"Oh no! Oh no!" Two sparrows exchanged cries of despair that the sun was disappearing.

"It's all right," Simon reassured them. "The sun will be back soon enough." This startled the birds and they stared at him with their beady, monoscopic eyes, tilting their heads this way and that, not believing him and not comprehending how this sort of terrestrial animal could speak.

Simon walked on. Gradually, he became aware that cars, buildings, and people were no longer in the forefront of his perceptions. He had never before thought about the way his brain prioritized how he saw the world, giving far greater importance to the creations of humans than to Nature. Now, he heard crickets singing to each other in complex cadences. Two male dogs passed each other on the sidewalk. The terrier lowered its eyes. Its submissive posture showed

111

it was a foreigner to the neighborhood. The shepherd was proud, with noble blood, and lived nearby. It slowed, daring the smaller dog to give offense. A sudden shift in the wind made Simon stop and sniff. He filtered out the gasoline and tire smells, detecting the distinct aroma of a decaying chicken. It could not be more than a minute's walk away. This possibility oddly interested him. Now, the cry of a seagull demanded as much of his attention as a car horn honking. It struck him that this could make it hazardous to cross the street. He would have to remember to watch for cars.

As Simon was pondering the confusion of living among humans, something struck him on the head. Although it was dark now, he discovered he could see surprisingly well. He reached down and picked up the small object that hit him. He smelled it and smiled. He licked it. Simon rolled the object around in his hand, feeling its rough husk. It pleased him. He looked up at the tree and thanked it for sharing one of its almonds with him. He placed the raw nut in his pocket next to his car keys. The metal of the keys felt oddly foreign. Simon had the peculiar impression that the almond had great importance and he switched it to his other pocket.

"I am gathering magic," Simon said out loud, as if surprised himself at the realization.

"You'll need it," said a voice in the shadows behind a Dumpster. It was a voice Simon knew well, a kindly, wise voice, heavily seasoned with a New York accent.

"Professor Campbell, can you tell me what's happening to me?" Simon blurted out to the formless apparition, like a child complaining about a scraped knee. "What am I supposed to do?" There was a long pause. Simon began to think he was imagining the encounter and maybe the rest of the evening's visions as well.

"You must do three things before you can complete your task," said the voice, finally. "Die." Another long pause. "Fight a demon." A longer pause. "And get a job."

"In that order?" asked Simon. "But I'm not ready, Professor Campbell."

"Oh, for heaven's sakes!" said the voice, clearly disgusted. "Don't be such a chicken. People get jobs every day. There's nothing to it."

"I mean about fighting the demon and dying and solving Steve's murder."

"Oh," said the voice.

"And I already have a job."

"Working for that putter company is not a job!" the voice roared so powerfully that the Dumpster rang like a bell. "Besides," the voice chuckled, "you were born for this quest as a monarch butterfly is born to migrate to Mexico, as an acorn is born to become an oak tree. As far as being ready, don't concern yourself. You'll be ready when the time comes."

"But sir, I don't even know where to start."

The voice sighed. "Don't you remember your studies of the Grail legend? What paths did each knight take?"

Simon thought a moment and answered, "Each knight chose his own path—"

"And so the path you choose will be your path," the voice interjected impatiently. "Once you start, just follow the signs."

"What signs, Professor Campbell?"

"Goethe said, 'All things are metaphors.' And Jesus said, 'They that have ears to hear, let them hear.'" The Socratic message carried an imperative tone.

"So," Simon began tentatively, "the signs could come from anything—a rock, a billboard . . ."

"Yes, yes, yes—anything—a cat, a trash can. Just pay attention! And remember, no hero succeeds alone. To complete your task you will need greater love than you deserve, greater wisdom than you can reach, and greater courage than your body contains."

Simon looked troubled. "Sir, I'm afraid that this task will be more than I can handle, since it is clearly important enough to bring you back from the dead."

"And I am afraid, sir, that you are gravely mistaken." There was a pause. "That was a joke, young man! You'll do fine and I have to go."

Simon stood in a daze by the trash container. Overhead, a 747 rained white noise down on East Los Angeles. Revelers were leaving a neighborhood bar and one of them was throwing up wetly in the street. Simon strained to hear a bird or a cricket, but he could not. He knew the spell had been broken.

Chapter 20

Simon expertly scanned the menu. It was festooned with gold trim and elaborate floral patterns and circuitous vines that drew a diner's eye from one exotic entrée to the next. "Kenny, what you need is more 'prana,' more life force, in your life."

Despairing over the uncompromisingly organic menu, Kenny muttered that his prana would be much improved with a large anchovy pizza and a beer.

"Come on, Kenny," Simon whispered. "This is an Ayurvedic restaurant. Ordering pizza and beer here would be like walking into a Hassidic restaurant and ordering pork rinds. Your dosha—your body type—is kapha, the earth quality. You need more fire in your diet. How about a nice spicy Rainbow Risotto?"

"Looking at all this fake tofu burger, cranberry pilaf stuff, I was beginning to think I could skip lunch altogether. You shouldn't have mentioned pork rinds. Now I could eat a whole range-fed tofu, complete with the hide and horns."

Simon ordered the Field Greens with Miso Barley Soup for himself and the Risotto for Kenny.

"Are you sure you're buying today?" Kenny asked. "All this is pretty expensive."

Simon shrugged. "I'm so rich it's embarrassing. I've made five sales this morning alone and I'm getting commissions on all the business we do with Chen. I don't even count it anymore. And it's all in cash." He reached into the pocket of his pinstripe suit and pulled out a fistful of paper currency.

"Put that away!" Kenny hissed. "You want to get us mugged?"

"I really don't think muggers would bother us. It's funny. I used to get hassled when I drove into East L.A. or Hollywood. Now, even gang members walk on the other side of the street when they see me coming."

"Maybe it's the violin case," Kenny suggested.

"Maybe it's Chen." Simon sounded serious. "He's convinced I saved his life. Sometimes I get the feeling I'm being followed. You know, I think he's having somebody watch over me."

Kenny took a large bite of his Rainbow Risotto and nodded his approval. "That's so cool! Your own underworld bodyguard!" He took a gulp of ginger tea, shuddered, and pointed his fork at Simon. "So what's this all about?"

Simon pulled a manila folder from his violin case and extracted a couple of grainy eight-by-ten photos that he slid in front of Kenny. "These are pictures of Steve Merritt."

"The dead guy? Jesus, Simon! Are these police photos? How'd you get them?"

One was a full-length picture of Steve crossing the street. The other showed Steve talking with a middle-aged Asian man at a newsstand without looking at him.

"This is Steve's personnel file. I grabbed it while Zelda was looking up my Social Security number. There isn't much in it that's useful. I know these look like surveillance photos. Maybe Going Platinum likes to check out its employees. But I was hoping you could help me with his physiognomy?"

"Sure. I'm happy to help you out. If only I knew what the hell you are talking about."

Simon tapped a photo with significance. "Physiognomy.

You know. The study of a person's essence based on what they look like. More than anybody I know, you can look at someone's body and see into their character. Look at these photos and tell me, what kind of person was Steve Merritt?"

Kenny scratched his head and shifted uncomfortably in his seat. He bent closer to the picture of Steve crossing the street and pointed. "This may be nothing. But check out his posture. Most people slouch a little when they walk. His back is ramrod straight. And see how he picks his feet up when he walks. He's practically marching. Maybe he's ex-military. Maybe a dancer. Certainly he's in great shape and I don't mean just a naturally fine physical specimen. He's in training. His build has symmetry. Probably works with a professional. Ordinarily, a person develops certain muscle groups more than others, depending on what sports they play or the work they do. This kind of physique doesn't happen by accident. And let me see that close-up again." Kenny studied Steve's face. "The detail isn't very good here, but notice the skin tone. No wrinkles, no sagging. He's no drinker. Your old rival may have complained about being poor, but this guy wasn't living on cheeseburgers and fries. He was eating a low-carb, low-fat diet."

"A bodybuilder?" Simon asked.

Kenny shook his head. "His face doesn't have that gaunt, leathery look most bodybuilders have. His muscles look more rounded and smooth. He's not going for bulk. Bodybuilders tend to look stringy and lumpy in clothes. Steve doesn't have that hard look. And there are little things like his sideburns. They're razor cut and the ends of his hair are uniform. He gets a haircut at least every two weeks—and probably a facial. Even his casual clothes fit perfectly. They're all tailored designer stuff. Trust me, this guy has bucks—had, I mean."

Simon was jotting down notes. "So he worked out, took good care of himself, he probably had money. He had good taste in clothes and he ate well. I realize this is a leap, but can you tell me anything about his social life?"

Kenny leaned his considerable bulk back in the booth. The wooden joints creaked with the strain. "Well, I'm no fortune teller. I don't see auras." Simon quickly scribbled down something else. "But I'd guess Steve was a loner. There's something cold about his eyes. He's a greedy little bastard, you can tell that." Kenny pointed again to the close-up. "And see, he's got a kind of smug expression. He's self-contained, not used to compromising or accommodating another person. Probably not gay. Definitely, not married."

"Do you think he really was a salesman?" Simon asked.

Kenny took a pull from his ginger tea and swallowed hard. "Either a salesman or a hired killer."

The man at the counter gave Simon the once-over and made a kind of sneering grin. "What is this, a shake-down?" The man had a large shock of thinning, bleached blonde hair. He was wearing a Hawaiian shirt that had enough material to make a pup tent. Blue veins snaked across the top of his bulging well-tanned forearms. He looked like a World Wide Wrestling Federation wannabe.

Simon adjusted the wide lapels of his gangster suit. "This is sort of a company uniform . . ."

The man slapped his palm down heavily on the counter. "You're one of those golf club guys on TV. Hey Mike!" he shouted to a side of beef in a three-piece suit standing by the dressing rooms within easy access of a full-length mirror. "Look what we got here. It's one of those platinum golf club Mafia guys!"

"What are you talking about, Jim?" Mike asked, evidently somewhat annoyed at being interrupted while stealing a glance at his own heroic profile.

"From TV," prompted Jim. "You know, that Russian Mafia guy who sells platinum golf clubs."

This last morsel of information was enough to distract Mike from his reflection and start him in the direction of the counter. Quickly, he made his way past the posters of Frank Zane and Arnold Schwarzenegger and past the racks of clothes designed to set off the physiques of overdeveloped men.

"Mike loves golf," Jim confided to Simon and gave him a big conspiratorial wink.

"Mike Ironside," Mike announced, extending his hand in Simon's direction. It was a lumpy-looking hand, decorated with a large high school ring and a rather feminine pinkie ring. There was a hard ridge of calluses across the top of his palm and another along middle joints of his fingers. To Simon, it felt more like a foot than a hand. "It's a pleasure to meet you. I've enjoyed your commercials. Corny, but fun in an amateur sort of way. Say, you wouldn't have one of those platinum putters with you, by any chance?" He motioned toward Simon's oversized violin case.

Simon popped the case and extracted one of the gleaming golf clubs, elegant and precise as a surgical instrument. Mike held it up to the light as if examining a diamond for flaws. He stepped aside to give himself some room and took a tentative putt at an imaginary ball. "Nice balance," observed Mike. "Do people actually use these, or are they just for show?"

"These clubs have been known to improve a few games," Simon said coyly.

Mike took another practice swing and licked his lips. "I

suppose these things cost a bundle."

Simon smiled. "What do you think?"

"Go get me a golf ball, Jim. There are a couple in my desk." Mike stared at the scintillating head of the club in front of his wingtip shoes, as if afraid to make eye contact with Simon while his sales resistance was so low. Jim fetched two balls, which he handed to Mike, and a coffee mug, which he placed on its side at the opposite end of the room.

"I'll bet you ten bucks you can't sink either one," Jim said, grinning like an ape.

Mike gave his employee a fierce look. "Do you have ten dollars you weren't planning to stuff your face with?"

Jim sucked in his bulging middle a little and sulked as Mike took aim at the stained coffee cup. Simon had to stifle a laugh, looking at the huge man hunched over the tiny putter with such intensity. A trickle of sweat ran down Mike's temple and dripped off his chin onto his shoe. He blinked hard, then practically tore off his jacket and tie and unbuttoned the top button of his voluminous white dress shirt. Again, Mike centered himself over the ball. His entire upper body swung back like the bust of a Greek god reeling at the wrath of Vesuvius. Then he struck. With a small metallic thunk, the ball crept across the floor. With a surety of purpose that was almost biological, it entered the not-very-immaculate porcelain womb and bounced out.

"Nice shot," said Jim. "Double or nothing?"

"Up your ass," he practically whispered as he bent to place the other ball in position. "Fifty bucks."

Jim was squirming against the wall with his huge arms folded, trying to get comfortable. "Yeah, okay. I'll do fifty."

This time Mike did not hesitate. He drew back and tapped the ball and it rolled straight into the cup as if it were on rails. Mike beamed. He waved to a make-believe

PGA crowd and kissed the putter. "It's magic," he said, his voice choked with emotion. "This platinum putter is pure magic."

Simon said, "Well, two weeks ago, I did sell a whole set to a billionaire who was very impressed with them."

Mike gripped the putter a little tighter. "No shit? A billionaire? You know I've got to have this club, don't you? I'm in no position to quibble. Just tell me, how much?"

Simon rubbed his chin thoughtfully. "Maybe we could work something out. Actually, the reason I came here is that Kenny from the spa thought you could help me."

Jim said, "Kenny's a good guy. You know Kenny from the spa, Mike?"

"Sure I know Kenny. He set up my workout program. What can I do for you?"

Simon pulled out the close-up of Steve and held it out for Mike and Jim to see. "I'm looking for a guy I used to work with. He worked out a lot and dressed well. I thought you might have seen him in the store."

"He does look kind of familiar," Mike said.

Jim spoke up. "Yeah, that sporting goods store on Sepulveda, The Final Buzzer, they do alterations for athletes. I think that's where I saw him."

"No," said Mike, "I think it was that sporting goods store on Melrose. We saw him there together about a month ago, remember?"

"No—oh, right, right. Now I remember, Mike. You're right. Melrose. That was it—"

"So, why don't you leave me your number?" Mike addressed Simon, cutting Jim off. "If I think of anything else, I'll give you a call."

Simon was about to say something when he felt a tickle in his throat. For an instant, he thought he could see Mike's face looking in two directions at once. The face looking at him was sincere and friendly. The other face appeared worried. It was semi-transparent and was looking in the direction of the telephone. The second face suddenly dissolved like fog in the sunlight. Simon coughed and handed Mike his business card.

"Now about this platinum putter," Mike said with relish.

Simon retrieved the golf club and replaced it in its fitted case. "This is a demo unit," he said hoarsely. "Thanks for your help." He snapped the violin case shut and walked out the door.

"You dumb ass!" said Mike viciously. "What do you got to open your big mouth for all the time?"

Jim looked hurt. "What'd I do? We did see that guy at The Final Buzzer."

Mike looked exasperated. "Do you have to say out loud every little thing you think?"

Jim took in a sharp breath as if to say something, but set his Neanderthal jaw and stared at the floor.

Mike continued, "This guy we saw is some kind of heavy hitter. Eddie at The Final Buzzer said he is bad news and we should stay out of his way—like don't talk about him."

"Well, I didn't hear that. Eddie never told me nothing," Jim said sullenly.

"Of course he wouldn't tell you. Because Eddie knows your head is like a tuba. Anything that goes in the little hole comes out the big hole even louder."

Mike stalked over to the coffee cup and snatched it off the carpet. Violently, he jammed the two golf balls inside. "That golf club gangster suspects something now. That's why he wouldn't sell that platinum putter."

"I'm sorry," said Jim.

"Shut up. You owe me seventy bucks." Mike picked up the phone and punched out a number. "Hi Eddie, it's me, Mike. You know that cocky little bastard—the sharp dresser—you said was bad news? Well, there was some golf club salesman at the store named Simon asking about him and Jim here blabbed that we saw him at your place." Mike listened a minute. "What do you mean he's dead?" He listened some more. "Of course, I know what 'dead' means. All right. If I see him again, I'll call you." Mike hung up the phone. "You did it now," he said to Jim.

"What'd I do?"

"That guy we weren't supposed to talk about got himself whacked and now people are sniffing around here."

Jim's suntanned face clouded over. "You think it was that gangster Simon who killed him?" Mike shrugged. "Hey, wait a minute!" Jim said, as if somebody thought they could pull a fast one on him. "If Simon killed that guy, why would he be looking for him?"

Mike rolled his eyes. "Well, maybe he's not really looking for him, you dumb ass. Maybe he's looking for anybody who might know he did it so he could kill them too."

Jim's massive jaw dropped as he processed this information. Suddenly, he had a thought. "Mike?" he asked.

"What is it?"

"Ten plus fifty equals sixty." Jim looked very pleased with himself. "I only owe you sixty dollars."

Chapter 21

His Grandma Louise was the one person who kept Simon from being branded as the peculiar member of the family. For the last 20 years, Louise had lived alone. She had bought a house in Venice Beach back in the days when a cottage along the ocean still cost less than $20,000. Her little place was worth many times that now. She could sell it and live comfortably off the interest, but she said she would miss the ocean breeze and, of course, the odd and often well-off folks who lived in Venice and provided Louise with a steady source of income and amusement.

Grandma Louise had been a seamstress, a short order cook, a circus acrobat, a faith healer, a Kirby vacuum cleaner salesperson, and a gossip columnist. There was even a story that she had been a Pony Express rider, but Simon was pretty sure she'd started that rumor herself. She once told Simon that all those jobs were not real careers at all, but only preparation for her true chosen profession. Grandma Louise tried to assure Simon that his many jobs were not wasting his life. "Education takes time," she would tell him. "Look at me. It took me sixty years of training before I had enough education to start my career." Grandma Louise was a channeler. And as much as Simon enjoyed his grandmother's company, it was for her professional talents that he came calling today.

They sat around her Mission coffee table, strewn with starched doilies, a crystal bowl of stale mints, and photos of the recently deceased Steve Merritt. The late afternoon sun filtered through the bamboo blinds, throwing horizontal striations of light and shadow undulating over the simple wooden floor in rhythm with the ocean wind. In spite of Aunt Louise's colorful past, her house was an old lady's house. It was cluttered with pictures of her grandchildren and stiff-looking photos of herself and her late husband, Grandpa Tom. There was a black Art Deco telephone with a rotary dial and a striped cloth-covered cord. There was a plastic AM radio from the fifties and a complete set of Fiestaware she had collected piece by piece from the days when it was given away free with a box of laundry soap. There was a shelf full of old *Look* magazines and *National Geographic*s with the pages stuck together from years of humidity and mold. The whole house smelled of mold and seaweed and homemade gingersnap cookies whose scents had soaked into the woodwork and the floors and the antique wool area rugs. To Simon, it smelled old and familiar and deliciously comfortable.

Grandma Louise looked up from the photos of Steve Merritt. "I could just slap the shit out of you, Simon!" she said. "You've gotten involved in some pretty shady characters in the past, but these fellows take the cake." She wore a silk Japanese tiger print jumpsuit. Her thick white hair was held in place with a cranberry-colored scarf. Louise had stopped doing handstands after her seventieth birthday, but occasionally could still be persuaded to perform a cartwheel.

"You look good, Grandma," said Simon.

"Don't change the subject, young man!" she scolded. "I had always hoped you'd amount to something. But being murdered was not the sort of fame I had in mind for you."

"I don't think it's as bad as all that, Grandma."

"Don't bullshit a bullshitter!" Grandma Louise's steel blue eyes flashed. "I know real trouble when I see it and boy you've got it! Folks pay me good money to put them on the path to happiness and protect them from evil. I act like I'm real concerned about their pampered little lives, but most of the time, they don't have much to worry about. But you—you've got evil swarming around your head like hornets." Grandma Louise smiled. "You want a cookie?"

Simon selected a plump macadamia nut chocolate chip cookie from the bright red Fiestaware platter. "That's why I was hoping you could help me out."

"Oh!" Grandma Louise acted surprised. "So now you want my help? You never asked for my help before. You know, not one member of our family has ever asked for help from Crazy Louise."

"Please, Grandma?"

She shrugged. "Well, I suppose I could try. If it's not too late."

It was true that her family had snickered at Grandma Louise's business of summoning spirit guides. They had grown up listening to stories about her circus days and how, like any "carnie," she would sometimes fill in for the half-woman, half-reptile lady or the ticket taker or the palm reader. Grandma Louise had been a performer all her life and it was no trouble for her to switch from one act to another. She settled in Southern California because she figured it was the only place where her show business/psychic background would actually be a professional asset.

Grandma Louise pulled the black drapes closed. She lit a cone of sandalwood incense and placed it inside a small, ornate porcelain dragon. Smoke poured from the fierce little dragon's nostrils and curled about its face. Soon, the kitchen was filled with the heady aroma of sandalwood.

"You understand I'm not making any promises about this," Grandma Louise cautioned. "We may not even get an answer. But you need a heavyweight spirit in your corner and I'm going for the biggest one I dare to call."

Simon munched the last of his cookie. "Okay. Go for it."

"One more thing." Grandma Louise's intense blue eyes locked onto his. "Once I call this rascal up, I may not be able to put him back."

"What do you mean?"

"I have no authority over spirits. They come and go as they please. Spirits, especially the old ones, are not usually comfortable in our world. But if one should become . . . attached to you, well, that's that."

Simon straightened up in his chair. "What? My spirit guide could become a parasite?"

"A parasite, or a tiresome guest that won't get the hint and go home. Or a little voice of reason in the back of your mind. And as far as that last one goes, you could do worse."

"Grandma!" Simon protested.

Grandma Louise arranged an assortment of crystals on the table and put on a kind of rainbow-colored fez, decorated with moons and stars. "All I'm saying is that it wouldn't hurt you to get a dose of reality once in a while."

Simon smirked. "Look who's talking."

Grandma Louise pointed to her magician's hat in surprise. "What, this?" She grinned. "It gets me in the mood."

"What about you?" Simon asked. "Did you ever have a spirit that wouldn't leave you alone?"

Grandma Louise got a wistful look on her face. "You know, Simon, it's been over twenty years since your Grandpa Tom died. I never remarried. I loved him that much. But a girl gets lonely." She winked. "My own spirit guide doesn't interfere a lot in my life, but it's a comfort to know somebody is watching over me."

With that, Grandma Louise took a deep breath, closed her eyes, and dropped her chin. She was still for five minutes or so. Simon was beginning to think she might be taking a nap when she made a low grunting sound, as if clearing her throat. Her head twitched and a shudder went through her body.

"Don Fernando!" Grandma Louise's voice sounded hollow and warbling, as if she were singing through a vacuum cleaner hose. Simon looked closely for signs that she might be somehow doing this for his benefit. "Don Fernando, we need you." Again, there was silence for several minutes. "Don't talk so fast!" she said, now in her own voice, still with her eyes closed. "You know I can't understand thirteenth-century Spanish. Speak English, for Christ's sake! All right, all right. I'm sorry. Listen, my grandson Simon needs your help. He's being accused of a murder he didn't commit and he needs to find the real killer. What do you mean you know all about it? Have you been spying on me again? I know I called you. But don't you have anything better to do than eavesdrop on an old lady? Mercy sakes! Get a life, will you? Oh, sorry. It's an expression. So it wasn't you who was watching, it was—translation please. Your . . . soul mate? Your heart of the mind? What? Well, then just tell me his name." She paused. "Have you been drinking your bathwater? Ben Hogan? The golfer? I'm sure he is a very dear soul. No, I'm not saying there is anything funny about that. It just seems a little surprising to me that a former Spanish Inquisitor would get chummy with an ex-pro golfer. You say he makes you feel good about yourself? You're right. I don't understand. But about my grandson?" Grandma Louise seemed to be listening. "So you're not going to help me at all? Even though I put you in touch with Pope Innocent IV? Yes, I'm sure Simon would like Mr. Hogan, but he really has to find the murderer and you've got the juice to do it. Sure, I'm flattered that a man of Ben Hogan's character would like to take charge of this case, but what experience does he have with murder? No, I'm not being snide. I understand the Church ordered you to kill those folks. Well, couldn't you assist him? Give him pointers? Come on, I didn't think dead golfers could get insulted. All right, all right. Well, thanks Don Fernando. I owe you. And next time you come over, knock first, okay?"

Suddenly Grandma Louise collapsed on the table, toppling over several of the taller crystals. She groaned and stretched all over as if waking from a deep sleep.

"Takes it out of you, huh?" offered Simon.

She snorted. "Are you kidding? I feel like I just did two weeks in a Swiss health spa. What do you think keeps me going?" She stretched her neck luxuriously. "Oh, baby! My secret's out now. Raising the spirits of the dead—Grandma's little helper." She clapped her hands and rubbed the palms together. "So, did you follow what was going on?"

"Yeah," said Simon. "My spirit guide is an old golfer."

"Not just any old golfer. Ben Hogan."

"You don't have to sell me on him, Grandma. I'm in no position to be particular. But what should I expect? Will he appear floating through the air and point the way I'm supposed to go? Will he whisper in my ear?"

"I'm stuffed if I know," said Grandma Louise. "Speaking of which, I'm starved. How about a nice cheese sandwich?" She scooped off her fez and threw on an apron. "Every spirit is different. Maybe you won't even know he's there. Maybe he'll watch and not do anything. Maybe he can't do anything." She cut a block of creamy white cheese into thin slices and slathered mustard on some whole grain bread. She carefully cut the sandwiches in half and handed one to Simon, along with a tall glass of milk. "Here, this will fix you up." She took a big bite of her sandwich and chewed ecstatically.

"Why would Ben Hogan be interested in finding a salesman's killer?" asked Simon.

"Lord, I love French cheddar!" enthused Grandma Louise. "Honey, I'm sorry. I tried to get you Don Fernando. But I'm afraid it's up to you from here." She brushed the crumbs off her apron. She shuffled through some papers in a kitchen drawer and pulled out a card. "Maybe this will help," she said. "Madame Samantha is the best astrologer I know. You'll get none of this New Age baloney from Sam. She'll tell you straight and, if she likes you, maybe she won't overcharge you."

Chapter 22

Detective Pat O'Reilly slumped in the passenger seat. "Hell, Bob, I don't see what you have against this guy Simon. It's not like we really have anything on him."

Detective Bentley gave O'Reilly a condescending sidelong glance from the driver's seat. "When you have more experience, you'll develop a nose for criminals. Maybe we don't have much hard evidence against Simon yet, but from the moment we met, I smelled criminal all over him. You mark my words, when we get to the bottom of this murder, we'll find Simon right in the middle of it."

"All I'm saying," O'Reilly argued, "is that it would be nice to have a motive and, as far as I can see, Simon had no reason to kill Steve Merritt."

Bentley wheeled his car into the parking lot. "First of all, we don't need a motive to investigate or even arrest somebody. And secondly, Merritt was everything Simon was not—he was focused, ambitious, aggressive, athletic, professional looking, and competitive as hell. Think about it. During their training at Going Platinum, Merritt must have walked all over that New Age pansy. I mean, Simon hadn't had a real, paying job in months and Merritt was going to humiliate him and steal his one opportunity to get ahead. A man can take only so much of that."

The car stopped and O'Reilly and Bentley got out. O'Reilly said, "That's motive to resent him, not murder him."

"When you're looking for motive," Bentley said with a

knowing look, "watch out for two things: money and women. Simon was about as broke as you can be in L.A. without actually living in the street. But more important, his girlfriend is a friggin' lawyer who is making six figures. And what's more, her old man is a big time lawyer."

"So she's used to the good life," O'Reilly suggested.

"Exactly! And as much as she might enjoy slumming with artistic types like Simon, she's going to want a man who can give her the kind of lifestyle her daddy gave her."

"An acorn doesn't fall far from the tree," O'Reilly chimed in.

"Exactly," said Bentley.

"But you really shouldn't be rousting Simon by yourself. If the captain gets wind of that kind of Lone Ranger stuff, he'll bust you down to Traffic Control."

Bentley stood over the spindly O'Reilly as if trying to decide whether or not to eat him. "Look here, you pencil-necked piece of shit. If the captain even sneezes in my direction, I'll assume it was you who put him up to it."

O'Reilly was unshaken but held up his long, spidery hands in defense, hairy as two tarantulas. "Okay, okay. All I'm saying is that, as your partner, I wish you'd keep me informed about what you're doing. For instance, why we are checking out Ironside's Big and Tall men's store. Merritt was buff, but he was only about five-foot-ten and one hundred eighty pounds."

Bentley had already regained his composure. "Well, we know that Merritt was a golfer. We know he has a record for selling steroids to bodybuilders and professional athletes. We also know that Mike Ironside was Mr. Orange County two years in a row and whenever somebody mentions golf, he practically pisses his pants with joy. I figured, maybe they've met."

Bentley pulled open the heavy steel and glass door to Ironside's store and the two detectives walked inside. Three beefy men were talking loudly by the dressing rooms. With them was a blonde woman in her late twenties, wearing iridescent yellow Spandex bicycle shorts and a black leather bustier. Blue veins popped from her neck and forearms, and her skin looked hard enough to bounce quarters. Jim was trying to engage her in conversation.

"So I says, 'I bet you twenty dollars you can't bench four hundred pounds' and he says, 'I bet I can.' So he has three hundred pounds on the bar and it's sitting in the rack, see?"

"Uh huh," said the woman, containing her enthusiasm.

"But it's loaded with twenty-five-pound weights and if he's going to put on four hundred pounds, he has to take off the little weights and put on the fifty-pound weights."

At this point the front door closed and everybody but Jim was looking in the direction of Bentley and O'Reilly.

"And what does he do then?" Jim continued, unaware of the distraction. "He takes all the weights off one end of the bar and the other end tips and the whole thing comes crashing to the floor! Ha! Ha! Ha! What a dumb ass!" Jim delivered the punch line to the woman's prominent cleavage, as if expecting from it some kind of appreciation.

"Is there something you want?" she said, icily.

Startled out of his performance, Jim followed the woman's eyes to the front door and the two detectives.

They approached the group and showed their badges. "I'm Detective Bentley and this is Detective O'Reilly. We're looking for Mike Ironside."

"Uh, Mike's not here," Jim said.

Bentley lifted the collar of Jim's colorful Hawaiian shirt and flipped it derisively. "Who are you, Don Ho?"

"I'm Jim Wilson. What can I do for you?"

"You can start by telling me who's selling you your steroids."

"Have you got a search warrant?" the woman spoke up.

Bentley turned a lascivious eye toward her. "I don't think you have anything to worry about, Wonder Woman. I can see you have nothing to hide."

"Oh, look at the time," said one of the men. "Come on, Sherry. We better get going."

Quick as a boa constrictor, Bentley grabbed the man's twenty-inch bicep and stopped him in his tracks. "Did I say you could go?" said Bentley, almost in a whisper. The other bodybuilder was shorter, but there was something dangerous that shone in his eyes and he seemed ready to spring. Bentley released the man's arm and smiled. "Like I said, we're looking for Mike Ironside. Actually, we were hoping Mike would know something about a golf pro named Steven Merritt." He whipped out a photo and held it up for them to see. "Maybe one of you knows him. He's about five-foot-ten, dark hair, sharp dresser, sells steroids and sometimes a little coke?"

"Hey, we're not into that," said Wonder Woman.

"No, I suppose you're built like Mike Tyson because you eat right and do aerobics twice a week," Bentley fired back.

"Come on, Detective," said the man with twenty-inch biceps. "We don't know this guy Merritt. We're just here to buy clothes."

Bentley said, "I hear the circus is in town. Maybe they'll sell you a tent, Fat Boy. All right, take off. We need to talk with our friend Jim here."

The three waddled out the door, their overdeveloped triceps holding their arms out at their sides and their huge thighs swishing together as they walked.

Jim shrugged his mountainous shoulders. "Geeze, I don't

know what else to tell you, Detectives. Mike's not here and I don't know this dead guy. I'm not from around here anyway," Jim rattled on nervously. "I came down from Mankato, Minnesota last year to check out the scene at Muscle Beach. You know, sun, sand, and babes in bikinis? Sorry I can't help you."

Bentley looked him squarely in the eye and smiled. "Geeze, ya know, I don't think we said anything about Steve bein' dead," he said, mocking Jim's Minnesota accent.

Jim got a stricken look on his face. "Well, I—I assumed he must be or you wouldn't be—you know . . ."

"Well, I think you do know him," Bentley pressed on. "I think you or somebody you know has bought steroids or cocaine from him. And I think you know somebody who didn't like him."

"I never bought anything from him. Honest."

Bentley softened. "Hey, we know Merritt was a first class prick. You're right. He's dead. And he probably had it coming. But we have to find out who did it. And your name is going to stay on the list until you give us a name to replace it."

Jim stood frozen with his big hands stuck halfway into the inadequately small pockets of his jeans. He stared into Bentley's eyes like a deer caught in a car's headlights.

"Hey, what do we have here?" O'Reilly pointed to something glinting behind the counter. He reached down and pulled out a gleaming silver-colored golf putter.

"Well, well, well," said Bentley. "You don't see one of these every day, do you?" He took the club from O'Reilly and held it up admiringly in front of Jim. "I could sure go for something like this, Jim. Where in the world could I get one like it?"

"I don't know," Jim said, still staring. "This one belongs

to Mike."

"And Mike knows Steve Merritt, doesn't he?" said Bentley. "And maybe Mike knows Steve's killer. And maybe you do too?" Bentley shook the club under Jim's nose. "So where the hell did he get this thing?"

Jim's voice shook. "There was a guy who came here. He was dressed like a gangster—"

"And he sold the putter to Mike," Bentley interrupted.

"No!" Jim practically wailed. "The guy wouldn't sell it to him. I thought he was going to. But suddenly, it seemed like he got mad at Mike for some reason. I don't know why. And then he just left."

"Then he and Mike met later and made a deal?" said Bentley.

"No. Mike had to drive to the home office, near a golf course someplace, and buy it directly from them."

"But this gangster-looking guy and Mike knew each other from before," Bentley pressed.

"No, I don't think so."

Bentley pantomimed a putt in Jim's direction. "But you are going to tell me where Mike is now. And you are going to tell me where you know Steve Merritt from, aren't you Jim?"

Jim sighed heavily. "Mike's at the spa over on Crenshaw. You can ask the big fat guy, Kenny, where he is. Like I told you, I didn't know Steve Merritt. I saw him once at the sporting goods store, The Final Buzzer. He was talking with the owner, Eddie Minetti. I don't know what it was about. Mike says Merritt was nobody to mess with and I never had nothing to do with him. Honest. But Mike will kill me if you tell him I told you any of this."

"Then if you turn up dead, Mike will be our first suspect." Bentley tossed the platinum putter to Jim and the two detectives turned and left. When they got into the car, O'Reilly chuckled.

"It looks like Simon is one step ahead of you."

"Well, he would be. He *is* the goddamned murderer!" Bentley growled.

O'Reilly nodded. "Either that, or he's looking for the murderer too."

Chapter 23

Even in the living room in apartment 210, the air was scented with the smells of garlic and ginger, fried pork and teriyaki. But in the kitchen, the smell hung thick as fog in Long Beach harbor. Mrs. Nhey spoke only Cambodian, but through her interpreter, her eight-year-old grandson, she expressed her great displeasure at having her kitchen sink stopped up. Simultaneously translating, the boy explained that it was not her fault that water from her sink ran over onto their kitchen floor and through the dining room ceiling in the apartment below. She had been calling all day, but nobody answered. The landlord buys cheap garbage disposers, so what does he expect?

"Please tell your grandmother I am very sorry for the inconvenience and I will fix her disposer as quickly as I can," said Simon. He knew he had been neglecting his duties as maintenance man for the apartment complex. Before, when a tenant called about a problem, he was usually at home, reading the *Bhagavad Gita* or the *Tibetan Book of the Dead* and he could be on it right away. But now, he had to work in repairing leaky faucets and jammed locks in between selling platinum golf putters to Chinese underworld figures and investigating a murder. Having a regular job was proving inconvenient.

The boy spoke in an even, adult manner to his grandmother and listened gravely to her reply. He turned to Simon, "My grandmother says you are not to blame. No

one can blame a crazy man who talks to his cat—ah! Sorry."
The boy corrected himself. "I mean, a man who discusses
with his cat." Mrs. Nhey added something and the boy
smiled. "She says you talk and the cat talks back. So you are
a little crazy and a little . . . uh . . . holy, I think she means."
Simon bowed in Mrs. Nhey's direction and she shuffled
back three steps. She muttered something else. "My grandmother says it is her duty to make noodles tonight, so please
hurry."

Simon opened the cabinet under the kitchen sink to get
access to the garbage disposer. But it was crammed with
bottles of detergent, a shiny, square three-liter can of soy-
bean oil, rags, a bar of soap bearing Hindu letters, and
roughly a bushel of onions, some of which were sprouting.
He turned to Mrs. Nhey to ask her permission to remove
the things, or to ask her pardon. He suppressed the impulse
to say it in Spanish because he couldn't speak Cambodian
and merely bowed again. Carefully, Simon laid out the
items one by one on the kitchen floor. Mrs. Nhey hovered
over him and scowled.

Simon scooted under the sink on his back. Holding a
small flashlight in his mouth, he inserted a hex key into
the opening in the bottom of the garbage disposer. It
turned, but with difficulty. He noticed that the red circuit
breaker button was out. There was no getting around it.
The thing was jammed and he was going to have to get inside it. He reached into his pocket to see if he had remembered to bring a crescent wrench, but there was nothing in
there but a thick clump of hundred-dollar bills from the
day's sales.

"Damn!" he whispered to himself.

"You can't curse in this house!" the boy enunciated
loudly.

The grandmother became agitated and they conversed in rapid sentences.

The boy looked sheepish. "My grandmother says you may curse if you like because you are touched with the spirit." He glared resentfully in Simon's direction. "That means you're crazy," he said.

"Please accept my apologies," Simon said to the boy who was clearly not a mere boy at all, but an officious little adult embarrassed to inhabit the body of an eight-year-old. "I'm Simon. May I ask your name?"

"I know who you are and you couldn't pronounce my name if I told you." Then, as if suddenly aware of his bad manners, he added, "You can call me Ek."

"Well, then, Ek, how long has the disposer been broken?"

Ek considered the matter carefully. "I think nine or eleven days," he said. "Do you have a cold? You talk funny."

Simon was breathing through his mouth to keep from inhaling the fetid air that hung over the sink, which was nearly overflowing with putrid water. Disposers always contained some decaying food. It came with the territory. But this one had been clogged and rotting for over a week. Simon sighed, unplugged the unit, and wriggled out from under the sink. He stood over the filmy, gray water, half expecting to see a salamander lurking beneath the surface. The smell was so thick and powerful he could practically taste it. In order to unclog the pipes, he was going to have to stick his arm into the water and into the decaying sludge of the disposer.

"Don't be such a wimp."

Simon turned to the boy who regarded him with a blank expression. Clearly, it wasn't Mrs. Nhey who had spoken.

"Did you say something?" he asked Ek.

"Of course I did. I asked you if you have a cold. Well, do you have a cold?"

I've been working too hard, Simon thought. I have been sleeping so little that my subconscious voice sounds real. "Maybe I'm a little stuffed up," he said. And, once again, he regarded the festering sink with dread.

"So now you've got a pocket full of easy money, you think you're too good to work for a living?" said the voice.

Simon closed his eyes and said a silent "Aum" to clear his head.

"Look, the lady has to fix noodles for a family of seven. It's her job. So why don't you do your job and stick your arm into that muck and fix her sink?"

Simon gazed into the murky water. "Who are you?" he asked.

"My name is Ek!" said the boy. "I told you that already. You're weird."

Simon gripped the edge of the sink to keep his balance. He took a deep breath.

Mrs. Nhey said something. Ek said, "My grandmother wants to know if you have to make pee."

"Uh, no. No thanks," said Simon.

"Will you stick your hand in the blasted sink already?" demanded the voice.

Simon plunged his arm through the gray water and into the cavity of the disposer. His fingers slid into a slimy mass of tightly packed particles that felt like maggots. He drew back his arm with what proved to be a handful of rotting rice. The smell was overwhelming.

"Pe—euw!" exclaimed Ek.

Exerting great self-control, Simon carefully tore off a paper towel from the holder on the wall, placed it on the counter, and deposited the rice on it. He repeated his expedition into the disposer until all the rice was removed and lying in a reeking heap on the paper towel.

"Now that wasn't so bad, was it?" said the voice.

"Are you nuts?" Simon said.

"Are you calling me 'nuts'?" demanded Ek.

Mrs. Nhey reached over Simon's shoulder, snatched up the towel with the rice, and disappeared outside with it. Again, Simon crawled under the sink. He plugged in the disposer and started to slide out.

"Don't forget to reset the breaker," said the voice.

"Oh, that's right," said Simon and pushed in the red breaker button.

"You are calling me nuts?" said Ek in disbelief.

"Sorry," said Simon. "I was just talking to myself."

Ek snorted. "I have a gerbil. You want to talk to him?"

Simon flipped the disposer switch. There was a muffled whir and the murky water churned and drained away, leaving behind a heavy scum and a swampy smell. He ran a little fresh water over his hands and wiped them off on a paper towel. Mrs. Nhey reappeared and glared at him.

"Please tell your grandmother that her sink is fixed and she can make noodles now," said Simon to Ek.

The boy translated and his grandmother replied. "My grandmother says she changed her mind about the noodles. She wants rice for dinner." Simon felt his stomach convulse. Ek grinned. "Only joke." Mrs. Nhey cracked a sly smile.

"All right, then," said Simon. "Well, thanks for your help." He extended his hand to Ek.

The boy looked in disgust at the hand that had been covered in rotten rice. "I don't think so!" he said.

Simon bowed awkwardly and headed back to his own

apartment. There, he washed his hands again and flopped into his favorite chair next to Cayce.

"Who is the man?" demanded Cayce.

"What man?" said Simon.

"You brought a man into our house. I don't know him. Is he a friend?"

Simon arched his back, sore from crawling under Mrs. Nhey's sink. "There's no man, Cayce. What are you talking about?"

Cayce crept around to the front of the chair as if hiding from something. "The fog man. Behind you!"

Simon whirled around to face the fog man but saw nothing. "Cayce?" Simon said cautiously. "Why do you call him the 'fog man'?"

Picking up on Simon's apprehension, Cayce let out a low growl. "I can see through him. Like fog."

"Oh, where are my manners?" said Hogan, suddenly materializing. Despite being translucent and slightly out of focus, Hogan had a substantial quality about him. He was of medium height and compactly built. He stood squarely with his arms akimbo, hovering a little above the carpet. He was wearing a white tam with a knit shirt and short golfing trousers with argyle socks. He smiled triumphantly.

"Oh, boy," said Simon, sliding out of the chair and backing toward the door.

"Don't get up," said the voice. "It's okay, Cayce. I am a friend."

"You can talk to cats, too?" asked Simon, temporarily forgetting that he was having a conversation with a ghost.

"Oh, yes. I enjoy talking with cats. I used to like dogs, but now I find they don't have much interesting to say."

"Stupid dogs," Cayce concurred.

"By the way," said the voice, "my name is Ben Hogan."

"Meow," said Cayce.

"The pleasure is all mine," said Mr. Hogan.

"You're my spirit guide?" asked Simon.

"Well, I used to be a professional golfer. But since I died, I've had to retrain."

There was a knock at the door. Simon hesitated, but decided to answer it. When he opened the door, there was Detective Bob Bentley and he did not look happy. Bentley strode in without being invited.

"I just wanted you to know, it's only a matter of time until I get you. You left a trail a mile wide and I'm closing in fast." He sniffed. "Christ! What's that smell? Are you hiding a corpse in here someplace?"

"You don't smell all that good to me either," quipped Mr. Hogan. "Don't worry, Cayce. He can't hear us."

Simon held out his hands. "Sorry to disappoint you, Detective. I just cleaned out a garbage disposer and I'm afraid it was a little ripe."

"I could get a search warrant," Bentley threatened.

"You'll never take me alive," said Hogan, cracking up.

"Do you mind?" Simon said to Hogan, getting annoyed.

"It's no trouble, believe me," said Bentley.

Cayce jumped down from the chair to get closer to the action. "Berk!" he exclaimed, landing heavily on his front paws.

"Cute cat," said Bentley.

"Big feet!" enthused Cayce, examining Bentley's size fourteen wingtips.

Simon stuck his hands in his pockets. "What exactly did you come here for?"

Bentley got a sly look in his eye. "Let's just say I can practically prove that you have been consorting with known criminals."

144

"Well, so have you," said Hogan.

"Will you please stay out of this?" Simon said to Hogan.

"Don't fight!" said Cayce.

"And that goes for you, too, Cayce. I'm trying to talk with Detective Bentley."

Bentley looked around the room for a clue as to whom Simon might be speaking. Suddenly, he brightened. "Oh, I get it," he said. "You're talking to imaginary playmates, planning to set up an insanity defense. Well, you can forget it. I'm way ahead of you."

Hogan walked over to Bentley, paused, then stepped inside him. Cayce ran and hid under the chair. Bentley shivered. "Jesus! Why don't you turn off your air conditioning?" As Bentley spoke, Simon could see his breath. He twitched and shivered again. "Well, uh, I've got to go." Bentley backed unsteadily toward the door, leaving Hogan standing in his place. He turned and practically fled out the door. "And don't leave town!" he called over his shoulder, sounding a little shaky.

Hogan said, "You know, if you did leave town, I think he'd miss you."

Simon sat down heavily in his chair and Cayce came out of hiding and hopped in his lap. "Well, I wouldn't miss him. He's starting to get on my nerves."

"Was I supposed to bite him?" Cayce asked.

Simon rubbed the bristly spot between Cayce's ears. "You did just fine." A car drove up the lane to the apartment complex parking lot and its headlights swept past Simon's door and right through Mr. Hogan. "What exactly was that trick you did with Bentley?"

Hogan pushed back his hat. "Oh, that was nothing much. I was sort of getting under his skin, you might say. I was curious about just how guilty he thinks you are."

"You mean you could read his mind?" asked Simon.

"No, nothing so precise as that. Only a gut reaction that he has more questions than answers about this case. I also got the feeling that he is not a half-bad fellow. Wouldn't you say, Cayce?"

"Me too," Cayce concurred.

Simon frowned. "That's easy enough for you to say, Mr. Hogan. He's not trying to put you in prison for murder."

"In any case, we've got work to do!" Hogan tried to clap in an expression of enthusiasm, but there was no sound from his ghostly hands. He looked at them in dismay. "I don't mind all that much not being alive," he said. "But I still do miss the little things."

Chapter 24

Zelda sat at her desk with her spindly arms outstretched, as if trying to cover all the ledgers and loose papers at once. She was wearing a snakeskin print rayon sheath dress with matching shoes. The dress hung loosely on her gaunt frame, perhaps too formal for office wear. At forty-eight, Zelda was not an altogether unattractive woman. She had large, hypnotic violet eyes that could still stop a man in his tracks. Her voice was melodious, almost soothing, when it suited her purpose. Zelda had lovely straight black hair, probably dyed, that hung past her shoulders, and brilliant white teeth. An ever-present cigarette smoldered in the ashtray, sending a sinuous plume of smoke slithering under her chin and up the side of her hollow cheek. She smiled coyly up at Mr. Z who stood over her, attempting to steal a glance down the scoop neck of her dress.

"Really, Yakov!" Zelda chided, cigarette smoke leaking from her thin lips. "I couldn't possibly burden Pater with all this stuff."

"But bookkeeping needs your end-of-the-month statement so we can file our quarterly report," said Mr. Z, still leering.

Zelda batted her artificial eyelashes. "I'll tell you what? I'll sort through all these boring old papers and make a file of everything that might be useful."

"You have so much other work to do, Zelda. Why not let Pater go through the papers and pick out what he needs?"

Zelda hunched her shoulders as if in a gesture of in-decision, making the neckline of her dress bow outward. "Well, I suppose I could. But you know I don't mind going the extra mile for you, Yakov." Again, she batted her violet eyes.

Mr. Z peeked down her dress past her prominent collar-bone to her lacy black bra, which appeared barely convex and hopelessly opaque. Zelda watched for a reaction to register on his face.

Mr. Z flushed. "I guess I don't see why not," he said. "In fact, you could bring the papers to my house tonight. I'll make you my special mutton sausage goulash. It's a little spicy. But if it makes you too hot, I have a nice Hun-garian wine that should help." He chuckled nervously.

Zelda still held Mr. Z transfixed with her eyes. "That's very gracious of you, Yakov, but you know I can't leave my daughter Crystal alone."

"She's twenty-nine years old!" exclaimed Mr. Z, a bit louder than he intended.

Suddenly, there was something touchingly melancholy in those violet pools. Tears welled up, threatening to make their color run. "I've told you how vulnerable she is," said Zelda, her voice wavering. "Ever since her father died, Crystal has been susceptible to the charms of artistic young men who, shall we say, lack professional ambition."

"And money?" offered Mr. Z.

"I'm afraid so," said Zelda. "So I'm sorry I have to de-cline your kind offer as long as Crystal and I are forced to fend for ourselves alone." She managed a pitiful smile and her perfect teeth glistened.

"All that girl needs to bring her out of her shell," said Mr. Z, "is a real man."

Zelda dabbed her eyes with the corner of a tissue. "Perhaps you're right, Yakov. But where can a woman find such a man?"

Alternating glances between Zelda's eyes and the front of her dress, Mr. Z adjusted his tie. He was breathing heavily now and spoke in short bursts. "Zelda, my lamb. I can solve your problem. I know just the man. Crystal will like him. He has money. You must give me a chance—I mean, give him a chance."

"Who is he?" demanded Zelda, the softness suddenly gone from her voice.

"Oh, my little cabbage! Wait and see. I'll bring him tonight. Then you and I can be together. At your house. I'll cook for you. We'll balance the books. Even if it takes all night!"

The limpid pools of Zelda's violet eyes iced over. "Nobody had better mess with my little girl."

"I swear to you," implored Mr. Z. "He is a gentleman. He has a future. I'll bring him tonight at eight o'clock. You'll see."

"Yes," said Zelda, her long, artificial nails, digging into her palms. "We'll see."

Chapter 25

Madame Samantha sat behind her massive oak desk and scowled. Her oversized horn-rimmed glasses made her look like a disgruntled owl. She was around fifty years old, with a healthy glow to her slightly plump cheeks. She was wearing a floppy Land's End hat and a loose-fitting sweatshirt with a picture of a bear sending smoke signals. The caption read, "Send more Indians." Two sides of the office were lined with books. On one wall hung complex-looking astrology charts and a couple of posters of photos taken from the Hubble telescope, along with several photos of herself with famous actors and a state senator. There was also a diploma from M.I.T.

"Louise said you were in trouble," said Madame Samantha to Simon flatly. "Something about a murdered colleague." She took off her owl glasses and glared at him. "I'll tell you right now, I don't get involved in open murder investigations. I don't care who your grandmother is. And if you were thinking I am the Good Witch of the North and I'm going to just click my ruby slippers and whisk you back to Kansas or Iowa or wherever you're from, you can forget it."

"I'll pay you five hundred dollars. In cash." Simon laid five crisp hundred-dollar bills on her tidy desk. "Grandma Louise said you were the best."

Madame Samantha stared at the money and sighed. "Oh, what the hell!" she said. "Sit down."

Simon handed her the personnel file he had on Steve Merritt. Madame Samantha took the whole file without reading a word of it, tapped the pages on the desktop to straighten them, and dropped the stack into the sheet feeder of a scanner. As it whirred into motion, she slid back a panel on the wall to reveal a computer the size of a side-by-side refrigerator. Simon gaped at it.

"You like it?" asked Madame Samantha. She punched a few buttons and waited for a response from the machine. "It's got twelve parallel processors and enough juice to generate climate prediction models or beat what's-his-name Kasparov in chess." She grinned. "I made it myself."

"It's just that . . . that . . ." Simon stammered.

"It's just that you wouldn't think an astrologer would use a computer? Think of it as my crystal ball."

In a few minutes, the printer shot out a stack of pages, containing text, flow charts, Venn diagrams, and streams of mystical-looking astrological symbols. Madame Samantha sat studying the pages and tapping her front teeth absentmindedly with a silvery Cross pen.

"Caput Algol," she muttered to herself.

"A ghoul, what?" Simon startled out of his reverie.

"Algol," enunciated Madame Samantha. " 'The demon.' It's Arabic. There's a nasty character behind this business and it's not your friend, Steve Merritt. Oh, he's no prince, believe me. I mean, look at his Mars—it's out of bounds. He probably exhibited some wild behavior. And there's Saturn conjunct Jupiter in the Seventh House. Pluto—conjunct the part of commerce." Madame Samantha was getting excited. "Somebody he knew killed him for money."

"Isn't that the usual reason?" Simon saw nothing to get excited about yet.

"I think I'm beginning to see who this guy was," said

Madame Samantha, ignoring Simon. "He has Leo on the Tenth House, Pisces on the Fifth. Probably did something escapist or recreational for a living—maybe near water, or a golf course." Simon perked up. "He worked out a lot— probably alone. He was not what you'd call sociable. He was smooth, but people didn't trust him." She tapped significantly on Steve's Zodiac chart. "Aries, the sign of self-promotion. This guy was some kind of hustler." Madame Samantha skimmed over a couple of pages and stopped. "And here! I was wondering when we'd get to this. Stevie had a girlfriend. And she was old enough to be his mom!"

"Where do you see that?" demanded Simon, looking over her shoulder.

"And is she ever a piece of work!" Madame Samantha continued. "Rigid, controlling . . . Capricorn . . . with Leo . . ." She seemed to be reading the symbols as if they were sentences. "And she was a jealous old bitch, too! Of course, she didn't really love him any more than he loved her. But she wanted to own him."

"What did he see in her?" asked Simon, as if the astrologer actually knew Steve and could discuss the intimate details of his life.

Madame Samantha shook her head. "I don't know. She had something he wanted, all right. It looks like she was into banking or bookkeeping. Maybe he was using her to get at some money. Maybe he just liked older women."

"Did she kill him?"

"Hard to say. It looks like they had some good fights. Over other women, I'd say. She probably gave him money, bought him clothes, heaped guilt on him, and made his life a living hell. But kill him? She'd have to have a better reason than jealousy. No, this was about money."

"You can tell all that from those squiggles?" asked Simon incredulously.

"Oh, Jesus!" exclaimed Madame Samantha. "Look, his Moon in Taurus is in close aspect to his Mars." She waited for a reaction. "Taurus is the sign symbolic of the throat." She gulped. "Did Steve have his, you know, throat cut or something?"

Simon looked pale.

Samantha shuffled her papers and muttered to herself. "Scorpio is on the Ascendant. Eighth House. Venus in the Seventh House in mutual reception with Mercury. Mercury in Aries."

"You think you could connect the dots for me here?" Simon asked impatiently.

Madame Samantha glowered over her owl glasses. "I'm an astrologer, you know, not the six o'clock news. I deal in cosmic forces, not facts. But I'll tell you one thing," she said significantly. "If you find the killer's nosy neighbor, you'll find the killer."

"What?" exclaimed Simon, exasperated. "That's like saying if I find the killer's bedroom slippers, I'll find the killer. If I'm close enough to find the nosy neighbor, it's no great navigational trick to find the killer too!"

"All I'm saying is that the stars indicate that the killer probably has a nosy neighbor who has clues about the crime."

"Okay, so how do I find this neighbor?"

Samantha slipped the five hundred-dollar bills into her desk drawer and gazed evasively at one of the Hubble photos. "I know somebody who's a dowser."

"If the killer's neighbor is an artesian well, we're in luck!"

"There's a palm reader who owes me a favor."

Simon stood in front of the Hubble photo. "I don't think you understand my situation. I'm about to be arrested for a murder I didn't commit. My girlfriend left me for consorting with criminals, and I'm being followed around by the ghost of a legendary golfer."

Madame Samantha's eyes narrowed. "Your grandma warned me you were a strange one. She gave me your birth date and I took the liberty of running your chart."

"Isn't there something you can tell me—I mean about Steve?" Simon pleaded.

She studied Steve's chart a moment. "I don't know if this helps you, but Steve had the materialistic star Canopus in the Twelfth House. That might indicate some kind of addiction. I'd say gambling."

Simon shrugged. "Well, I suppose that's something." He turned for the door.

"Just one more thing," Samantha called. "You're a cop, right?"

"I sell platinum-plated golf putters," he said, puzzled.

"FBI?"

"No."

"CIA?"

"Nope."

Madame Samantha took off her oversized glasses. The dark circles under her eyes made her gaze particularly penetrating. "Look," she said, "you can't fool me. You've got Aries on your Sixth House cusp with Mars in Aries. That means a profession, not a hobby, in law enforcement. And your Pluto is in the First House of Sagittarius—you're a searcher, but trouble finds you. You're a cop all right," Samantha declared. "Or you ought to be."

Chapter 26

Detective O'Reilly ran his long hairy fingers over the computer keyboard and squinted at the columns of numbers. "It doesn't add up," O'Reilly declared. "Even if you don't count the income he must have made from selling steroids, it doesn't add up."

Bob Bentley shifted his bulk impatiently, towering over O'Reilly's desk. "It doesn't take H&R Block to figure out this guy Merritt was cooking his books. Why are we wasting our time on accounting? We should be tailing that weirdo Simon."

O'Reilly clicked away on the keyboard with remarkable speed, ignoring his partner's protestations. "It shows here that Merritt declared his income as a golf pro and even an additional eight thousand dollars in miscellaneous income he got from a part-time job selling powerboats."

"What a shame he died before he got a good citizenship award. Now can we hit the street?"

O'Reilly pointed to the screen. "Here's a guy making almost ninety thousand dollars a year and he's driving a ten-year-old Monte Carlo and living in a four-hundred-dollar-a-month dump in Inglewood. And look here: he's got two hundred fifty dollars in his checking account, no savings, and his credit cards are maxed."

"Coke don't grow on trees," observed Bentley. "And we know he was a sharp dresser. He ate good. Come on, the guy was high maintenance."

"Merritt wasn't a user. He may have sold the stuff occasionally, but the autopsy showed no sign of drug abuse of any kind. And as far as the clothes, remember Mike Ironside said he donated all of Steve's clothes as a promotional write-off."

"Yeah, and I suppose Merritt donated steroids to Ironside's customers. What's all this number-crunching supposed to prove?"

O'Reilly leaned back in his chair. "Well, I don't know that it proves anything, Bob. But I'm just saying, the guy doesn't have much to show for his money."

"What about broads?"

O'Reilly twisted his spindly frame to face Bentley. "Did you say 'broads'? Where do you pick up this stuff—Humphrey Bogart movies?" O'Reilly lowered his voice to a whisper. "You can't say 'broads.' What if a female officer overheard you? There'd be a lawsuit and you'd be busted down to directing traffic."

Bentley sneered. "Sometimes, O'Reilly, I think *you* must be a female officer—and a goddamned hairy ugly broad at that."

"In any case," said O'Reilly, "everything we found so far would suggest that Merritt was mostly a loner."

Bentley shrugged. "Drug dealer types like Merritt all have Swiss bank accounts or money stashed in the Cayman Islands. Anyway, who cares? The poor bastard's dead while his killer is walking around free."

"All I'm saying is that there is more to this than meets the eye. I say, follow the money and we find the killer."

"And all I'm saying is that if we follow Simon, we find the killer—and probably a dozen other major criminals. The captain should assign a whole department to that guy."

Bentley stepped back and cocked his head. "Wait a minute. Turn sideways. Now arch your back." He whistled. "You know, O'Reilly, if you'd shave your wrists, you wouldn't make a bad-looking broad at that."

Chapter 27

Simon adjusted the white tie on his gangster suit and pressed the doorbell. He hadn't had time to change and came right from work. Mr. Z had said something about dinner, but seemed uncharacteristically formal, almost apologetic about it. In spite of all the money Simon was bringing in for the company, Mr. Z had never before invited him to a social occasion.

Simon had never given much thought to Mr. Z's home, but he would not have guessed his boss would live in a place like this. The modest three-bedroom stucco was painted a stony dark gray. Steel bars covered the doors and downstairs windows. Even the door to the attached garage was fitted with an elaborate grid of bars and armor plating, making it look more like a drawbridge than a garage door. Instead of flowers and decorative shrubbery, the perimeter of the house was lined with cactuses and other spiny plants. The whole effect was curiously gothic.

Near the front door was a large, artificial pond that gurgled thickly from under a layer of unhealthy-looking green algae. Simon peered into the Zen-looking, stone-faced pond, straining to see in the dimming daylight what might be living in its murky depths. An enormous black catfish, the size of a Thanksgiving turkey, slid slowly into view and suddenly caught Simon's gaze in its fierce, cold-blooded eyes. Simon jumped back as if the giant catfish had been guarding the door and about to leap for his throat.

"Who's there? What are you doing?" a voice called out from the vicinity of the second-story balcony next door.

"The fish . . . I . . . it was looking at me and . . ." Simon stuttered.

"What did you say?" the voice demanded. "What do you want?"

"I'm here for dinner with my boss, Mr. Z, and—"

"Oh, you mean that big Russian who sells golf clubs. Why didn't you say so? Watch out for those people. It's a strange household. Believe me, I know!"

Simon heard a window slam. Just then, the front door opened and Mr. Z stuck out his head. "Simon, my boy, come in, come in. What's the matter with you? Who were you talking to? What are you doing over there?"

Simon staggered toward the door. "Uh, the neighbor. Do you know there's a sea monster in your pond?"

Mr. Z dragged Simon inside. "As usual, I have no idea what you're talking about," he said. "But we have a nice Bulgarian goulash for you—no meat! I made it myself!" Mr. Z sat Simon down in a straight-backed wooden chair. "Wait here, I want to introduce you to somebody."

A circular antique iron chandelier hung from the ceiling. Instead of light bulbs, it was lit with four yellowish candles that sputtered softly and gave off a sallow glow. The walls in the narrow living room were covered in a mossy, dark green flocked wallpaper. No pictures hung on the walls, but several small paintings, as well as an authentic-looking Russian icon and a set of leather-bound books, were enclosed in a massive display case that nearly reached the nine-foot ceiling. Formal Victorian chairs, none facing each other, were pushed against the walls. There was a delicate eighteenth-century mahogany display table on top of which rested what appeared to be a stuffed iguana.

The floor was made of irregular flagstones, accented in the center by a hand-woven Oriental rug. Simon had gotten up to inspect the lifelike lizard when he noticed that the round tabletop bore an intricately carved and painted design. At first glance, Simon thought it was a model of a Mayan calendar. But upon closer examination, it appeared to be a Tibetan mandala. He picked up the iguana to get a better look.

Now he could make out the four concentric circles that surrounded the eight Buddhas, representing the various points of the compass. In the center was the symbol of the Buddha. Guarding the center were the four gatekeepers, carved fierce and forbidding. From his studies in college, Simon recognized this as a Vairocana mandala, containing merely thirteen deities, instead of a hundred or more, common in many Tibetan mandalas. It is connected with the Buddha Vajrasattiva, who represents the origin of crystalline purity.

Simon recalled that a mandala is an imaginary palace on which a meditator contemplates, in some ways, like a rosary. The meditator is guided in his contemplation by the symbols of the mandala. Before arriving spiritually at the gates of the palace, he must pass the outer circles of purifying wisdom, the vajra circle, the circle of eight tombs, and the lotus circle.

The mandala was beautifully carved and, like much of the room's other furnishings, probably not as old as it appeared. The four outer rings—the fire ring, the vajra circle, the tombs ring, and the lotus circle—were made of brightly colored enameled brass. The purifying fire ring was colored with alternating bands of red and yellow. The vajra, symbolizing strength and fearlessness, was decorated with colored symbols: a blue diamond, a red Dharma wheel, a yellow bell, a green thunderbolt, and a white lotus. The tombs circle depicted the eight states of consciousness which the meditator must transcend: seeing, hearing, tasting, smelling, the consciousness of the body, of thinking, of the self, and basic consciousness. The symbols were irregularly spaced and there seemed to be more of the "self" symbols (depicted as human faces in different profiles) than the others. The lotus circle was made up of small bands, each of a different color.

Next to the mandala, written in gold in a careful hand, was the ancient Sanskrit Hymn to Vairocana. It began:

> *Om, homage to the glorious paradox!*
> *Follow me now, and look,*
> *We pass through the gateway*
> *At the crown of Golden Manjusri*
> *And enter the vast mandala of the Conquerors . . .*

Simon had studied the hymn in college, but smiled to think he would still remember so much Sanskrit all these years later. He touched the fire circle to feel the glossy enamel. To his surprise, it turned. In fact, the ring turned with remarkable ease, gliding apparently on ball bearings, as smoothly as a bicycle wheel.

Curious, Simon tried the other wheels. The vajra turned with some difficulty and clicked to a stop as each symbol came to rest beneath the central deity at the top of the mandala. But the tombs and lotus circles both turned freely. Simon spun the fire circle and watched the bands blink red and yellow. Why did the artist go to such great pains to make the mandala's circles spin? What purpose could it serve? he wondered.

Absentmindedly, he spun the fire ring again, but faster

this time. The red and yellow bands flickered hypnotically. Slowly, he read the second stanza.

> *We enter the vast mandala of the Conquerors,*
> *And we turn its great turning—*
> *We follow the sun's turning*
> *On through dawn of unshakeability*
> *On through the midday of heart that gives all*
> *On through the dusk of deep love and stillness*
> *On through the night of no fear, the hand across the void*
> *We follow the turning of the sun.*

Simon relaxed his eyes so that they ceased to track the individual bands of red and yellow, until the colors blended together to form a smear of green. He stared until the momentum of the fire wheel wore down and its individual colors returned. Looking at the three other circles, Simon noticed that the lightning bolt in the vajra circle bore the same verdant green as the fire wheel's blended colors. Of course, he thought. The thunderbolt was once the symbol of Indra, the god of storms, pictured with four arms, one of which carries a net of illusions. A fitting player in such a riddle, thought Simon. He rotated the vajra circle until it reached the top of the mandala. It clicked. But Simon was disappointed, expecting something more. "We follow the turning of the sun," he said to himself, repeating the recurring theme in the hymn. "East to west," he said. On impulse, he rotated the vajra wheel from left to right one full revolution until it once again stopped at the top of the mandala. It clunked solidly like the sound of lock tumblers falling into place.

Excitedly, as quickly as he could, Simon read the rest of the hymn for other clues. But nothing seemed to jump out at him. One stanza began:

And outside the cave, in brilliant blue and sunlight
Sits the Illuminator
In the sunlight sits the Illuminator on a throne of white,
   white, gold
And he is so white
Almost you cannot see him . . .

The last stanza did sound promising, but if it contained any answer, he missed it. Part of it read:

All homage to the Illuminator
Who, smiling, holds wheel, spiral, and mandala
Like a puzzle, in his hands of truth
And turns it, like a key in the lock of our heart's eye . . .

It was a puzzle all right! In frustration, he spun the tombs circle and watched the blur of symbols. Simon happened to glance up at the green lightning bolt and noticed that if he stared at it, he could see the individual symbols blur by. As the wheel slowed, he found that the "self" symbols made a kind of movie, like a deck of those novelty cards he played with as a kid, with slightly different individual pictures that seem to move when flipped in sequence. The head, in profile to the right, appeared to turn toward him until it faced him. Eerily, it seemed to stare at him a moment, then looked off to the upper left on the mandala. This pattern repeated until the wheel lost momentum and the tomb circle's other seven symbols again came into view.

Simon figured there must be some significance to where the "self" was looking. But the upper left corner was blank, as if the artist had abandoned the project before it was finished.

Simon spun the lotus circle and watched as the rainbow of colors streaked dizzyingly around the mandala. He spun it faster and the colors began to blend together. He stopped the wheel with his hand. Then with one hand on each side, while still holding the stuffed iguana, he spun the lotus wheel with a quick snapping motion. Instantly, the many-colored lotus circle went white.

Simon was stricken with a kind of panic, like vertigo. If he had taken the time to think about it, he would have remembered that white light is made up of all colors. But he felt as if he had just fallen through a trap door and wasn't thinking calmly.

Simon stared transfixed at the rapidly spinning lotus circle, now a whirl of white light. It was all he could see at first. He had lost his bearings. It was like a seizure. Like a subject in a sensory deprivation experiment, Simon felt he was floating and his mind yearned for some sensory stimulation to fix upon. He thought of the brightly colored mandala, that fanciful palace with its elaborate gates, the home of gods and the treasury of spiritual bliss. In his mind, Simon saw the two-dimensional representation of the palace take shape as a solid, three-dimensional structure. The fire circle was a hedge of real fire. Inside it, the vajra glistened hard and still as diamonds. The tombs circle was made up of lifelike statues, tall and forbidding, whose eyes followed him as the circle revolved slowly around the palace. The lotus circle was a wall of pure white.

Simon suddenly found himself inside the mandala. He was not so much surprised to discover that he had entered the imaginary building as relieved that he was somehow transported inside the impenetrable-looking rings. He stood at the foot of a long staircase, made of crimson marble, that led to one of the four palace gates. Not knowing what else to do, Simon climbed the stairs, which required considerable effort because the stairs were unusually high, as if made for someone much taller than himself.

Upon reaching the top of the stairs, Simon paused to catch his breath and marveled at the glistening walls of orthoquartzite, illustrated with scenes from the *Bhagavad Gita* in gold and onyx and lapis lazuli. A section of the wall was covered in a strange script that resembled Sanskrit and was inlaid with ruby that burned red, as if lit from behind. Could this be the legendary language of the gods he had read about? The mysterious words pulsed and shimmered on the wall. Simon couldn't read the message but felt uneasily that it contained a warning.

Around the top floor of the palace ran a widow's walk with a railing and narrowly spaced spindles of beige sandstone. As Simon looked away, he thought he saw, out of the corner of his eye, something move between the spindles. But he looked back and it was gone.

Towering above the palace grew minarets of rose quartz, slender and tall as palm trees. The translucent towers seemed to sway with the wind, but Simon could see that this was an illusion made by the wave-like quality of the light in the sky. Gazing up so high made Simon dizzy and he steadied himself against the cool quartzite wall. Off to his left, he heard a low growl.

Simon's knees nearly failed him. The doorkeeper was tall and well formed, like a man, but with the head of a wild boar. The beast wore the clothes of an Indian aristocrat of the twelfth century, with silks and fine cotton and delicately hammered gold armbands. It stood squarely in front of the door's entrance—its bare feet on either side of the door, its toenails long and cruelly curved. The creature put its hands together as if in prayer and bowed deeply. Then it drew its scimitar, six feet long from the leather-wrapped pommel to the gleaming tip of the blade, which, in the middle, was as wide as a man's back.

Simon's body felt as if it was turning to liquid. He had no thought of running, nor had he the ability to do so. The palace was absolutely still. Hardly a breath of wind disturbed the silence. It suddenly struck Simon that he had never before experienced such beauty. The creature's deep chest expanded and contracted slowly with each silent breath. It held the great sword in two hands without so much as a tremor. Its feral black eyes remained fixed on him. Deliberately, Simon took his hand from the wall and steadied himself. He placed his palms together as the creature had done and bowed. Upon straightening up, he slowly reached into the right front pocket of his pants and withdrew his closed fist. The doorkeeper's black eyes narrowed slightly as it regarded Simon's hand. Simon opened his fingers to reveal the almond he had carried since the night Cayce first spoke to him. With a quick movement, Simon flicked the almond in the direction of the doorkeeper. In a wide arc, the almond fell toward the head of the creature, which caught it in its savage mouth with a loud clack of its tusks. And with that, the creature sheathed its scimitar and stepped back from the doorway.

By this time, having regained the use of his legs, Simon walked through the entrance, making an effort to not steal a glance at the doorkeeper as he passed by. The first thing he noticed as he stepped inside was the smoke. It wasn't sweet like the smell of burning leaves or a wood campfire. Nor was it especially thick. It smelled slightly of decay, and the wisps of smoke were just dense enough to catch the dim light of the corridor.

Simon moved down the hallway cautiously, not sure of what his options might be if he encountered any danger, not wishing to take his chances again with the doorkeeper. The quartzite walls and floor glowed with a gold light from what Simon assumed was the sun filtering through the translucent stone. With the glare and the smoke, he found it difficult to see details as he edged along the hall.

Simon turned a corner and came upon a massive stone door secured with a heavy brass padlock. The door had no handle, but there was a window the size and shape of a silver dollar made of some semi-transparent mineral. He wondered what unearthly treasures might lay behind such a door. If he stood on his tiptoes, he could just see in. Simon shaded his eyes against the bright light coming from within the room, squinting to see through the small milky window. He had to blink at the dazzling whiteness of the room to clear his eye. Like the hallway, it seemed to be lit from all sides, but it was so bright, he could hardly see anything but the throbbing light. As his eye adjusted to the glare, he could make out the edges of the walls and ceiling. Because the window was so small, he had to move his eye around, straining to see the totality of the room. The room was small and, like the hallway, made of quartz. It had no windows or doors or other features. And it was quite empty.

Simon walked away marveling at the empty room and felt the floor of the corridor climb. And as he climbed, the smoke grew thicker and more acrid. Simon's dress shoes slipped on the steep stone and he panted through the smoke. Now, he was feeling his way along the wall, his eyes burning from the smoke and the glare. He began wondering if he was falling into a trap—a trap within a trap. He reproached himself for not studying harder, for not learning more about Tibetan mandalas. Surely, if he knew more about

Vairocana, he could figure a way out of this place. He thought of calling on Ben Hogan for help, then smiled bitterly. "I guess this isn't exactly a sand trap," Simon muttered to himself.

As the climb grew steeper, the smoke became thicker and the air hotter and harder to breathe. He unbuttoned his collar and loosened his white tie. By this time, Simon was crawling on his hands and knees, feeling along the wall as he went. He felt the corridor spiral upward and, as he negotiated a turn, he felt another door. With some difficulty, he wedged the fingers of his right hand into the crack of the door's vertical edge to keep his balance and stood up. Simon stretched to reach the small round window and blinked hard to clear his watering eyes. The room inside was luminescent like the hall but free from smoke. As his vision returned, Simon saw a beautiful young woman sitting in the middle of the floor. She had long, straight black hair and dark, almond eyes. She wore a simple floor-length gown of layered white silk and a thin band of gold around her forehead into which was set three rubies, the size and shape of her eyes. She wore soft leather sandals that laced up her ankles, and around one foot was a heavy silver chain anchored to a large brass ring set into the stone floor. Her face was downcast in despair.

Simon tried to shout to her, but only coughed from the thick smoke. He rattled the massive brass lock, but failed to get the woman's attention. Desperately, he kicked the lock, which clattered ineffectually against the stone door. This time, the woman looked up at the tiny window, but there was no hope in her eyes. Again, Simon kicked the lock, causing him to lose his grip on the door and fall, sliding down the corridor until he came to rest at the curve. He fought his way back up to the door again, but the smoke was sapping his strength. He called out to the woman that he was going to get help, but he was all but certain that she did not hear him.

After rounding two more turns, the pitch of the corridor leveled off and Simon struggled uneasily to his feet. Now he could see that the smoke was coming from an open doorway at what looked like the end of the hall. He advanced cautiously and felt the floor begin to pitch downward the closer he came to the smoking doorway. The smoke was not steady, as from a raging fire. It appeared to come out of the doorway intermittently in great puffs. Curious, although hardly able to breathe, Simon walked up to the doorway and looked in. There he saw no fire, but heaps of gleaming jewels and golden goblets and ornamented swords and shields, all twinkling through the haze of the lifting smoke. He saw a ceremonial bronze battle-ax that might break open the lock where the young woman was bound. Not seeing anyone in the room, Simon entered to get a better look. There were fragrant spices and subtly carved boxes of precious African wood. There were piles of Roman gold coins and bolts of Chinese silk, intricately woven with threads of gold and silver and copper. There were scrolls in ancient Arabic and Greek and some forgotten Hebrew dialect. The glitter of the gold and jewels was muted by a thick layer of dust. Ancient abandoned spider webs hung between a pair of Egyptian alabaster unguent jars. Pomegranates and grapes, long dried and decayed into little more than a stain and a few seeds, littered plates of solid gold. Lying on top of a Spartan helmet filled with sapphires was a moldy, leather-bound book written in the same script as the writing on the palace walls. Simon bent to pick up the text and heard a deep whistling sound like a faraway gasp, coming from the back of the room.

The scaly green tail flashed through the haze and Simon saw the dragon rear its ancient head and spray flame and smoke onto the ceiling. The dragon was no more than eight feet long and around two hundred pounds. It took two steps toward Simon and inhaled.

"This is not happening," said Simon out loud. "None of this is real." But when the dragon was about to breathe fire in his direction, Simon instinctively, in self-defense, raised up his hands, one of which, he was surprised to notice, still held the stuffed iguana. The dragon's emerald eyes fixed upon the stuffed lizard and there appeared to be a flicker of recognition in its murderous reptilian face.

Simon took this opportunity to dash out the door and down the steeply declining hallway, followed quickly by a wave of fire and smoke. As he ran and slid down the corridor, the entire palace began to shake. The quartzite walls and floor cracked and undulated. Sharp splinters of quartz whined past his head like hornets before shattering against the wall. He could hear the dragon bellowing a challenge behind him. Although his heart was racing and his lungs burned from the exertion, Simon was disgusted with himself for taking any of it seriously. A particularly large shard of quartz crystal knifed the air beside him, slicing cleanly through the padded shoulder of his zoot suit. "This is an illusion!" he called out to nobody in particular.

Suddenly he came to the ground floor of the palace and the doorway into the courtyard. Simon sprinted out to the open space and turned to see three minarets fall—not like tall trees—but crumble to dust as if their weight somehow became too much to bear. The earth around him shook and wide cracks ran up the palace walls. The majestic quartz columns cracked and gave way. Spandrels slumped and split, dumping a gilded onion dome into the courtyard, where it disintegrated into a cloud of dust. A wave of debris rolled toward Simon and he had only enough time to back up two steps before it covered his shoes. "Sand!" he marveled. "The whole place is turning to sand!"

To keep from being buried alive, Simon ran toward the rings. The white lotus ring was the nearest. It was smooth as glass, impossible to climb, and too high to jump over. He looked toward the crumbling palace and up through one of the pendentives under a dome in time to see the door guardian crumble into sand and spill out onto the steps below. It soon became clear to Simon that the courtyard was too small to contain the enormous volume of sand into which the palace was dissolving. Hoping to climb the mounds of sand and escape over the rings, Simon scrabbled against the lotus ring but discovered the fine sand would not support his weight.

Already up to his waist in sand, Simon found it difficult to move and with the collapse of every wing of the palace, the tide of sand rose higher. "How am I going to get out of this one?" Simon panted, desperate.

"If it was me," said Ben Hogan cheerily, "I'd use a sand wedge."

With considerable effort, Simon pivoted to see his spirit guide hovering above the advancing sand and found himself eye-level with Hogan's argyle socks.

"Do something!" Simon pleaded.

Hogan looked thoughtful. "There we have the heart of the problem. If you took the time to consider the matter fully, I'm sure you'd figure it out for yourself, but you see, I'm a ghost. I can't actually do anything." And he passed his own hand through his Scottish knit wool sweater by way of illustration. "I'm not really here," he said and winked.

The powdery sand was now chest high on Simon and he

could feel the grit in his mouth and eyes. "Well, I can hear you just fine," he said. "So in some sense, you must be here."

Hogan shook his head. "You're too deep for me. I'm just a simple golfer. Still," he said looking toward a new wave of sand as it slowly shifted in their direction, "if I were you, I'd be taking a serious interest in this matter."

"I am taking it seriously!" Simon shouted, causing an onset of sneezing from the sand in his nose. "Say, can you tell the future? Am I going to die here?"

"Your Grandma Louise is better than I at predicting the future. But I've always had a keen eye for measurement and I'd say that the next wave of sand should be about up to your eyebrows. At the British Open, we once had a contest in the clubhouse to see who could hold his breath the longest. I won. Three minutes! What's your record?"

The sand was now up to Simon's chin and he had to tilt his head back to speak to keep sand from running in his mouth. "You're an ethereal being. You found your way in here. Is there a way out?"

"Undoubtedly," said Hogan. "What do you suppose became of that damsel in distress who was chained to the floor?"

"You were following me the whole time?" Simon sputtered, now standing on his tiptoes to keep from drowning in sand. "Well, I imagine she turned into sand like everything else in that cursed palace." He was suddenly struck with a thought. "Tibetan mandalas are usually made from colored sand. When they're through with the ceremony, the monks pour the sand back into the river."

"How interesting," said Hogan, clearly not interested. "Oh look! Here comes some more sand."

"You mentioned that you are not really here."

"That's right," chirped Hogan.

The sand now covered everything but Simon's eyes and mouth. "So the damsel wasn't there either."

"Seems logical," observed Hogan.

"And neither was the dragon."

"You never really believed in it anyway."

"And neither was the gate guardian—or the palace itself, for that matter."

Hogan looked around from his superior vantage point. "Not much left of any of it now, is there?"

"None of that stuff was ever really here. And neither," said Simon, "am I." And with that, he exhaled and sank beneath the rising sand.

Chapter 28

Simon panted, his heart racing and feeling a little self-conscious about it, standing, as he was, in the living room, over the mandala, with a stuffed iguana in his hand. The mandala looked different to him now—not like a piece of artwork, but like a map of someplace he had been before. Maybe he had not seen the mandala's main feature, the Buddha, but he had walked within its walls and now felt a special familiarity with the palace.

Looking over the Sanskrit hymn, Simon read over part of a stanza that stuck in his mind.

> In the sunlight sits the Illuminator on a throne of
>   white, white, gold
> And he is so white
> Almost you cannot see him . . .

Simon studied the mandala, frowning as he counted the intricately carved figures that seemed to float in and around the mandala's palace. "Twelve," he said aloud. "The Vairocana Mandala is supposed to have thirteen deities." His eyes were drawn to the blank space in the upper left corner of the mandala where the "self" face had looked. "And so it does," he said and pressed the empty white square.

It clicked and depressed about a quarter of an inch. There was another, louder click from the other side of the room. The massive display case shuddered and slid slowly back on a track in the floor to reveal an old-fashioned wall safe, covered in spider webs, with a tarnished brass dial and a heavy, rounded steel handle. Simon pressed the white square again and the case glided back into place. And when it stopped, the four wheels around the mandala spun in different directions, resetting the mechanism.

A shriek erupted from the doorway.

"It's him!" screeched Zelda.

Simon jumped and the stuffed iguana flew across the room and landed softly on one of the satin-upholstered Victorian chairs.

"You deceived me!" Zelda shouted at Mr. Z, who stood cringing beside her.

"It was supposed to be a surprise," he offered weakly.

She glared at him with her violet eyes. "Well, it was!" Zelda took a deep drag from her cigarette and blew the smoke in his face.

Mr. Z strode across the room toward Simon. "Please forgive my awkward social graces," he said. "I thought it would be nice for the four of us to have a little dinner together—some goulash and a nice wine. Maybe get to know each other better."

"Four?" inquired Simon, taking a quick inventory of the people in the room.

Zelda had scurried behind Mr. Z. "What were you doing there?" she demanded. Simon started to answer but she cut him off. "Never mind!"

Simon picked up the iguana and was attempting to replace it when Zelda snatched it from his grasp. "This poor thing has been through enough," she said, slamming it down on the mandala.

"You have no idea," muttered Simon.

"Come Simon," soothed Mr. Z, taking Simon by the arm, steering him toward the dining room. "There's someone I'd like you to meet."

Zelda glared at Mr. Z and whispered loudly, "I want to speak with you alone!"

Mr. Z blushed and whispered back, "Later, my little cabbage!"

The dining room looked formal and purposeful—like a courtroom, thought Simon. The rough Arts and Crafts-style table was big enough to seat six and there were four straight-backed iron Spanish chairs. A large crockery tureen sat in the middle of the table and next to it, an old, carved wooden spoon. There was a loaf of dark bread on a platter. The plates were heavy brown English ironstone framed by ornate silverware.

Simon was trying to think of something polite to say about the meal when he looked up to see an awkward, large-boned young woman dressed in black with short dark hair and sad eyes leaning against the doorway.

"This is my daughter," said Zelda. "Crystal."

"How do you do?" said Simon.

Crystal did not speak but stared soulfully into Simon's eyes.

"Crystal is very spiritual," said Mr. Z, trying to sound encouraging. "You'll like her."

Zelda shot Mr. Z a warning glance. "Please, Simon, sit down." She tried to smile. "Welcome to my home."

Simon looked surprised. "Oh, I thought this was Mr. Z's home. You have some extraordinary things here, Zelda."

Mr. Z chuckled and he took his seat. "My place? Not likely. Too dark and gloomy for me. I have an apartment in the country club with lots of sunlight. But yes, Zelda has a regular museum."

Zelda stood stiffly behind her chair, looking at once elegant and severe in her opalescent dark green sheath dress. A long, winding trail of smoke from her cigarette slithered up her arm and around her gaunt outline. "The furnishings were collected by my late husband. He also built this house. He had some peculiar ideas about style. He was a peculiar man."

"Don't start, Mother!" Crystal spoke up in a high, whiney voice. She sat next to Simon and looked at him as though he surely must appreciate her long suffering.

"I hope you enjoy real Bulgarian food, Simon," said Mr. Z heartily. "You've been working so hard lately, I thought you could use a good home-cooked meal." He chuckled. "God knows what you normally eat. Nuts and twigs, I suppose." He reached a long, burly arm to the wooden spoon, scooped up a large dollop of goulash, and plopped it on Simon's plate. "Here. Eat this and you can fight off a wolf with your bare hands."

"In that case," said Zelda, half to herself, "I'll be sure to have seconds."

Mr. Z helped himself to a steaming mound of goulash and a thick slab of Russian rye, which he had buttered thickly and was about to devour.

"Don't you think we should say a blessing?" Crystal interjected.

Mr. Z stopped, the bread halfway to his mouth. "I don't know any prayers in English," he said.

"Crystal, dear, don't embarrass our guests," said Zelda.
Crystal pouted.

"Well, of course, you may say a prayer silently if you wish," her mother said.

"It's not a proper blessing for everyone if it's silent," insisted Crystal. "I'll say the blessing. I don't mind."

177

Zelda smiled tightly. "All right Sweetheart. But just don't make it too long. You know how carried away you can get."

Crystal suppressed a little triumphant smile. "First, we have to all hold hands." Zelda rolled her eyes. "Come on, come on," she coaxed, fluttering her moist, plump fingers in Simon's face.

Crystal took Simon's hand in hers, and self-consciously, he and Mr. Z reached across the table to clasp hands. Mr. Z took Zelda's hand under the table and rubbed his thumb significantly between her fingers. She dug her long red nails into Mr. Z's palm so that he rearranged his grip more reverentially.

When she was satisfied that everyone was in a thankful frame of mind, Crystal took a deep breath and closed her heavily made-up eyes. "Oh Gaia, great Mother, creator of heaven and earth . . ." Mr. Z opened one eye, hoping to get some clue from Zelda. "Thank you for the many blessings for all of us here and for all of womankind (and men too). We also thank the Spirit of the North and the Spirit of the South and the Spirit of the East and the Spirit of the West. Let us thank the four elements, Earth, Air, Fire, and Water. Let us thank the ancestors of all the great Indian nations who first walked this land and who were so badly treated by white men who killed their buffalos and built shopping malls on their holy land."

"This is beginning to sound like the Academy Awards," muttered Mr. Z.

"Let us thank the sun for giving life to all living things," Crystal continued. "And to the moon that guides our planting seasons. And to the stars that show us the way at night."

"I think she's stalling," whispered Mr. Z to Zelda.

Crystal gripped Simon's hand tighter. "And thank you

for the rainforest—what's left of it. And thank you for . . . Simon, wouldn't you like to add something?"

Simon squirmed a little in his hard iron chair. "Well," he said, "we could give thanks for the food."

Crystal opened her eyes and glared at him. "How do you mean?"

"Oh, I mean . . . that is, it would be traditional—in the aboriginal sense," Simon stammered, trying to placate Crystal, who was now practically crushing his fingers, "to give thanks . . . to the food."

Mr. Z let go of Simon's hand. "You want to thank the food?" he asked, incredulously.

"I think that's beautiful!" Crystal enthused.

Simon cleared his throat. "Early civilizations didn't consider humans superior to other animals. So when they made a kill, they thanked the spirit of the animal that gave its life for them."

Crystal gazed at Simon with something between reverence and hunger. "That is so respectful!" she said.

Mr. Z snorted. "So you want us to pray to the corn and beans?"

Zelda shook loose of Mr. Z's grip. "Surely we must have appeased enough of the most important pagan gods so that it is now safe for us to eat."

"Mother!" protested Crystal.

"My goulash is getting cold," said Mr. Z.

Reluctantly, Crystal released Simon's hand. "Oh, all right," she said. "Amen."

Zelda served Crystal and herself while Mr. Z poured the wine.

"None for me, thanks," said Simon.

"You don't know what you're missing," said Mr. Z.

Crystal snatched Simon's full glass. "I'll have his," she

said, gulping it down noisily.

"Now take it easy with that, dear," said Zelda. "You know what Dr. Johnson said about mixing alcohol with your medication."

"Mother, please! Do you have to tell the whole world about my personal medical history?"

"I'm just saying . . ."

Crystal filled her own glass and downed it in one swallow. "I am an adult, Mother. I know my limits. Besides, I wouldn't have to be on medication, if you weren't so controlling." She poured herself another glass and took a dainty sip.

"The goulash is terrific!" said Simon.

"What a shame you have to leave right after dinner, Crystal," said Zelda.

"What are you talking about?" Crystal demanded.

"Well, isn't this the night you and your little witch friends dance naked in the woods and make vortexes or something?"

"They're Druids, Mother. And you know perfectly well that's tomorrow night." Crystal smiled sweetly at Simon. "You want to come?"

Mr. Z gagged on his goulash and had to gulp half a glass of wine to clear his throat. "That went down the wrong way!" he wheezed. "So Simon, Mr. Chen tells me he is very pleased with your work. We're doing so well with our new arrangement that I thought you might like us to set up a Swiss bank account for you." He turned to Crystal. "Our boy Simon here is very important at Going Platinum—a very big success!"

"Sure. A Swiss bank account would be nice. Thanks," said Simon.

Mr. Z clapped his hands together with finality. "Well,

why don't you two young people get to know each other better? Zelda and I have to go over the monthly statements at my place. We shouldn't be gone more than a couple of hours."

"We most certainly will not!" said Zelda. "Crystal, you know how nervous you get around strangers."

"Mom!" Crystal whined. "I'll be all right. Besides, it seems like Simon and I have known each other for years. Isn't that right, Simon?"

"Why not let the kids talk? You know that financial statement can't wait." He whispered to Zelda, "You know I can't wait!"

Zelda lit a cigarette and her violet eyes melted him through the smoke. "I have everything you need here. I suppose we could do a few short pages."

"Yes, yes." Mr. Z was eager to accept a compromise. "A few short pages. Yes. We'll be back before you know it. Yes. We must start tonight. Yes. Now. Now!"

Zelda and Mr. Z slipped out of the dining room and there was the sound of rustling and a muffled slap.

"You have to get me out of here!" whispered Crystal. "You don't know what it's like. The things I go through! Do you have a house or an apartment?"

"Well, I—"

"I love the ocean, don't you? Let's go for a walk along the ocean. We can look for sand dollars and discarded wedding rings. I actually found a ring one time. Have you ever found anything on the beach?"

"Once I found an almond . . ." Simon reached into the pocket of his jacket and felt around in vain.

"Ah!" Crystal gasped and clutched at her plump bosom. "We can take Muffy!"

"We can?" asked Simon, not sure if he wanted to know more.

"Muffy loves the beach. Muffy's my German shepherd. He's my widdo boy," she said in what would have been a good imitation of Shirley Temple in her prime. "I take him everywhere. The Druids love him. Muffy's very spiritual. Do you believe in reincarnation?"

"Well, the concept of reincarnation is an extension of cosmological renewal which is central to fertility rites. In the story of Osiris—"

"That's so erotic—and so true! I can tell you're into books and I read this book once that talked about this kid who made friends with the singer, Jim Morrison. And even though the kid was only twelve at the time, Morrison introduced him to philosophy and poetry and drugs and eventually the kid went to work for him as a roadie. And after Morrison died, the kid, who was older by now, was addicted to heroin and went to this acupuncturist to be cured who turned out to be Morrison's old photographer! So this acupuncturist said like, 'I'm not going to treat you until you go to a psychic and find out why you are still so obsessed with Jim Morrison.' So the guy goes to this psychic who does hypnotic regression—which I totally believe in—and the psychic tells the guy that he and Morrison were once brothers in another life! When I read that, I'm like—whoa! It sent a chill down my spine, I'm telling you. And in another life they were pirates together and in another life, they were in some monastery and Morrison was like the abbot and—get this—he was dying, just like he did in real life!" Crystal was dewy-eyed with emotion and exertion. "Evidence like that can make a real believer out of you, don't you think?"

"Incredible," said Simon.

"I know!" she said, nodding.

"Your father must have been an interesting man to build

such an unusual house. That mandala in the—"

"You have the bluest eyes, Simon," she said. "They're quite beautiful."

"Well, thanks. So about that mandala—"

"I believe the eyes are the windows to the soul. What do you see in my eyes?" she asked, leaning forward and opening her dark eyes wide.

Simon studied her a moment and said, "I see kindness and insecurity. I see a child who wakes up each day to a new world. And I see a woman who goes to bed each night with longing in her heart. I see a person with a great capacity for happiness."

Crystal swallowed hard. "You do?" she said. "Ask me anything about myself. Anything."

"Okay. What is one thing you can do that makes you feel competent?"

"Competent?" Crystal was momentarily at a loss. "Well, I can cook," she said. "Not that Mom cares. She never eats. I swear I don't know what keeps her alive. She's like a steam engine. She just pours in water and pours out smoke. Me, I eat all the time. I know I'm not model-thin, but the whole food thing is so complex, do you know what I mean? I mean, food is like love and comfort and survival and chemistry and magic and even art all rolled into one. And making a really good meal for someone makes them so happy—even if they don't even know you—even if they don't even like you. So no matter what else in the world is confusing or screwed up, if I can get the right ingredients and get the proportions right and the mixing right and the temperature and the timing right, the food will come out right. And there will be one thing I've done that's right and good."

Simon leaned back slowly in his chair and smiled. "That sounds like magic all right."

"You're pretty skinny. Looks like you could use somebody to cook for you."

"My girlfriend is a good cook," said Simon.

Crystal looked stricken. "Your girlfriend?"

"Well, she dumped me. But that's beside the point."

"Oh, I think that's exactly the point!" Crystal observed. "And now you're just wasting away. You like Italian food? How about a nice Risotto Milanese? Or Cajun? I can do a Jambalaya that will make you sweat and sing Hallelujah!"

"Well, actually . . ."

Mr. Z burst into the dining room looking very pleased with himself. "I hope you two have been getting along," he said.

Crystal gave Simon a conspiratorial glance. "We certainly have! Simon is such a good conversationalist."

Zelda slithered in behind Mr. Z, languorously smoking a cigarette. "It was nice having you for dinner, Simon. I hope you had a good time."

"Simon and I are going for a walk on the beach," Crystal chirped up.

A chill seemed to pass over Zelda. "Crystal, dear, do you really think that's wise? Just when your therapist said you were starting to make progress?"

Crystal jumped up in a huff. "Must you humiliate me every chance you get?" she bleated and stalked out of the room. A moment later she stuck her head back in. "Wednesday's okay for you, isn't it, Simon? About seven?"

"Seven?" said Simon.

"Then it's a date!" She crinkled her button nose, pantomimed a "toodeloo," and disappeared.

"Wednesday," said Mr. Z as if mentally consulting his calendar. "What a coincidence! I think I also have Wednesday free. We could work some more on the financial

184

statement—maybe do a few more little pages?"

"I'm going to be busy," Zelda said flatly.

Mr. Z whispered, "I'll make you busy sure enough!"

"I will not be available."

"But Zelda!" pleaded Mr. Z. "Besides, we really must complete the financial statement. We're already behind and my poor cousins are getting nervous."

"Your poor cousins!" Zelda scoffed. "They'll do what you tell them. They don't understand American business. They won't be happy until they start grazing sheep on the golf course."

Mr. Z chuckled. "It's true. They think the old ways are best. But we'll show them. We'll make them rich, won't we Simon?"

"We're certainly headed in that direction," Simon concurred.

Mr. Z put his arm around Simon. "I'm so glad you could be here tonight, my boy. You have no idea how glad. And I think Crystal was glad too. Tomorrow is your day off. What will you do? Eat three grains of wild rice and meditate standing on your head? Read a book on philosophy?"

"I think I'll go to the horse track," said Simon.

Chapter 29

"Of course we get losers here," the man behind the ticket window said, smirking. "Making losers out of people is our business."

Detective Bentley had a lot of experience with wise guys. They were often the best informants. Wise guys love to talk. He handed the man a photo. "Maybe you've seen this individual—cocky, sharp dresser, kind of a good-looking kid. Maybe a high roller."

The ticket taker shrugged. "I seen a lot of guys like that. They all look alike to me."

"Yeah, I hear you," Bentley said. "Walking around in their thousand-dollar suits like their shit don't stink. Throwing around money like it's water. This guy was a piece of work, I'm telling you. Into drugs and who knows what else."

"Yeah?" said the ticket taker, still on his guard. "Maybe he was good to his momma."

Bentley continued. "The thing about this guy is that he hated to lose. You know the type. Big shot gambler. Makes a big show of living on the edge to get the girls breathing hard. But just can't take losing."

"Life is such a bitch, ain't it?"

"It is," Bentley agreed. "And I suppose it's only natural that a guy like that turns to cheating. Only that's not so easy to pull off in a place like this without an inside man."

"What are you talking about?" The ticket taker's smirk was starting to crack.

"Ever heard of Lasix?"

"Yeah, they make paint out of it."

"No," said Bentley indulgently. "You're thinking of latex. Lasix is some kind of super diuretic used to dope horses and make them run faster. Thus the term, 'piss like a racehorse.' Only it also makes them dizzy and bleed under the skin and die. Slipping that poison to a poor dumb animal is just the sort of thing a little rat bastard like you would do for a couple of bucks."

"You're fishing." The ticket taker was starting to sweat under his green eyeshade.

"Yeah, and I think I got me the big fish on the hook right here."

"Hey, I ain't no big fish."

Bentley leaned his bulk over the counter and grinned. "Well, you know that's funny because your name keeps coming up."

"Look, man why don't you give me a break? I don't know nothing about no Lasix. The line's backing up. We're losing money here. I'm going to lose my job."

Bentley shook his head sadly. "Life's such a bitch, isn't it?"

O'Reilly had his badge out, waving customers back as if directing traffic. More than fifty people were standing in line, grumbling and growing agitated.

"What do you want from me? You need to talk to my boss." The ticket taker pressed a button under the counter. "You got to let me go back to work. Please."

A middle-aged man with steel-rimmed glasses emerged from a side door, wearing an immaculate gray suit that perfectly fit his blocky build, except for a slight bulge under the left armpit. "Can I help you gentlemen?" he asked smiling.

Bentley signaled to O'Reilly and showed the man his badge.

"My name is Rich Hunter," the man said. "Please, step into my office."

He led the detectives into a spacious room overlooking the racetrack. The walls were lined with photos of horses and jockeys and himself pictured with various celebrities. He took a seat in a large leather swivel chair and motioned them to sit in the two wooden chairs by his desk.

"I didn't think I'd see you folks again so soon," he said.

"What do you mean?" asked O'Reilly.

Hunter chuckled. "You guys crack me up. Your man grills me for an hour about this guy Steve Merritt, who has been losing money all over town, not just here. And now you're back for more. I told the other guy everything I know, honest. Now, come on. I got a business to run."

"What other guy?" asked Bentley.

Hunter grinned. "What other guy? That clown in the zoot suit. He was here yesterday and I told him Merritt dropped a couple of grand here every week. He wanted to know if anybody was lending him money and I said I didn't know. And he asked did Merritt ever come with anybody else and I said I thought he always came alone. What's the matter, don't you boys ever compare notes?"

"Son of a bitch," said Bentley.

O'Reilly took out a pad and a pen. "This other guy, did he show you a badge? Did he give you a name?"

Hunter snorted. "What? Are you telling me this guy was a civilian? Listen, the minute he walked in, I smelled cop all over him—no offense. He didn't have to show me a badge. He was smooth in a kind of quirky way. Some kind of genius, I figured. I felt like he was reading my mind anyway, so I told him what I knew. Said his name was Simon."

When the detectives got back to their car, O'Reilly spoke up. "This guy Simon is staying one step ahead of us. What do you think he's got, a crystal ball?"

Bentley spat. "Well, the reason he's got the jump on us is that we're investigating a homicide and he's covering his tracks."

O'Reilly started the engine and pulled into traffic. "Simon did give Hunter his name."

"He's slick," observed Bentley. "I'll give him that."

O'Reilly said, "Well, we know now that Merritt was spending more money than he made."

"As far as we know. Unless he had another source of income."

"Right," said O'Reilly. "As far as we know. But he didn't have enough free time to have been making that kind of money honestly. If he was borrowing it, there's somebody out there still carrying the guy's markers. Maybe the murderer."

"He'd have to be a loan shark who hated Merritt enough to forfeit his debt."

"True," said O'Reilly. "So let's assume Merritt's money man didn't kill him. Who did? And why?"

"I still say if we follow Simon, we get our killer."

"Another thing that bothers me," said O'Reilly. "What in the world was Steve Merritt doing applying for a stupid sales job at Going Platinum?"

"So who says it was a real sales job? There's some fishy stuff going on in that place. Look at Simon. I know a uniform who works Crenshaw says he eats lunch at this little Thai restaurant in the neighborhood. Simon comes in there once or twice a week. Pays cash, nothing smaller than a fifty. He says he saw Simon go to pay for a bowl of rice and a cup of tea and pulls out this wad of hundreds. Now are you going to tell me that schmuck is making that kind of money selling those platinum-plated golf putters?"

O'Reilly shrugged. "I don't know. They're pretty nice. I'm thinking about getting one myself."

Bentley sneered. "Well, if a moron like you would buy one, we should be seeing platinum-plated golf putters on the Home Shopping Channel any day now."

"I'm just saying they could actually be selling a lot of them."

"And I'm just saying you spend too much time thinking about toys and not enough time thinking about catching bad guys. I never saw a grown man so obsessed with gadgets. You've got computers at work, computers at home. You've got that squinty little pocket computer with a wireless Internet connection."

"That's the future of police work," said O'Reilly.

"Shoe leather. That's the future of police work. Let me see the bottom of your shoes," Bentley demanded.

"I'm driving for Christ's sake!"

"Show me your left shoe, then."

With difficulty, O'Reilly twisted his skinny left leg to expose the sole of his shoe.

"Just what I thought!" exclaimed Bentley. "Hardly any wear at all. If you walked more and typed less, we'd have something to show the captain by the end of the week."

"Geeze, Bentley. These are new shoes—which, I may say, are at your disposal if you've got any brilliant ideas about where we ought to be walking."

"O'Reilly, that's the first intelligent thing I've heard you say today."

Chapter 30

Kenny fluffed up his white carnation and adjusted the white tie he had borrowed, along with the violin case, from Simon. He stood by the elevator, a 300-pound guy in a gangster outfit, trying not to look conspicuous. An attractive thirty-something woman in a power suit gave him the once-over as she stepped into the elevator.

"Big concert tonight," he said, patting the oversized violin case. "Beethoven."

The woman tried to ignore him by studying the buttons in the elevator.

"I'll get you a back stage pass if you play your cards right—you know what I mean?"

She checked her watch as the elevator doors started to close.

"I know Yo Yo Ma," he called. The doors shut. "Yo yo mama!" Kenny muttered to himself.

"What floor do you want?" A trim, elegant looking older man was suddenly standing behind Kenny.

Kenny jumped at the sound. "You sure know how to sneak up on a guy," he said, recovering. "What do you re-sole your wingtips with, mink?"

The second elevator arrived. The doors opened and the man stepped inside. "What floor?" he asked, although it sounded more like a command than a question.

Kenny did not move. "Thirteenth," he said.

The man smiled. "There is no thirteenth floor."

191

"Yeah?" said Kenny. "That's the way my whole day's been going."

"Get in," the man said. "I'm J. D. Harriman." Harriman pushed the button and watched the digital dial as the elevator passed the second floor. "Talk fast. When we reach the penthouse, your time's up."

Kenny grinned. "I'm a fast talker anyway. You know what company I represent. My name's Kenny and because I like you so much you can call me 'Kenny.' "

"What's on your mind, Kenny?" Harriman watched the dial as they passed the fifth floor.

"I'm with customer service—don't laugh. Even we need customer service. I'm just following up on an incident involving one of our salesmen. Maybe you remember him, Steve Merritt."

Harriman kept his eyes on the dial and said nothing.

"We have reason to believe that your contact with Mr. Merritt ended unsatisfactorily."

"For me or for him?"

"We're interested in your satisfaction, Mr. Harriman. Mr. Merritt's satisfaction is beyond our reach. Dead, you know."

"You think I killed him?" Harriman watched the dial, which read 15.

"Did you?"

Harriman turned to Kenny. "The little prick tried to shake me down, pretending he was a government agent. He wanted a share of the diamond shipment. I told him to get lost."

"Good for you," said Kenny.

The elevator bumped to a stop at the penthouse and Harriman got out. "I've never seen you before. Did Z send you?"

Kenny stepped out, towering over Harriman. "You don't see me unless there's a problem. And it's my job to keep our problems to a minimum." He emphasized the last word as he glared down at Harriman. "We'll make sure our salesmen are nice to you in the future. And you make sure you're nice to them. You know who I mean." Kenny pointed the violin case at Harriman's belt buckle and assumed a wide-eyed, crazy look that had once impressed him in a Jimmy Cagney movie.

Just then, the other elevator arrived and the bell startled Harriman and Kenny both. The doors opened and two men emerged in the middle of an animated discussion about the Lakers game. Without taking his eyes off Harriman, Kenny backed through the elevator doors. Inside, he stood facing the doors.

"Oh, my God!" he said, tearing off his tie. "I am such an asshole!" Kenny turned around to find the woman in the power suit staring at him, horrified. "What?" he said.

Chapter 31

"What were you thinking?" Simon laughed.

"I guess I got carried away," said Kenny. "Besides, I don't like the way he treated you. Serves him right to sweat a little."

Simon poured Kenny a tall glass of orange juice and sat next to him on his dilapidated couch. "I doubt if J. D. Harriman has sweat glands. And you! You big lunk—you're lucky you made it out alive! There's something really scary about him. I don't believe he'd think twice about killing Steve Merritt."

Kenny drained the orange juice in one breath, making a kind of flushing sound. "But you don't think he did it."

"I don't."

"Well, at least we found out Harriman is running diamonds."

"And not drugs," Simon added. "I'm not sure which is more dangerous. I only hope Harriman doesn't get curious about your visit."

Cayce jumped up on Kenny's lap. "What do you think, Cayce? Who killed Steve Merritt?"

"I like you!" said Cayce, nuzzling Kenny's chin. "Where is Amy? I miss her!"

Kenny rubbed the bristly spot between Cayce's eyes. "What do you hear from Amy?" he asked.

"You remember, she dumped me. She won't return my calls. She's stubborn. I don't know what to do."

"Stay home with me!" said Cayce. "We could read and pet and eat."

"You could quit your job," said Kenny. "Amy would come back to you. She's just worried, that's all." He scratched Cayce behind the ears. "And Cayce would like it too."

"I can't quit yet," said Simon. "There's been a terrible wrong done here and I feel it's my responsibility to put it right."

"The man with the big feet wants to help," offered Cayce.

"Come on, Simon. It's a police matter. Let them do their job."

Simon looked quizzically at his cat. "This whole thing goes deeper than Steve's murder. I can't explain it. It's just a feeling I have. Something out of balance. I feel that if I don't do it, it might not get done."

Kenny held Cayce with one hand and started rummaging in the kitchen cupboards for something to eat with the other. "I don't know," he said. "Maybe you're right. But I definitely sense something out of balance in your life." Not finding anything to his liking, he shuffled over to another cupboard and almost tripped over a grocery bag full of cans.

Cayce let out a yowl of distress. "Messy house!" he exclaimed.

"Sorry pal," said Kenny, stroking Cayce's back. "Our Simon has a messy house, doesn't he?"

Simon chuckled. "You and Cayce have quite a connection. I never realized."

Kenny nodded. "Yeah, we seem to speak the same language."

Cayce jumped down and trotted over to sit by Simon. "Kenny's nice," said Cayce. "I wish he could talk."

Kenny bent down to set the bag upright and picked a

stray can, which he held up for Simon's inspection. "Canned spaghetti?" He held it at arm's length with two fingers as if in danger of contamination and re-deposited it in the trash. "You would never have sunk to this if Amy was around."

Simon looked morose. "I know. I'm working long hours, plus doing the investigation, and I've been letting a lot of things slide. The pool filter's clogged again and the gas cylinder on the grill is empty. The back door to apartment 5 sticks."

"Eddie put his bubble gum in it again?"

"No," said Simon wearily. "DentuGrip."

Kenny shook his head sympathetically. "Maybe I could talk to Amy for you. We could do something together tonight, like old times."

"I've got a date tonight," said Simon.

"What?" said Kenny, shocked.

"Well, not really a date. The secretary's daughter sort of cornered me into taking her and her dog to the beach. She's really kind of sweet—you'd never know she was Zelda's daughter. You'd like her. But their house is really interesting and I'd like to know more about Zelda's ex-husband. He was an architect and a collector of Asian curiosities."

"Divorced?"

"Dead. And whenever his name comes up, you can just feel the tension in the room."

"Whoa! Maybe he's buried in the basement!"

"Yeah, maybe." Simon stood up. "Well, Kenny, I'd better get going. Wish me luck. I don't know much about dogs. Or women either, for that matter."

"Nothing to it," said Kenny. "Just let 'em sniff your crotch."

Simon chuckled. "Dogs or women?"

"Whatever."

Chapter 32

Muffy stuck his cold, wet nose over the car seat and into Simon's ear and sneezed.

"Ah!" exclaimed Simon, nearly driving off the narrow alley into a telephone pole.

"Don't scare Muffy!" Crystal scolded. "He likes you. Don't you like Simon?" She reached into the tiny back seat of Simon's Honda and patted Muffy's tawny head. "Simon wet you wide wif him. You're such a good boy!" She clutched Muffy around the neck and kissed him repeatedly. Muffy, in turn, licked Crystal full on the mouth. "Muffy wuvs Mommy!"

Simon wheeled the little car around a tight corner and squeezed into a space that would have been insufficient for a normal automobile. "So, you say your friend has a store right on Venice Beach?"

"Well, it's not a store, really. More like a booth. Even so, the space costs a fortune." Crystal giggled. " 'Costs a fortune.' Good thing she's a fortune teller."

Muffy was starting to whine loudly with his big head between the front seats.

"Do you have to go potty?" she asked Muffy and looked expectantly at him for his answer. "Now don't piddle in the car. This isn't our car."

Simon looked stricken.

Crystal said, "I think Muffy smells the ocean." She stuck her head out the window and inhaled deeply. "Don't you love the smell of the ocean, Simon?" Crystal immediately began gathering up Muffy's water dish and special bottled water, along with his favorite toys and his blanket, and stuffed them all into a blue backpack with the name "Muffy" embroidered on the flap. She then attached a collar around Muffy's neck and attached a retractable leash to that.

By this time, Muffy was practically howling and thrashing around, banging violently into the roof and side windows.

"Is he okay?" Simon asked, concerned that Muffy might tunnel through the seat and escape out the trunk.

"Here, you hold this," she said, handing Simon the re-tractable leash. "If he starts to run away, push this button," indicating a black button with a stiff spring. Crystal let Muffy out of the car and, instead of racing off, he slunk low and whined pitifully. She directed Simon to stand on a patch of grass, which Simon weakly argued was probably somebody's lawn, while Muffy prepared to do his business. "Go potty! Go potty!" Crystal called out, well within ear-shot of Muffy and the rest of Venice Beach. But Muffy only circled Simon and moaned, finally taking refuge in a shadow by the wall. "He's shy," said Crystal with affection. "Is widdow Muffy too shy to make piddo?" They waited an-other five minutes. "Go potty! Go potty!" Crystal shouted, as if Muffy was deaf and not modest or constipated.

"Maybe he doesn't have to go," Simon suggested.

"I should know my own dog!" she snapped. "He has to go all right. He's just doing this to embarrass Mommy!" Crystal enunciated the last sentence as if to shame Muffy into demonstrating that he was well bred after all and per-fectly capable of peeing on command.

A second-story window opened and a long-haired surfer

dude stuck his head out. "Hey man, what's going on?" he called to Simon. "What are you doing under my window, dude?"

"Potty," said Simon.

"Oh, man! You can't do that!"

"You're telling me," said Simon.

"Oh, let's go!" whispered Crystal, stalking off toward the beach in a huff.

Muffy, sensing that his mistress was mad at him, began moaning piteously.

"Oh, hey man," the surfer called out, "I didn't know you had to go that bad. I'm sorry. Let her rip, dude!"

Although it was starting to get dark, the Venice board-walk was bustling with activity. There were two street musicians playing a ragtime tune. There was a tall man wearing a long robe and a turban, roller-skating while playing some kind of ethnic music on a cheap electric guitar. Two young Oriental men in identical sharkskin suits stood holding orange slushes and not drinking them. Simon nodded and they nodded back. There were a lot of people on roller skates and skateboards and mountain bikes, all whizzing past pedestrians who were eating soft pretzels or ice cream cones and not paying them the least attention.

Muffy was particularly interested in a young man who was juggling buzzing chainsaws while telling jokes to a small crowd. The man pretended to drop one of his chainsaws and a little girl squealed. Muffy, with police dog in his blood, charged.

"Stop Muffy! Stop!" Crystal called ineffectually.

Simon, remembering the button on the retractable leash, pressed it hard. All sixty pounds of Muffy reached the end of his free rein and came suddenly to a stop, jerking Simon off his feet and sending him flying through the air to land at the feet of an athletic-looking young woman wearing very short shorts who was lacing up her skates. Muffy, having forgotten all about rescuing the little girl or eating the chainsaw man, trotted back toward Simon and immediately started nuzzling the skater.

"What a pretty boy!" the skater said, patting Muffy's head. She glared at Simon, as if to dispel any notion that she might have been referring to him.

Crystal caught up to Simon and took the leash from him. "Are you all right, Muffy?" she said, pulling the dog a little roughly away from his new friend. "Muffy doesn't like strangers," she told the skater coldly and proceeded down the boardwalk with Simon trailing behind, dusting himself off as he went.

Other vendors were closing up their booths and little stores. Two men hurriedly folded up hinged plywood panels containing hundreds of pairs of sunglasses and fitted them into the back of a new SUV. An old woman sat looking into the sunset. Beside her were stacks of brightly colored, handwoven fabric from Guatemala and a black velvet display with exquisite silver jewelry.

When they came upon the fortune teller's stall, the sinking sun cast long shadows across the beach and the booth was bathed in darkness. They approached cautiously. Muffy flopped down and promptly went to sleep.

"Hey Mel," Crystal called out timidly.

A form emerged from the shadows that looked like a shadow itself. She was dressed in a long, tiered skirt made of many layers of filmy deep blue fabric, making it look almost like feathers. She wore a loose black silk blouse covered by a brick red shawl. Her hair was dark and thick and hung in ropey braids.

"Crystal," she said. "I'd almost given up."

200

"Melanie, this is Simon. Simon, Melanie."

Melanie didn't look in Crystal's direction. She looked into Simon's eyes, as if searching for something that was lost. Her own light green eyes did not seem to blink and darted back and forth like a bird's.

"Like I told you before, Simon works at the same company as my mom," Crystal said, already conscious that she was being ignored. "Simon's into all kinds of New Age spiritual stuff and it's like we've known each other for centuries."

"You are an old soul," Melanie said to Simon. She looked him up and down, her bird eyes never resting on any one place for long. "You need answers," she declared.

"We're just going for a walk," Crystal interjected. "We thought you might like to come."

"You were destined to find me," said Melanie.

"But if you're busy . . ." said Crystal.

"You're in grave danger," Melanie announced.

"Don't mind Mel," Crystal said to Simon. "She takes this Druid thing very seriously. She doesn't mean to scare you. Do you, Mel?"

Simon said, "That's okay, Crystal. Do you read palms or something, Melanie?"

"She casts runes," said Crystal. "She makes them out of real bones. And she's a vegetarian, too. I don't know how she stands it. You're still a vegetarian, aren't you Mel?"

"Sit down," Melanie told Simon. She lit some sage, which smoked with a faintly illicit smell. "What is your question?" she asked.

Simon thought a moment and answered, "How do I put things right?"

There was a flicker of a smile from Melanie's thin lips.

"Most people ask about money or romance," Crystal interjected.

Melanie waved the burning sage in the air and traced around Simon's body with the smoke, all the while mumbling in some unknown tongue. She drew out a clean white linen cloth and spread it on the ground and passed the burning sage over it. She opened a small soft brown leather pouch and stirred the contents with her hand, her fingers long and slender with sharp, natural nails. The runes clicked dryly in her hand. She turned to the north and suddenly stopped chanting, as if the words caught in her throat, and tossed the runes onto the cloth. The nine rune bones landed on the white cloth that seemed to gather what light was left in the sky. The runes were inscribed with crude black symbols. One of them bounced out and landed face-down on the sidewalk. Of the remaining eight, two rested face-down. The others, with their stark, angular black lines, appeared to float on the white linen, like characters on a computer screen.

Melanie walked around the cloth, chanting softly to herself, sometimes bending low to make out one of the runes in the failing light. As she circled the runes, her hands fluttered at her sides and the evening breeze off the ocean made her layered skirt flutter too.

"She's memorizing the runes and their positions and which ones are up," Crystal whispered. "The runes represent the universe. They show how everything is interconnected. The idea is that fate is the consequence of stuff you've done, but it can be changed. Casting runes isn't witchcraft, more like psychology with some intuition thrown in. Personally, I think Melanie is a little psychic too. I don't know if it's traditionally okay, but if it comes to her, she incorporates that in her castings." Simon was watching Melanie's every movement with intensity. "She's also a little weird," Crystal added. "And hasn't had like a real date in over a year. So watch yourself."

Melanie's quick bird eyes landed on first one rune and then another. Finally, she turned up the ones that were down and studied them for several minutes. She stepped up to Simon and took his hand, leading him to where the runes lay and knelt beside them, Simon following her lead. Crystal stood over them, trying to see what was going on. Melanie pointed with a long sharp finger to a rune that looked like a capital F angling upward. "This is your 'Fehu,' " she said. "It literally means 'cattle' and represents wealth. It seems you are a wealthy man. But money is not important to you. Your wealth is your friends—and see how it lies against your 'Algiz,' " she said, indicating what looked like a capital Y with a line up the center. "This is your protective sanctuary. Your friends are also your fortress. They hold you up and keep you safe. But if they fall, you fall."

Melanie pointed to two other runes. "And see here. These two are also touching: weapons and God's light. There are powerful forces behind you." She nodded to the rune that had bounced off the linen. "And that is your 'Hagalaz.' " She looked furtively into his eyes. "You also have powerful forces gathering against you. In your future, there is great danger and you are walking to meet it like a lamb to the slaughter." She drew a deep breath and closed her eyes a moment. She opened her eyes and pointed. "Note the arrangement of these two here. You are soon coming upon a series of events that will develop faster than you can react. They will overrun you. If you prevail, your 'Ansuz,' your karma, will greatly benefit. If not, the consequences for thousands of people will be grave."

Melanie squeezed Simon's hand and let out a little gasp. She convulsed and seemed to slip into a trance. "The one you seek is near and although the way is clear as glass, you cannot see." She shuddered as if fighting something off.

"Answers to your questions await you in the ancient relics. But also betrayal and death." Melanie released his hand as if it burned her and staggered to her feet. She picked up the burning sage and waved it over her whole body as if scrubbing herself clean. "I've done all I can," she said, not looking at Simon. "Now go."

"Just like that?" Crystal asked.

"Uh, no." Melanie said, sounding distracted. "Give me a hundred dollars."

"Huh?" said Simon.

"Come on, come on," said Melanie, still looking away. She fluttered her thin, pointed fingers, palm up.

Simon shrugged and peeled two one-hundred-dollar bills off a roll, deposited them in her hand, and stuffed the rest back in his jeans.

Crystal roused Muffy and they walked back to the car in silence.

Crystal looked at Simon sheepishly. "It's been a fun first date, huh?"

Simon nodded. "You sure know how to show a guy a good time."

"Listen, I don't know what got into Melanie. I've never seen her go so totally psycho. At first, I figured she thought you were just like cute, you know—and was acting silly. Melanie never was what I'd call a smooth talker. But I mean really! What was that deal about the forces of darkness gathering against you? A line like that has got to be bad for business. Speaking of which, I'm surprised you still paid her. Besides which, if I recall correctly, her regular fee is twenty-five dollars."

"She looked scared to me," said Simon.

"Well, yeah. She was trying to charge you four times her normal rate."

Muffy had fallen asleep in the back of the Honda and was snoring loudly.

"I wonder what she meant about finding answers in ancient relics," said Simon.

Crystal shrugged. "I don't know, but Melanie once told me that casting runes pulls stuff out of the customer, out of thin air, and out of herself, too. So, talking about relics made me think about shopping. Okay, so most things make me think about shopping. But Mel and I go shopping together at odd places like the kite shop on Melrose and the consignment places on Sepulveda. Our favorite place—her favorite place—is this little antique store, across from the old gas station in Santa Monica. They have got like the coolest old kimonos and those huge antique Chinese pots. You could hide in one—like what's his name, Ali Baba."

"It does sound like a good place," said Simon. "But it doesn't sound like a place of murder and intrigue."

"Maybe not, but they do have some old books and great brass stuff from India and these old prayer wheels from Tibet that my dad . . ." Crystal's voice trailed off. "Well, all I'm saying is that they have some genuine antiques and the guy who runs it knows a lot about the history and stuff. We should go some time." She grinned. "Come on. Would I steer you wrong? And as you can imagine, I'm looking for any excuse to get out of the house."

Chapter 33

"Did Simon send you?" Amy asked warily, speaking through the narrow gap allowed by the security chain.

"Come on, Amy," said Kenny. "Do I have to have an ulterior motive to visit an old friend?"

Amy sighed wearily, unlatched the chain, and opened her door. Kenny stepped in and stood awkwardly on the threshold for a few moments, looking forlorn as a puppy in the rain. "Oh, come here, you big galoot," she said and opened her arms. They hugged, Kenny engulfing the petite woman.

"We miss you, Amy," he said, his voice quavering.

They disengaged and Amy held Kenny at arm's length to get a good look at him. A single tear ran unashamedly down his big face and dripped off his chin. "Now you cut that out," she said, turning away toward the kitchen, surreptitiously wiping her own eyes. "I've got some jambalaya here. It's still hot."

"Okay," Kenny said brightening.

They sat at the kitchen table. When Kenny was through, he wiped the sweat from his forehead with a linen napkin. "Oh, that was good! Good and spicy. I'm a new man," he declared.

"What a shame," said Amy. "I kind of liked the old man."

"Simon didn't send me, you know," Kenny said, looking suddenly serious. "He wouldn't like it if he knew I was here. I know he would have come himself if he thought you'd take him back. He hasn't been himself since you broke up."

"Suffering, is he?"

"It's the little things that give it away. His apartment is a wreck, there's stuff piled everywhere."

"And this is new?"

"You should see what he's eating—canned spaghetti!" Kenny made a face. "And I actually saw some white bread in his cupboard!"

"No! Did you call the suicide hotline?"

"Not only that, but he's been working sixty hours a week. Our Simon, working!"

Amy nodded. "Well, that *is* disturbing. Working every day—that proves he must be out of his mind with grief. I didn't dump him, you know. I gave him a choice: give up his job with those crooks at Going Platinum or give me up. And he chose that job over me. So I say good luck to him. And if he ever quits that job, well, he knows my number."

Kenny placed his two enormous paws over her hands, completely covering them. "Don't be such a hard case, Amy. He needs you now. More than ever. He's gotten into something really bad this time."

"Have him call the lawyers' referral service."

"There's only one lawyer who can help him now. And I'm looking at her."

Amy stared at him a moment. "Oh, geeze, Kenny. How can I say no to you?" She extracted one of her hands and laid it on Kenny's. "You're a good friend. Sometimes I think Simon doesn't deserve you. Or me either. What do you want me to do?"

Chapter 34

The Tibetan shop in Santa Monica was smaller than Simon expected. The front window displayed tempera paintings of mandalas and there were some items of jewelry that were stylish, but not rare or otherwise valuable. Inside, there were a few of the large Chinese pots Crystal had promised. Reproductions were mixed in with the genuine antiques. A fierce-looking Himalayan mask hung on the wall with a spiky projection coming out of the top of its gruesome head. The price tag was turned to the wall and it was too high to reach without a ladder.

Even if there were a lot of tourist knock-offs, the place smelled old. It had the tangy smell of old brass and the musty smell of moldy leather and old wooden packing crates. It smelled foreign too. Judging by the clutter by the side door, their suppliers used straw and native wood shavings for packing, not bubble wrap and plastic peanuts. There was no computerized cash register at the counter, just a pad of rough-looking off-white paper and a fountain pen tethered with a brass chain.

Near the back of the store was a glass display case containing what Simon suspected was museum quality art. Elegantly framed, the collection included a silk tapestry of a mandala depicting Mara, the fearsome goddess of the underworld. An iron vajra, the symbol of one of the circles of the mandala, resembling a mirror image of eagle claws, back to back, rested on a special stand. It looked heavy and useful, more like a tool than art. It was subtly decorated with bronze inlays of human skulls and severed heads.

One shelf displayed a series of bronze castings of Buddhist deities, each shown in the process of vanquishing lesser gods. There was Bhimsen, wearing a Newari headdress, about to strike a deadly blow to his divine enemy. There was Vajrapani, the god of unpromising causes, trampling a snake god beneath his feet. Chakrasamvara, with twelve arms standing for the twelve links in the chain of causality, was shown tearing an elephant in two with one pair of hands, playing a drum with another. With his other hands he was holding a skull bowl of blood, a trident, and cradling the severed head of the god Brahma.

"Pretty sick and twisted stuff if you ask me," observed Crystal.

Simon nodded. "It looks nasty, all right. But it all has subtle symbolic significance. And every one of these pieces is a national treasure of Tibet, probably looted from temples and monasteries after the uprising in nineteen fifty-nine. You have to wonder what the authorities in Lhasa would do if they knew these things were here."

"You've studied this stuff. Who's this bad boy with all the arms?"

"He's Chakrasamvara, also known as Heruka, which is Sanskrit, roughly translated as 'more or less pissed off.' "

Crystal whistled. "I'd hate to see him really pissed." She pointed to a three-bladed ceremonial dagger. "What's the story behind this thing?" she asked.

"It is a phurbu," said a voice behind them. "It is a Tibetan exorcist dagger, used by lamas to drive out evil spirits." He was a short, compact man of around sixty with thick gray hair and bright blue eyes. He wore a gold talisman of Chinese origin around his neck and an old scar behind his right ear. "Forgive me for sneaking up." He chuckled. "How are you Crystal? Nice to see you have brought a friend." He extended his hand to Simon. "I am Do Kham, the humble owner of this establishment."

Simon shook the hand, which felt as dry and hard as if it had been carved out of wood. "Pleased to meet you," he said.

"Do you like the phurbu? It is a nice piece, don't you think? See how the three blades emerge from the mouth of the Makara. It is a very fine casting from the seventeenth century. On special today for the low, low price of eight thousand dollars American. Shall I wrap it up?"

Crystal giggled. "Don't you have any new ones? I don't know where this one has been."

Do Kham chuckled mirthlessly, the sound like that of gravel under heavy boots. "Very wise, too," he said. "Let me show you something a bit more pleasant."

He handed Crystal a necklace of squarish pieces, bearing carved symbols, tinted purple. "This is a well-crafted example of eighteenth-century Tibetan folk art, carved from yak bone and strung with tightly-woven human hair."

"It's lovely," said Crystal.

Simon looked over her shoulder. "Very interesting," he said. "I don't know much about the history of Tibet, but in the eighteenth century, was there an influx of Japanese goods?"

Do Kham's blue eyes caught fire.

Simon pointed to one of the decorated squares. "Isn't this the Japanese character for 'horse'?"

Do Kham smiled. "So it is. How did this get mixed in with the antiques?" He deftly tossed the necklace into a wooden barrel that contained toy prayer wheels and photos of the Dalai Lama in plastic frames. "Perhaps I could interest you in something merely beautiful." He produced a necklace about twenty-five inches long with large blue oval stones and held it in both hands for Crystal to see.

"Oh, my God!" said Crystal. "This is gorgeous. What's it made of?"

Do Kham made a little bow. "This is a Tibetan necklace made of lapis lazuli and silver. Although it is a modern piece, it is reminiscent of more ancient renderings found in museums. Do you see how the smaller lapis stones are echoed by the small silver beads?"

Crystal examined the necklace carefully. "I can't believe this," she said. "The pattern on the silver is almost like the pattern on my anklet!"

This revelation stopped Do Kham in the middle of his sales pitch. "How interesting. Might I have a look at it?"

A little self-conscious, Crystal lifted the hem of her long dark cotton skirt to reveal her silver anklet. She unhooked it from a pudgy ankle and held it up for Do Kham's inspection.

He looked it over quickly, then pulled out a small magnifying glass and studied it more closely, turning the individual beads over one by one. The muscles in his lean face tightened and twitched. His breathing grew noticeably shallower. "This is nice," he said, casually. "May I inquire where you obtained this?" Do Kham asked, unable to completely mask his excitement.

Crystal shrugged. "I don't know. I got it from my dad a long time ago. I've worn it every day since he died."

"Your father?" he said nonchalantly. "Oh, yes. I believe you mentioned once that he traveled to Tibet or China or thereabouts."

"India," Crystal corrected.

"Ah, yes. My poor memory. India, as you say." Do

Kham held the anklet like a bird, fragile and likely to fly away at any moment. "Would you care to sell it?" The look of anguish on his face betrayed that he knew he had spoken hastily.

"No," said Crystal. "It was a special gift from my father."

"Yes, yes, quite so," Do Kham seemed to agree. "Sentimental value. Hard to put a price on that, isn't it? Still, I could give you a fair price. In truth, it's not worth very much, but there are certain buyers who ask for such things."

"You don't happen to play poker, do you?" Simon asked. "Oh, never mind."

"I don't think so. But thanks," said Crystal. "And how much is this necklace?"

Do Kham smiled. "A beautiful thing, is it not? Why don't you put it on?"

Crystal shivered with glee as Simon fastened the strand of blue stones and silver around her neck. "How do I look?" she asked Simon shyly.

"Stunning!" said Do Kham. "It sets off your dark eyes most splendidly. I am taken quite off my guard. The necklace was meant for you. Truly."

Simon nodded. "It really does look good on you."

"How much?" asked Crystal.

"I don't want to embarrass you, Crystal," said Do Kham evasively. "I'm afraid it is rather a lot. I know you are not currently employed. It is not financially in my best interest, but a beautiful woman should have beautiful things. Perhaps a trade? This exquisite necklace for your little silver anklet?"

Crystal looked to Simon for support. "Ooo, what should I do?" She giggled and moaned and pranced around in circles.

The bell on the shop door rang, indicating a customer

had entered. They were standing behind a row of shelving and could not see the door. Do Kham was clearly irritated by the interruption, but he bowed and turned to see to the door.

"Excuse me," said Simon. Do Kham stopped. "The anklet?" He held out his hand.

Do Kham gave a gravelly laugh and pointed to his forgetful head. "Quite so, quite so," he said. He deposited the anklet in Simon's hand and hurried off to the door.

Simon examined the anklet to see why it held such fascination for Do Kham. The hook was stainless steel and the anklet was probably not more than a hundred years old. Some of the individual beads bore slightly different markings and might have been older. It was likely the anklet had been restrung. He could see no reason why Do Kham would trade it for the lapis necklace.

As he was pondering this question, Simon thought he heard a familiar voice coming from the front of the shop. Out of context, it took him a moment to identify it. But there was no mistake. It was the voice of Detective Bob Bentley.

"What kind of place is this?" Bentley was saying. Do Kham explained that he dealt in Oriental antiques, specializing in Tibetan religious artifacts. Apparently thumbing over the merchandise, Bentley exclaimed, "Six thousand dollars for this ugly mask? You gotta be shitting me! I'd be afraid to go to bed with this thing in the house. Would you look at this creepy thing, O'Reilly?"

"It's old," said O'Reilly.

"I can see that it's old," argued Bentley. "But as ugly as it is, I can't see how it got to be so old."

Do Kham said, "Then perhaps there is something else with which I can help you? I am at your service."

"I want you to take a look at this photograph," said Bentley, "and tell me if you recognize him."

"No. I'm so sorry. Is he a collector?"

"No, he's dead," said Bentley. "His name was Steve Merritt."

Crystal let out a little gasp. "Why are they looking here?" she whispered.

"That is a very good question," said Simon. "I thought they were looking for me. They think I killed Steve—you've probably heard that by now."

Crystal stroked the necklace. "Yes, but I never believed it."

"Thank you," said Simon

Bentley pressed on. "So you've never seen this man or heard his name mentioned."

"Not that I recall," said Do Kham.

There were several seconds of silence. Then Bentley spoke. "Well, you know that's funny, Mr. Kham. Because it was reported to me that you were seen in Mr. Merritt's company on several occasions."

"I'm a businessman. I see many people and hear many names."

There was the click of keys of O'Reilly's pocket computer. He spoke up. "On the afternoon of June fourth, you were seen in the New Health Fitness Center on Sepulveda, working out with free weights next to Steve Merritt."

"I believe in keeping fit," said Do Kham.

O'Reilly continued. "On the morning of June twenty-sixth, you were seen in Mike Ironside's Big and Tall store at the same time Mr. Merritt was there."

"And you don't look all that big to me, Mr. Kham," said Bentley.

Do Kham did his raspy chuckle. "In my country, I am

considered larger than average. You Americans are so big! But no. I was looking for a gift for a big friend."

"Then maybe you can tell us," said Bentley, "what you were doing on June twenty-ninth at three p.m. at the Going Platinum Country Club."

"The customary thing. Golfing of course."

"Alone?"

"Yes, I was alone."

"Did you speak to anyone at the club or on the golf course itself?"

"I am not anti-social, officer. I'm sure I must have spoken to someone."

"And you did speak to Steve Merritt."

"I suppose it is possible," Do Kham said loftily.

Bentley could be heard sighing heavily. "Because your caddy told me that you and Steve Merritt had a long conversation on the fourth hole and when Merritt left, he did not look happy. In fact, he didn't even finish his game. Now what can you tell me about that?"

"Ah, yes! My poor memory. Forgive me. The unfortunate gentleman did not mention his name. And, excuse me, Caucasians all tend to look alike to me. Ha, ha. But yes. Now I remember him. He was a very good golfer. Very fast and I am regrettably slow. The gentleman wanted to—how do you say—play through. It was not polite of me, I know. But I have so little time for recreation. I needed to get back to the store. I told him no. I am ashamed of myself to remember it. Especially now that the poor man has passed away."

"Not exactly 'passed away' Mr. Kham. Steve Merritt was brutally murdered."

"Oh, I am so sorry to hear of that," he said.

"Was Steve Merritt ever in your store?" asked O'Reilly.

"I don't believe so," Do Kham answered. "But an employee might have waited on the unfortunate Mr. Merritt in my absence."

"Show us the computer where your POS data are stored."

" 'POS'? What is that? I have no computer."

"Point Of Sale," O'Reilly enunciated as if Do Kham had suddenly gone deaf. "You don't know Point Of Sale? No computer? How do you keep track of inventory? How do you figure your taxes? That's unbelievable!"

Do Kham laughed like grinding gears. "This is an antique store. I also am an antique. All our records are made with pencil and paper, I'm afraid. I keep them in the back. You are welcome to look."

"This is going to take forever!" said O'Reilly, exasperated. "Everybody has a computer."

"Why don't you lend him one of yours?" said Bentley. "You must have a spare or two on you."

"We might as well get started," said O'Reilly.

Simon whispered, "I'd really rather not have them find me here."

Crystal said, "They'll probably head for the storeroom where they have all the file cabinets. I've seen it before when he let me use the restroom. We can hide in the office behind the door to the left."

Simon and Crystal slipped into the office seconds before Bentley and O'Reilly reached the back of the room. Do Kham had a puzzled look on his face when he did not see them in the back. He accompanied the detectives to the storeroom.

Simon and Crystal closed the door behind them. They could still hear the detectives banging file drawers and complaining. The office seemed stark for an ongoing business.

The small desk was uncluttered, with only a couple of pieces of mail stacked neatly on one corner. There were no pictures on the walls. Only a few back issues of trade journals on the bookshelf.

"So do you think I should like get the necklace or what?" Crystal asked, still whispering.

"Definitely," said Simon. "But something tells me you shouldn't trade your anklet for it."

"He does want it pretty bad," she acknowledged.

"Did your father ever say anything about it? Is there something special about it?" Simon handed the anklet back to her.

Crystal glanced at it, shrugged, and stuffed it in her cluttered purse. "No. Well, actually, he never said anything about it at all. It was in a box of stuff he bought at an estate sale in India at a house he remodeled."

"What else was in the box? Whatever happened to it?"

Crystal ran the bumpy beads of the necklace slowly over her teeth. "Don't you think it's kind of risky and romantic, hiding in the office of a mysterious foreigner while the police are looking for evidence against you in the next room?"

"It makes me kind of nervous," said Simon.

"Exactly!" Crystal's whisper became louder. "It makes me kind of hot!" Her dark, heavily shadowed eyes grew wide.

"About this box—" said Simon.

"Yes?" Crystal leered. "Oh, all right! The box. It just had a lot of old stuff in it. I never got a good look at it really. Mom took care of it. In fact, I remember, she was mad. Dad was always sending home these goofy brass knick-knacks of Hindu gods and dragons and mandalas and incense burners. Junk. Mom said with his connections, Dad could have smuggled back some really valuable things. But he always bought junk that nobody would want. Actually, Mom was so mad she threw the entire box of stuff in the trash the week we had our roof replaced. I sifted through the nails and broken shingles and pulled the anklet out of the Dumpster. Now I'm glad I did. It's all I have to remember Daddy by. So you really think I shouldn't trade it for the necklace?"

Simon had been pacing around the office and stopped to open a small cupboard. He stood in front of it, transfixed.

"What?" asked Crystal. "Is it like drugs or gold bullion or a shrunken head? What?" She tried to see around Simon.

"I'd never actually seen one of these before," said Simon distractedly.

"What is it, for heaven's sake?" demanded Crystal, forgetting to whisper.

Simon seemed to come to his senses and stepped aside to show Crystal what looked like a metal saucer about eight inches in diameter, decorated lavishly with gold and silver skulls and severed heads. The center of the object was dominated by a large and deep triangular relief. Beside the saucer was an ornamented iron tool like a gardening trowel about a foot long, with a flat triangular blade that appeared to match the indentation in the saucer.

"Cool!" Crystal enthused. "What the hell is it?"

"Well," said Simon. "I've only seen pictures before now. But I believe you are looking at holy relics used in the secret Homa ritual. I'd say sixteenth or seventeenth century."

"Get it down. I want to see it up close."

"I'm not touching that thing!" said Simon.

"Oh, don't be such a chicken!" said Crystal. "I thought you were tight with the Hindu gods."

Simon looked surprised. "Are you kidding? I'm a Methodist. And this is nothing to mess with. I understand that the actual ritual is a secret, but it has something to do with a fire sacrifice to Vaisaravana, the god of wealth. These relics should be in a museum back in Tibet, under armed guard."

"You don't believe in that stuff, do you?"

Simon took a step back. "I believe that evil and the power of greed are real."

"So did they, like, sacrifice humans to get rich?"

Simon arched one eyebrow. "Does that sound so far-fetched? As I said, I think the ritual was a closely guarded secret, but I've seen scraps of it that have been included in textbooks. As I recall, the Master, the one who performs the ceremony, prepares two kinds of foods, cut into triangles: one white for the gods who eat vegetables and the other red for the gods who eat meat. There are incantations of protection and incantations for the god of fire." Simon thought a moment. "I remember there was this bit about driving away some kind of evil spirits. It goes, *'Om Sunbani Sunbani HUM HUM Peh! Om Krihara Krihara HUM HUM Peh!'* "

"What are you doing here!" Do Kham shouted savagely, suddenly appearing in the doorway.

Crystal let out a squeal and clutched Simon's sleeve.

"I'm terribly sorry," said Simon.

"We were just looking for a place to wait until you were through with your other customers," explained Crystal.

Do Kham's face was red and the veins in his temples were swollen. The scar on his neck had turned purple. He strode to the cupboard and slammed the doors shut. He drew a deep breath and composed himself. He motioned to the door and ushered them out. Once outside the office, he closed and locked the door. "Please forgive my little outburst," he said. "Security is my responsibility and if my insurance company knew of my negligence, they would cancel our policy. I was only angry with myself."

"What's all the noise out here?" Bentley called, emerging from the back room, followed by O'Reilly. He caught sight of Simon and stopped dead. "Well, I'll be damned!"

"Hello, Detective Bentley," said Simon.

Do Kham looked warily, first at Simon, then Bentley.

"What brings you out this way, Simon?" asked Bentley.

"Shopping," Simon answered cheerily.

"Do tell. What'd you get?"

"We're getting this lovely necklace," Simon said. Crystal smiled sweetly. "How much?" he asked Do Kham.

The proprietor glanced involuntarily at Crystal's feet and said, "Three hundred fifty American."

"Sold!" said Simon and handed Do Kham the cash. Crystal made a little gasp and blushed.

Bentley snorted. "I knew there had to be somebody who could afford to shop here. So the platinum putter business has been good to you."

Do Kham looked surprised.

"I can't complain," said Simon. "You might check out the Himalayan demon mask for yourself. It could work wonders for your attitude. Well, we'll be seeing you, Detective Bentley." Simon took Crystal by the arm and started walking out the store.

"What's wrong with my attitude?" Bentley appealed to O'Reilly, palms up.

Outside the store, Simon breathed a sigh of relief.

"I don't know what to say," said Crystal, fingering her new necklace. "That was so generous of you!"

"Not at all," said Simon. "You've helped me out today more than you know. Consider it payment for services rendered."

"Pretty scary back there in the office, huh?" said Crystal.

"I thought I was going to pee my pants when Do Kham sneaked up on us. Geeze! You were looking in that direction and you didn't even see him walk in. I'm like, 'Where did he come from?' "

"Where indeed?" said Simon.

"This neighborhood creeps me out!" said Crystal. "Look." She pointed to the street. Simon caught a glance of the homeless man he had last seen in Century City near Harriman's "office" scuttle into an alley. This was the first time Simon got a good look at his face. Somehow, he had not noticed before that the man was Asian.

Chapter 35

Zelda smiled and cigarette smoke sifted through her perfect teeth and veiled her luminous violet eyes. "Really Yakov, I don't see how we can do anything on the, um, financial statement. Crystal insists on staying home tonight."

Mr. Z pouted. "What about her little naked witches?"

Zelda wore a sequined silk tube dress that accentuated her waifish figure. She posed herself languidly upon the banister that led up to her bedroom. "Crystal said that Melanie, the head Druid, has been feeling 'scrambled' ever since she and Simon visited the booth on Venice Beach. The group hasn't met since."

"And where is our boy Simon? I thought they were getting along so well. Why isn't Crystal out with him tonight?"

Zelda's sensuous expression iced over. "If you must know, I have forbidden Crystal to see Simon any more."

"But why?" Mr. Z practically wailed.

"You know I never approved of Simon in the first place. He's trouble, I tell you. That business with poor Melanie, and now Crystal tells me that they were practically thrown out of an antique store."

"So big deal," scoffed Mr. Z. "Maybe some people find him odd. I admit I do myself. But he's a good boy. And Crystal likes him."

"Crystal will do what I tell her!" Zelda snapped. "And mark my words, Simon will end up making trouble for Going Platinum, too. Did you see that strange woman hanging around the clubhouse this week? Well, she turns out to be Simon's ex-girlfriend's mother."

"I don't see what that has to do with Simon. And what harm has the woman done, anyway?"

"What about Mr. Harriman?" Zelda persisted. "He was in this week, asking a lot of questions about Simon. It seems Simon sent some big goon to intimidate him."

"J.D. didn't say anything about it to me."

"You know Mr. Harriman. Nobody pushes him around. He means to get to the bottom of this."

"Maybe I'll deliver J.D.'s shipments personally for a while," said Mr. Z. "He's a little hot-headed. Only a few weeks ago, he came in and complained about Steve Merritt."

Zelda perked up. "He did? What was that about?"

Mr. Z shrugged. "He said something about Steve trying to get money out of him for some reason. I don't know. He talked so fast I really didn't understand him. Anyway, it's all sheep under the fence now that Steve is dead—God rest his soul." Mr. Z crossed himself.

Zelda placed a bony hand over her mouth. "You don't suppose Mr. Harriman . . ."

Mr. Z straightened. "You think J.D. killed Steve Merritt? Maybe I'll have a talk with Simon."

"That's right!" said Zelda, a little too forcefully. "You fix his wagon."

"Yes, if Simon has a wagon, Yakov will fix it, all right. I wouldn't want anything to happen to him."

"What? I thought you were going to fire that New Age freak!"

Mr. Z laughed out loud. "Fire Simon? Fire my golden goose? That boy makes more money for Going Platinum than I do. Fire Simon? Really Zelda, you are so funny. Now come, let's finish our financial statement."

Zelda looked coy. "Yakov, you are such an animal! But not tonight."

Mr. Z tapped the banister. "No, I mean the real financial statement. My cousins are angry with me. They say our books don't balance. Our putter supplier stopped a shipment last week because we did not pay our bill. I had to pay him out of my own pocket. I told my cousins everything is fine. We are making money so fast we can't find it, that's all. I promised I would finish the statement and show it to them this week. They trust me, but they are growing impatient."

Zelda slunk up two steps, turned, and bent low toward Mr. Z. "Well, maybe we could do a few little pages, Yakov."

Mr. Z kept his eyes on hers. "You have made a fool of me long enough, Zelda. I want that statement on my desk by nine o'clock tomorrow." And with that, he turned and strode out the door.

Zelda took a deep drag on her cigarette and blew the smoke straight up. There was a cough from the top of the stairs. "Oh, it's you," Zelda droned without turning.

"Mother?" The voice was small and tender, like a child's. "What have you done? Have you embezzled from Going Platinum?"

Zelda whirled around, the candlelight glinting softly off her sequined green dress. "Do you dare to judge me, you silly little cow? You, who have never had a real job in your entire life? What did you think kept a roof over your head? What did you suppose bought those cheesecakes you continuously stuff down your throat? Since your father died, I have had to manage the best I could for us. Even before that, I was the one who had to look out for our future because that worm was only interested in paradise." Zelda spat out the word. "He squandered what little he made as an architect on that junk stolen from temples. The worst of it was, if he'd ever had anything valuable, he wouldn't have known it. And you—you're just the same, mooning over that idiot, Simon. He'll soon be broke again. That's his natural condition. And he'd take you with him into poverty if I'd let him."

"Simon is very nice," Crystal's voice quavered at the top of the stairs.

"So is a cocker spaniel," said Zelda.

"But I thought we were doing all right," said Crystal. "What do we need the money for?"

Zelda took a deep drag from her cigarette and smiled secretively through the smoke. "We're buying a country club."

"Will you have to go to jail, Mother?"

Zelda glared at the darkness above the stairs. "Not if you remember to keep your mouth shut, dear."

Chapter 36

Simon pulled off the Santa Monica Freeway, drumming on the steering wheel more or less in time with the Cairo Cats, an Egyptian percussion band, throbbing out of his new CD player. A row of tiny brass bells jingled merrily from the visor.

"Om—m—m—m—m," Simon intoned as he whipped around the corner onto a side street in time to see a car pulling away from the curb, leaving the only parking space within two blocks. Simon zipped into the space.

"You really think that Om thing helps you get parking places?" Ben Hogan inquired from the back seat.

"Works every time. Hi Ben," said Simon. "Nice of you to drop in." He glanced in the mirror to see Ben Hogan with his jaunty tam. Simon adjusted his gangster tie and carefully centered his crystal. He gave the "thumbs up" into the mirror. Simon scooped up his shoes and socks with one hand and his empty violin case with the other and hopped out of the car, closing the driver's door with his bare foot. Simon did a little hornpipe dance on the sidewalk and continued on at a brisk pace with Hogan wafting behind him. "So tell me, Ben, how do you like being back in the land of the living?"

Hogan wafted a bit faster to catch up to Simon. "To tell you the truth, I'm a little disappointed. Not having a body means you end up left out of most of the really fun things. Plus," Hogan drifted through a fireplug and three pedestrians who were walking toward them, "nobody hears me but you—and, of course, Cayce. It's lonesome. I tried talking with Cayce but he talks mostly about food, petting, birds, and you and your friends. He doesn't seem to know a thing about golf. And speaking of which, I can't hold a club or hit a ball anymore. I'd love to play against some of these new hot shots." Hogan looked sad and a bicyclist whizzed through him. "But those days are over."

"Oh, cheer up, Ben," said Simon. "You get to help solve a murder and restore mythological equilibrium."

"I'd rather play eighteen holes with Tiger Woods," he said glumly.

A scruffy looking man sitting at a bus stop, next to an empty coffee can, held a sign that read, "Prepare for the Kingdom of Heaven!"

Simon stopped and said, "The kingdom will not come by expectation. They will not say, 'See here, see there.' The kingdom of the Father is spread out upon the earth and men do not see it."

The scruffy man gaped. "What scripture is that, brother?" he asked.

"The Gospel of Thomas," said Simon. "Dead Sea Scrolls. You should check it out," he said cheerily and dropped a hundred-dollar bill into the coffee can.

"Thank you, brother, I will," said the man.

Simon walked briskly up the sidewalk to the Going Platinum Country Club. A stocky well-dressed Asian man with mirrored sunglasses lurked in the shadows by the entrance. "Good afternoon, Lin," Simon called to him. Lin nodded. "Where is the ever-vigilant Mr. Chow?" Lin tilted his head slightly upward. Simon glanced up to see Mr. Chow standing on the roof. He waved and Simon waved back.

Simon pulled open the door and swept in, his bare feet

slapping the vinyl floor as he went. "What do you think of our little country club, Ben?"

"I've seen worse," said Hogan. "The water hazard on the five hole is a pip!"

"That means it's good, right?" asked Simon.

"Right," said Hogan. "I guess I could say it's 'cool.' " He shuddered. "Horrid slang, you kids use!"

"Where are your shoes?"

"Good afternoon Zelda," Simon said holding up his shoes for her to see. "Lovely frock you have on today." Zelda growled something back.

"She hates you," Hogan observed.

"She likes me," said Simon out loud as they passed her desk.

Zelda punched her intercom. "Simon just arrived," she said. "He's talking to himself again."

Mr. Z's voice answered, "Thank you, Zelda. I'll be in a meeting with Mr. Chen for about an hour. Please hold all my calls. Have Simon leave his paperwork on his desk."

"I heard," Simon called to Zelda, waving to her over his shoulder.

Simon glimpsed Pater, the bookkeeper, entering Mr. Z's office and closing the door behind him. Simon opened a side door. "How do you like my office?" he asked.

"You get an office?" said Hogan, incredulously.

Simon made himself comfortable in an overstuffed swivel chair behind a large wooden desk. "Hard to believe, isn't it? Like other things around here, it's mostly illusion." He snapped open his violin case, withdrew the morning's paperwork, and stacked it neatly on the desk. "So tell me, Ben, how's the investigation going?"

Hogan hovered across from Simon's desk, arms akimbo, with a smug look on his face. "Well, I'm glad you asked because it just so happens I got some information that's going to break this case wide open. I've always wanted to say that."

"So come on, Ben—give—what have you got?"

Hogan rubbed his palms together—or tried to. "As you know, I have been spending a good deal of time down by the golf course, observing keenly the goings on there, noting who comes and who goes and what they are doing and—"

"Okay, okay, enough already. Cut to the chase."

"Well," said Hogan with relish, "I was at the seven hole yesterday and who do you suppose I saw? All right, all right. It was Do Kham. And guess what? The man is no golfer." Hogan nodded his head triumphantly.

Simon sat waiting. "That's it? That's all you've got? The man is no golfer? You come back from the dead, on the high recommendation of a prominent Spanish inquisitor, to provide me with precious information of a supernatural nature and all you can tell me is the man is no golfer?"

"I don't expect you to understand the subtleties of the situation, as you are not acquainted with the fine points of the great game yourself. But," Hogan chuckled, "that man is no golfer. Do you hear what I'm saying? He was putting with a nine iron, for mercy sake!" Hogan howled with laughter.

Simon waited patiently for him to settle down. "And what does this tell me?"

Hogan composed himself. "Well, sir, I don't know what that tells you. But it tells me that Do Kham has no business out on that, or any, golf course. Oh, he does have a strong swing. The man's in shape, I'll give him that. But his elbows are bent every which way, he slices every drive to the right. I could go on and on. The point is, Do Kham isn't golfing, he's pretending."

Simon absentmindedly drummed out a Middle Eastern rhythm on the desk. "I still don't get it."

Hogan wafted up to the desk. "Well, isn't it obvious? Do Kham is only pretending to golf so he can walk around the course. I took a good look at his scorecard. First of all, the man cheats—which is unforgivable! But second, his scorecard contains little sketches and arrows and Xs. It's like he's mapping the entire course."

"And why would he do that?" asked Simon.

Hogan shrugged. "Beats me, Detective. It's your case." He performed a pantomimed putt. "There is one other thing," he said. "There are these little holes all over the course."

"Gee, holes in a golf course—call CNN."

"I mean just random holes, all over. Not big enough for a golf ball."

"Gophers?"

Hogan sighed impatiently. "Look, Simon, I've spent more than half my life—and quite a lot of time since then—on golf courses. I've seen every kind of hole made by gophers, groundhogs, moles, and squirrels burying walnuts. These are clean—no dirt around the hole—no sod pushed up—nothing. It was like somebody drove a one-inch pipe through the turf. Weird, huh?"

Simon sat a moment, lost in thought, playing with the crystal around his neck. "Maybe not," he said. Suddenly Simon jumped up and clapped his hands together. "Well, it's back to work for me. Ben, you're a good man . . . er ghost . . . whatever. I knew I could count on you. Keep up your surveillance, if you wouldn't mind."

"I've got nothing but time," said Hogan.

"Who knows, you might run into the ghost of Payne Stewart or somebody and get a game in."

Hogan brightened at the thought and levitated a little higher off the floor.

Simon headed for the door. "Well, see you . . . or not. Anyway, take care," he called and stepped into the hall in time to see Pater emerge from Mr. Z's office, looking pale and shaken. Pater passed by the open doorway to Simon's office and glanced in. Seeing nobody, he gave Simon a quizzical look.

Simon headed back to the lobby where he saw Sabrina, casually reading a golfing magazine through dark sunglasses. Beside her was a legal pad half filled with notes.

"Hello, Mrs. Castor," Simon said. "What a nice surprise! I didn't know you were interested in golf."

Sabrina appeared alarmed to see him. "Shush!" she said, motioning Simon to look away. "You don't know me!" she whispered harshly.

"Yes, I can see that," said Simon. "Is there something I can help you with?"

"No! Go away!" she whispered.

The intercom on Zelda's desk crackled. "Zelda, come into my office immediately!" said Mr. Z.

Zelda coughed. "I'm not feeling well. I'm going home now. I'll check back with you when I'm better. Goodbye." Mr. Z tried to say something, but was cut off. Zelda grabbed her purse and hurried toward the door. As she passed Simon and Sabrina, she snorted in disgust.

"What's her problem?" asked Sabrina, still whispering.

"A cold, I guess. There's nobody else around, so you can talk out loud if you want," Simon offered.

"Well, I don't want. I'm gathering information and don't ask me any questions. It's a secret."

"Okay," said Simon. "I just wanted to say that I really miss Amy. I wish she would return my calls. I know we can work things out. I love her, Mrs. Castor."

"Yes, yes. Go away!" she said out loud.

"Goodbye, Mrs. Castor," Simon said and walked out the door, making little slapping sounds with his bare feet.

Simon headed back to his car and passed the scruffy man with the sign.

"Hey, brother," he said. "Your parking meter expired. Don't worry, I got you covered."

Simon shook the man's hand. "Thanks very much. That's thoughtful of you."

"Oh, and you got a note on your dashboard." Simon waved as he started back down the sidewalk. "You really should lock your car, brother. This is L.A.!" the man called after him.

Simon found twenty minutes on his meter and a note on pink stationery wedged between the window and the dashboard. It read:

Dear Simon,

My mother has forbidden me to see you. She has been quite out of her mind lately (more than usual). It has been torture not seeing you (I know it's only been two days). I fear something really bad is going to happen and I don't know how to stop it. Maybe you're the only person who can help. Although it breaks my heart, I have a most urgent secret to tell you. Come to our house at 7:00 p.m. tonight and you will set my tormented mind at rest. I'm making a nice Omelet Grimaldi with Tomatoes Gervais and a yummy Tarte Francaise for dessert.

Yours, Crystal.

Chapter 37

Simon made his way up the cobblestone sidewalk, carefully avoiding the giant catfish. The little pond churned as he drew near, but he looked away so as not to make eye contact with the spooky fish. He reached the door and was about to knock when he heard a window open.

"Oh, it's you again," the voice said. "Zelda's not home. Just that peculiar daughter. Which is probably just as well. Less shouting, you know. I'd stay away from this place if I were you. Don't say I didn't warn you." And with that, the window closed again.

Simon shook his head and knocked. He heard the deadbolt snap back and the door opened slowly to reveal Crystal dressed in black. She wore an ankle-length, hourglass shaped skirt with an outer layer of filmy cotton floral print with accents of deep violet and a matching top with a low scoop neck. Her hair was in disarray and she was carrying a half-empty goblet of red wine. She stared at him for several seconds through heavily shadowed, half-closed eyelids. Crystal reached out and took him by the hand.

"Oh, Simon, I was so worried you wouldn't come," she said, leading him into the kitchen. "Look at all this food!"

The small oak kitchen table was laden with covered silver platters, gilded gravy boats filled with aromatic sauces, little stacks of orange pinwheel pastries, and shell-shaped almond madeleines. There were cobalt glass bowls filled with grapes and fresh apricots. The room was lit by candlelight and shadows danced and flickered across the plain white Wedgwood plates.

Crystal selected a saucer overflowing with pastries and held it under Simon's nose. "These are Grape and Cheese Puffs," she said. "I left out the garlic sausage because I know you don't eat meat. I substituted marinated tofu. They're supposed to go well with wine." She took a gulp of hers. "There's some grape juice here for you."

Simon inhaled deeply. "This smells . . ."

"I couldn't find any fresh scallions," Crystal rattled on, whipping the cover off one of the chafing dishes. "Can you believe that? So I made a Truffle Omelet instead. Isn't it funny I could find truffles and not scallions? But then, I've always been lucky at finding good truffles. It's Mother's private joke. She calls me her little truffle pig. What do you suppose 'omelet' means in French—a little 'om'?" She removed the cover from another dish and frowned. "I hope the Tomatoes Gervais are still hot. I started them early because I knew the omelets wouldn't keep and—"

"It's all wonderful, Crystal," Simon cut in. "Really."

Crystal smiled sheepishly. "I tend to cook too much when I'm nervous. So," she waved her hand over the abundance, "you can see tonight I'm practically psychotic."

"Let's eat," suggested Simon. "And you can tell me all about this secret of yours."

Crystal divided the Truffle Omelet while Simon broke off a steaming piece of fresh sourdough baguette for each of them. The Mornay Sauce ran luxuriously into the omelet and Julienne Potato Cake. Crystal squeezed lime juice over Simon's fruit salad, and for several minutes she watched with rapt attention as he ate.

Simon took a breath. "Crystal, you are gifted," he said.

She smiled. "Do you like it?"

With his mouth full, Simon grunted in the affirmative.

They ate in silence, their knives and forks clicking and scraping on the porcelain plates. As they passed the dishes across the table, shadows from the candles cast silhouettes of feasting giants.

Together, they finished off the Truffle Omelet, the Tomatoes Gervais, the Spanish Orzo Salad, most of the Cappelletti in Ginger Sauce, and an entire plate of Raspberry Jam Rosettes. By the time they got to the Tarte Francaise, they were both prepared to surrender.

Simon threw down his napkin like a white flag. "Crystal, I haven't eaten this well since . . ." he stumbled over a reckless thought. "Well, since a long time," he said.

"I wanted to do something nice for you," Crystal said, a dreamy look in her eyes. "You mean so much to me."

Simon shifted uncomfortably in his seat. "Crystal, there is something I need to tell you."

She reached across the table and took both his hands in hers. "And there's something I need to tell you too, Simon."

Just then, there was the sound of a car door slamming in the driveway.

"Oh my God!" Crystal squealed. "Mother's home!"

Crystal grabbed Simon by the hand and dragged him upstairs. "We have to hide!" she said, scrambling around for a likely place.

"What are we hiding for?" asked Simon.

"If Mother finds us together, she'll kill us both!"

Crystal pulled open her bedroom door and out sprang Muffy, barking excitedly. "Quiet, Muffy! Good Muffy." She tried in vain to calm her bouncing German shepherd.

Downstairs, there was the sound of the front door opening. "Quick!" Crystal whispered. "In here!" She flung open a small broom closet and pulled Simon inside.

"Crystal?" Zelda called from the living room. "Are you home, dear?"

Outside the closet, Muffy moaned and scratched on the louvered door like a jug band musician playing a washboard.

"Crystal, do you have company?" Zelda's voice came from the kitchen and now it had taken on a more sinister tone. "Crystal, are you in your room? What's that sound?" Zelda started to climb the stairs.

Quickly, Crystal opened the broom closet door and let Muffy squeeze in. Once inside, Muffy appeared reassured that he was not being punished and reveled quietly in the close company of loved ones.

Zelda was halfway up the stairs when the doorbell rang. "Now what?" she muttered and headed back downstairs.

"I thought you said your mom wouldn't be home until late," Simon whispered.

"That's what her note said." Crystal shifted Muffy's head to keep him from slobbering on her dress. "It said she was going to the hardware store—which is kind of weird because I don't think Mother has ever actually been in a hardware store before. But then, she's been very agitated lately."

They heard the front door open and the sound of muffled voices.

"Well, what do you want me to do about it?" said Zelda loudly.

"Please Zelda, they're going to kill me!" It was Mr. Z.

"I'm sure if you sit down and discuss the matter with him—"

"Chen doesn't discuss. He shoots!" hooted Mr. Z.

The voices moved from the living room to the kitchen.

"What's all this?" asked Mr. Z. "Someone's having a banquet?"

Zelda said something about Crystal's food fixation.

"It would be a shame to waste it," said Mr. Z hopefully.

"That thing I had to tell you," said Crystal. "Well, Mother has been embezzling from Going Platinum."

"What?" said Simon out loud.

"Shush!" said Crystal. "I found out a couple of days ago. She says she's doing it for me because we're like poor or something."

"But Chen will kill him!" Simon whispered.

Muffy, sensing excitement, started to moan loudly.

"Be quiet, Muffy!" Crystal tried petting her dog vigorously, but that only reaffirmed his suspicion that all was not well. "Pet him!" she urged Simon. "Hurry, he's going to start barking!"

Simon scrunched down to pet Muffy. Unable to see in the low light and unable to fully bend at the waist, he made an awkward lunge and placed his hand on Crystal's upper thigh.

"Ooo!" Crystal squeaked.

"Excuse me," said Simon.

"Arf! Arf!" barked Muffy.

"Crystal must have locked that stupid dog in her room again," said Zelda. "Wait a minute while I let him out." She started up the stairs.

"Zelda, what's that on your shoes? Mud?"

Zelda walked quickly back down the stairs. "I must have stepped in something," she said dismissively.

Simon and Crystal could hear Zelda and Mr. Z eating and making small talk. Sensing that the immediate crisis had passed, Muffy stopped barking and, having been alerted by the smells of cooking on them, began foraging for food.

"You kind of surprised me there," said Crystal, fanning herself.

"Yes, sorry."

Crystal shifted in the narrow space, rubbing languorously against him until they were face to face. "Oh, Simon!" she breathed. Her eyes glanced downward.

Simon followed her eyes. "That was the dog," he said.

"Get away from there!" Crystal scolded.

There was an awkward moment while they listened to the sounds from the kitchen. Finally, Simon joked, "Now I almost wish I hadn't eaten so much."

"What you really mean is that you wish I hadn't eaten so much. You think I'm fat!"

"No, no, I only meant—"

"You're just like my mother!"

"You're a wonderful woman—"

"But I'm not skinny like your ex-girlfriend?"

"About my girlfriend . . ." Simon began.

"I don't want to hear about your slinky girlfriend!"

"I think you're very pretty—"

"In a Rubenesque kind of way?" said Crystal derisively.

"More like Gaugin," said Simon. "You have that primitive, rounded sensuality that leaves a guy defenseless."

"Yeah?" said Crystal brightening. "You think so?"

Simon felt his cramped foot falling asleep and shifted his weight a little. "In fact, it's all I can do now to keep from touching you."

Crystal giggled. "So you don't think I'm too fat?"

"Crystal," Simon said, "if you were really fat, we wouldn't be having this conversation."

"But you're still in love with your girlfriend," she said.

"I am," said Simon.

"I'm sorry, Zelda," they could hear Mr. Z say, "but

what else am I to think?"

"Well, I am very disappointed to hear that you could believe I would embezzle money from your company—after all we've meant to each other, Yakov," said Zelda.

"I only want you to put my mind at rest. Show me all your records. Three hundred thousand dollars doesn't just disappear."

There was a pause. "Did you tell anyone else of your suspicions?"

"No, I . . . what do you mean? You don't want anyone else to know? You *have* been stealing from me. I told you what Chen said he would do to me if our books didn't balance and you still did it. It's like you put a gun to my head yourself, Zelda. Why?"

Zelda laughed disdainfully. "Look who's moral and law-abiding all of a sudden!"

"I'm begging you, Zelda. Don't do this to me!"

"If you're so sure I'm stealing from you, why don't you go to the police?"

Mr. Z lowered his voice so that Simon and Crystal had to strain to hear. "If you don't return that money by this time tomorrow, you will wish I had gone to the police."

They heard Mr. Z get up from the table and walk out of the house.

"Quick, you'd better leave before she comes up here," whispered Crystal.

"Where?"

Sensing trouble and not knowing what he should do about it, Muffy began to moan mournfully.

"Out the window!" she said, flinging open the closet door and leaping deftly over Muffy. "Hurry!" Crystal slid open her bedroom window and motioned Simon to go through it. Simon looked out the window and saw no means of getting to the ground but jumping.

Opening the window was all the proof Muffy needed that a crisis was in full swing and the dog started howling for all he was worth.

"You want me to jump?" Simon asked, incredulous.

"What's that noise up there?" Zelda demanded. "Crystal, are you home? Is there someone with you?"

"Yes! Jump!" Crystal pleaded.

Simon got one leg out the window and Muffy began running in circles, barking and howling. "Crystal, how did your father die?"

"The Chinese executed him for smuggling."

"Crystal, I'm coming up there!" Zelda warned and started up the steps.

Simon got his other leg out the window and balanced on the ledge.

"For God's sake, jump!" said Crystal and pushed him out the window, slamming it after him and closing the curtains.

Simon landed softly in a flowerbed near the front door and a patch of prickly pear cactus. Raising himself up on his elbows, Simon found himself staring into the soulless eyes of Zelda's giant catfish.

"Ah!" Simon yelled.

"Did you hurt yourself?" the voice from next door asked.

Simon stood up and dusted himself off. "No, I guess not, thank you," he said, not exactly sure where the voice was coming from.

"I don't blame you for being in a hurry to get out of that place," said the voice. "Still, you might have broken your leg. It's getting so the neighborhood isn't safe, what with all the foreigners coming and going out of this house. Where are you from?"

"Iowa," said Simon.

"Good farm country. You're probably okay, then."

"Thank you very much," said Simon. "Have a nice day."

He heard the window shut hard.

Chapter 38

The afternoon sun filtered through the curtains and shimmered with the rippling reflection off the pool. Simon sat in his over-stuffed chair with books piled three feet high on all sides and Cayce squarely in his lap. Balancing on one arm of the tattered chair was Mircea Eliade's *Immortality and Freedom*, R. A. Venkataraman's *A History of the Tamil Siddha Cult*, and Kamil V. Zvelebil's *The Poets of Power*. Simon turned a page in a book titled *The Alchemical Body: Siddha Traditions in Medieval India*, and Cayce tensed. Simon started to turn the next page and, quick as lightning, Cayce slapped it back.

"You think that's funny?" said Simon.

"Enough reading," said Cayce and purred loudly.

"Okay," Simon relented and placed the tome on top of the nearest stack. He petted Cayce's back with long, even strokes. "Do you believe in magic, Cayce?"

"What's that?" asked Cayce, clearly not interested.

"Well, magic is something a person does that is so amazing you don't know how they did it."

Cayce closed his eyes. "All people do magic."

"I agree. But there are supposed to be some special people who can do things like move objects without touching them, and appear and disappear."

"Fog Man can do that," observed Cayce.

"Yes, he can," said Simon. "Is Fog Man here now?"

Cayce pretended to sleep.

"Cayce?"

"He's no fun," said Cayce. "No hands."

"But is he here?"

Cayce sighed. "In the kitchen."

"Tattle tale!" said Hogan, materializing beside the refrigerator. "I was here earlier, but I didn't want to disturb you. What are you working on? You act like you're studying for a test."

"You've been around. Have you ever seen a mystic or yoga master do incredible feats?"

"Like what?" asked Hogan, wafting into the living room and drifting through a table lamp.

"Oh, you know, moving from one place to another at the speed of thought, becoming invisible, achieving weightlessness."

"What's the big deal about that stuff? Everybody my age can do that. Trust me, in a hundred years or so, you won't think it's anything special either."

"Anything new at the country club?" asked Simon.

"Chen's back in town," said Hogan. "And for an amateur, he's not a bad golfer. He made par on the four hole. Of course, that's the only hole he plays. And you should see the beautiful set of clubs he has!"

"Any more little holes in the sod?"

"No," said Hogan. "Just one big hole. Somebody tried to cover it up and put back the turf, but it looks like the dickens."

"I was afraid of that."

"Yeah, it's not as if it was just a divot. Something that big is going to show."

There was a knock at the door.

"I wonder who that could be?" said Simon.

"Maybe I should disappear," said Hogan, disappearing.

Simon opened the door and stood staring.

"Hi, Simon," said Amy. "How've you been?"

"Amy! Amy!" meowed Cayce, bounding off the chair.

"I missed you, Ames," said Simon.

"Well, do I get to come in?"

Simon led her to the couch where they sat awkwardly for a moment. Cayce hopped up in Amy's lap.

"I'm so happy!" said Cayce.

Amy looked around at the grocery bags full of empty cans and the piles of books. "I like what you've done with the place." She turned her attention to Cayce. "It's good to see you again, Cayce," she said, rubbing his ears vigorously and kissing him on the top of his head.

"I don't know what to say, Amy," said Simon, feeling strangely stiff and inarticulate.

"Why don't you pet her?" asked Cayce.

"Good idea, Cayce," said Simon and put his arms around her and his cat. For a minute, they all seemed to purr together.

"I wanted to call you," Amy said.

"I know."

"I should have known you would be more stubborn than I would."

"I'm sorry," said Simon. "You're everything to me."

"I know," said Amy.

"I got in too deep with this job. You wouldn't believe what's going on there."

Amy disengaged herself from him. "Yes, I would," she said suddenly businesslike. "First of all, I have a confession to make."

"If you've been seeing someone else, I don't blame—"

"What? Are you crazy? I haven't been seeing anybody—and you better not either!" she said, giving him an affectionate shake. "No, my confession is that Kenny has been keeping me up with what has been happening, as far as he knows. And I have been doing a little research on the matter."

Simon grinned. "A conspiracy!"

"And you're outgunned so you might as well learn to live with it," she said. "By the way, Kenny told me you've been living like a pig and eating canned spaghetti, so I hope you don't mind that I brought along a few things." Amy opened the door and picked up two grocery sacks she had set there. She carried them into the kitchen and started unpacking Tupperware containers full of frozen food and deposited them in his freezer and refrigerator. She said, "You might be interested to know that your former colleague, Mr. Merritt, was never interested in working for Going Platinum. He was hoping to buy it."

"Why? How?" Simon was astounded.

"Why?" said Amy. "To get stinking rich, I suppose. You know now that Steve had been a golf pro. Well, for the past six months, Going Platinum's aspiring star salesman had been lining up sponsors, golf celebrities, and his otherwise-rich cocaine and steroid customers to be part of a Pro-Am tournament. He knew everybody in the business and already had enough endorsements to make a small fortune. All he needed were the facilities. And he figured he could get Going Platinum cheap."

"Well that little weasel!" exclaimed Hogan.

Simon gave the corner of the living room where the sound came from a dirty look. "What was he going to use for money? Steve was in debt to every bookie in town."

"Blackmail," said Amy, removing a bag of herb salad and a bottle of homemade vinaigrette dressing. "You mentioned that while he was in training as a salesman, Steve was asking embarrassing questions about the company's profitability and he must have figured out they weren't making it legitimately. After it became clear to Steve that he couldn't buy Going Platinum for what it was worth, he discovered, no doubt to his delight, that it was a crooked company and he could force them to sell cheap. Steve had been doing some background checks on Mr. Z and his cousins. He was probably mad that he didn't get the sales job because it interrupted his research. You will enjoy knowing that my father pulled some strings and traced certain inquiries Steve made with Interpol, Immigration and Naturalization, and the Drug Enforcement Agency, as well as the State Department. You said you saw him breaking into bookkeeping. Well, he must have found what he was looking for."

"And bit off more than he could chew," said Hogan.

Simon said, "I can't believe Mr. Z would kill Steve."

"There were millions of dollars at stake," said Amy. "Not to mention deportation or prison for him and his relatives. People are killed for less than that every day. Your boss Yakov is a career criminal. Still, as far as I know, he's a smuggler, not a shooter."

"About Mr. Z," Simon began. "Unless Zelda decides to give back the money she embezzled, Chen threatened to have him killed tonight."

Amy took out a can of kitchen cleanser and a roll of paper towels. "So Yakov's secretary has been robbing him blind. There's a certain justice in that, I guess. I wonder what made her think she was going to get away with it?"

"Maybe she won't," said Simon, choosing to stand back and give Amy room to transform his kitchen herself. "I overheard Mr. Z threaten her if she didn't give back the money."

Amy waved in the direction of the stacks of books on the

246

floor. "I'm curious. If you suspect that two human beings are in danger of being murdered this very night, why are you sitting around with your nose in a book?"

"It's a long story, but maybe there is something I can do. Anyway, did you happen to find out anything about Mr. Chen?"

Wearing rubber gloves, Amy removed a sopping, moldy sponge from the sink and, holding it at arm's length, dropped it into a trash bag. "The State Department is very tight with its information on Chinese nationals. But your benefactor, Mr. Chen, was a very bad boy in his native Beijing. The list of charges against him goes on and on like the Great Wall. But Chen was resourceful and rich enough to work a deal, so now he'd doing a kind of work-release program. And what he's up to, hanging around a two-bit smuggling operation like Going Platinum, I have no idea."

A flicker of a smile crossed Simon's face. "I think I do."

Amy stopped her flurry of activity and turn to face him. "Well, do you want to let me in on it? I am your lawyer, after all."

Simon put his arms around her waist. "Yes, you certainly are. And you make house calls, too. What's it going to take to keep you on retainer?"

"I can't explain," she said stripping off her rubber gloves, twirling them around her head, and flinging them behind her. "I'll have to show you."

Simon started leading her to the bedroom and looked around for any signs of Hogan. "I hope everyone else in the room is planning to keep his eyes to himself," he enunciated.

"Hey, you don't have to draw me a picture," said Hogan, wafting through the door, "I know when I'm not wanted."

Amy said, "I'm not worried. Cayce has seen me naked before."

Cayce climbed up on a stack of books and closed his eyes. "Everybody sees me naked," he said.

Chapter 39

Bentley and O'Reilly walked through the front door of the country club. It looked normal enough. There were two energetic young men talking excitedly and each carrying a set of expensive clubs. A small, well-dressed Asian man of about seventy was using the pay phone and a woman wearing dark glasses sat in the lobby scribbling notes on a legal pad. The detectives approached the front desk and caught a glimpse of Yakov Zhelev slipping in a side door. A thin, sad-looking man with a droopy mustache sat at the desk.

"May I help you gentlemen?" he asked with a thick Slavic accent.

"Where's the skinny broad who works here?" Bentley asked, flipping out his badge.

The thin man's expression did not change. "My name is Pater Zhelev. I am bookkeeper. Zelda does not work here any more."

"Why not?" Bentley demanded.

Pater regarded Bentley steadily. "Health problems."

"Then let me talk to Yakov," said Bentley.

"He's not here," said Pater.

O'Reilly stepped up to the counter. "Didn't I just see—"

Bentley kicked him subtly behind the counter.

"Ow! What was that?"

"Get out your little computer, O'Reilly," said Bentley.

"Yakov will be gone the rest of the day," Pater said, ignoring O'Reilly completely.

"What was the name of that golfer friend of Steve Merritt?" Bentley asked O'Reilly.

O'Reilly punched in a few characters on the hand-held device. "Mark Tyler," he said, still grimacing from the pain.

"Yeah, Mark Tyler," said Bentley. "I understand he might be here today."

Pater nodded. "He started ten minutes ago. He's wearing plaid slacks and a green knit shirt. Should be by the three hole by now. Take a cart," he said, throwing them a set of keys.

"Thanks," said Bentley.

The detectives headed for the door. The woman in the lobby removed her dark glasses and regarded them suspiciously, making notes as they passed by. By now, the man at the pay phone was gone and as they reached the exit, a young Chinese man in a dark suit opened the door for them.

As they walked toward where the golf carts were parked O'Reilly asked, "Since when do they have doormen in country clubs?"

Bentley grinned. "And since when have they started packing Uzi's under their thousand-dollar silk sport coats?"

O'Reilly stopped in his tracks. "Wait! We've got to go frisk him."

"You have my permission to frisk him, O'Reilly. Oh, and make sure you frisk his partner on the roof." Bentley chuckled. "Where would you like to have your body sent?"

"But, but . . ."

"Have you forgotten that we are conducting a murder investigation?"

O'Reilly pulled out his cell phone and started to dial.

Bentley grabbed it out of his hand. "Give me that, you

knucklehead!" He jabbed at the keys with his index finger. "Where's the 'off' button on this goddamned thing? If you call the station, they'll send a squad car down here with the lights and sirens going and spook our whole operation." He tossed the phone back to O'Reilly and sat behind the wheel of a golf cart.

"You know how to drive one of these things?" O'Reilly asked.

"What's to know?" he said and turned the key.

Bentley wheeled the cart around and careened blindly over a rise, narrowly missing a large gentleman wearing lime green slacks who was bending over to pick up his ball. "Whoa!" exclaimed Bentley, accelerating around a sand trap, "I gotta get me one of these!"

With the three hole flag in sight, Bentley shot down the fairway, trying to get a glimpse of Mark Tyler.

"What's that?" shouted O'Reilly.

Their cart hit a section of loose turf and stopped dead, pitching O'Reilly over the dashboard and flat on his back in the grass.

"You okay?" asked Bentley.

O'Reilly stood up slowly and surveyed the grass stains on his elbows. "Will you look at this? How am I ever going to get this out?"

"What are you doing wearing light-colored suits to work anyway? You look like a goddamned Good Humor man."

O'Reilly looked at the front of the cart. "What did we hit?" He bent over and lifted up a piece of loose sod the size of a trash can lid. Underneath was freshly dug earth. "Looks like somebody buried something in here," he said, sticking his fingers into the soft soil. "Ow!" he shouted and withdrew his bleeding hand.

There was a knitted golf club head cover in the back of

251

the cart and Bentley threw it to O'Reilly for a bandage. There was also the shaft of a broken graphite club which he used to probe the section of fresh dirt. After two or three tries, he hit something. Bentley dug gingerly into the soil and pulled out a pair of rusty hedge clippers.

"Geeze!" exclaimed O'Reilly. "What's that doing in there?"

An old duffer had pulled his cart alongside theirs when he saw the accident. "You found some buried treasure, I see," he said chortling. "You may not have heard this, but five or six years ago, this place was a landfill. Sometimes the ground heaves and stuff comes to the surface. Last year, they found a washing machine by the seven hole. Well, good luck." He pointed to the lump of sod. "And replace your divots!" He drove off laughing.

"The clubhouse said you were looking for me," said a fit-looking man wearing plaid slacks and a green shirt. "Mark Tyler," he said, shaking hands with Bentley.

"I'm Detective Bentley and this is Detective O'Reilly."

O'Reilly instinctively extended his right hand, bearing the bloody head cover. Tyler took a step back. "How do you do?" he said.

"We'd like to ask you a few questions about one of your acquaintances by the name of Steve Merritt," said Bentley.

"It's funny you should mention Steve Merritt," said Tyler. "I was supposed to meet him here today. The guy at the clubhouse said he died."

"Murdered," said Bentley. "What was your relation to Merritt?"

Tyler shrugged and gazed down the fairway. "I hardly knew him. We played in a couple of tournaments. He had a pretty good swing. I thought he had a chance at getting into the money, but I guess he never pursued it. Last year, he called me up out of the blue and said he just bought a country club and asked if I wanted in on this tournament he was putting together. The date fell between a couple of major tourneys and I figured I could use the tune-up. I said yes. He even talked about cutting me in for a percentage and if I came down, we could play a round and talk it over. So here I am."

"He said he bought the country club?" asked O'Reilly.

Tyler snorted. "The guy at the front desk thought that was funny too. How was I supposed to know Merritt was delusional?"

"I'm sorry he wasted your time," said O'Reilly.

"Yeah. Me and a lot of other people," said Tyler. "If he wasn't dead already, he would have been after this stunt. You need a ride back to the clubhouse?"

"If you let me drive," said Bentley.

"We'll walk, thanks," O'Reilly said quickly.

The detectives started back toward the clubhouse.

"So, is Simon still your number one suspect?" O'Reilly asked.

"Shut up. I'm thinking."

"It's starting to look pretty complicated to me."

"You probably think tying your shoes is complicated," grumbled Bentley.

O'Reilly panted as they climbed a hill. "Here's what we know: we know Merritt was deeply in debt when he applied for a salesman job at Going Platinum. He was asking a lot of questions about the company's business. We know he had been dating Zelda, the office secretary. Somehow, he thought he would have enough money to buy the country club, which, by the way, was not for sale. We know that the owners of Going Platinum have a criminal past and are probably involved in diamond smuggling."

Bentley nodded. "And I'd bet anything that slick bastard Do Kham is some kind of smuggler, too. I don't suppose Tibet allows its religious treasures out of the country to be sold piece by piece in Santa Monica, California."

"Right," said O'Reilly. "But what's his connection to Steve Merritt? Were they both smuggling diamonds for Going Platinum? Was Do Kham buying steroids from him? Was he a golf nut?"

"And what about this Zelda broad?" said Bentley. "She was boinking Merritt and now it looks like she was doing the head gangster, Yakov. And today, they say she's quit the company."

"And let's not forget what happened to her husband, executed by the Chinese for—guess what?—smuggling."

"Yeah," said Bentley. "And they won't say what it was he was supposed to have been trying to smuggle. But it must have been something important if they offed him for it."

"And Do Kham is Chinese or Tibetan or something."

"And those two with machine guns were Asian." Bentley was getting excited. "And so was that old guy on the pay phone in the lobby."

O'Reilly shrugged. "Could just be a coincidence."

"Bullshit!" said Bentley. "We're getting close to something. I feel like the answer is right under our noses."

O'Reilly stopped and looked at his bloody finger. "I wonder," he said.

"What do you wonder, Sherlock?"

O'Reilly blew on his finger and grimaced. "I wonder if whatever Zelda's husband was trying to smuggle ever left the country."

"And the Chinese are trying to get it back?" Bentley whispered.

The detectives crested the hill, panting.

"Hey, isn't that . . ." O'Reilly didn't have enough breath to say his name.

"Do Kham," said Bentley. "Look, he's trying a chip shot with a wood. Whatever he is, the man is no golfer."

"And who is that on the hill, watching him?"

"Just some bum," said Bentley.

O'Reilly squinted. "Just some Chinese bum," he said, pointing.

"Well, go after him! We have to talk to him."

O'Reilly took two stumbling steps and the homeless man disappeared over the hill.

"You spooked him when you pointed, you idiot," said Bentley.

"We could still question Do Kham."

"What's he doing now?" said Bentley.

Do Kham pulled a metal detector out of his golf bag and was swinging it back and forth. He stopped and pulled a long skewer from his bag. He knelt on the ground and stabbed the skewer into the sod over and over. He stood up and resumed swinging the metal detector. Do Kham glanced up and saw the detectives watching him. He replaced the metal detector and skewer in his bag and pretended to putt.

"Maybe we'll talk to him at that," said Bentley, plodding down the hill toward Do Kham.

"I could call for backup," O'Reilly suggested.

Bentley sneered. "What for? He can't get away. We outnumber him two to one. Three to one if we count you."

Do Kham looked up at them again and then crouched behind his golf cart, out of sight.

"Now what do you suppose he did that for?" said O'Reilly. "It's not like we can't find him."

Bentley held his side and panted. "I wish we still had a cart."

O'Reilly wheezed. "I hope the guy doesn't try to put up a fight."

With no small exertion, the detectives reached the bottom of the hill where Do Kham's golf cart was. They stopped a few yards away. Bentley unsnapped his gun holster. "Mr. Kham, we know you're there. Stand up slowly with your hands in the air."

There was no response. They waited for a minute, listening to the wind blow through the trees. Somewhere, a man's laughter could be heard and there was the sound of a radio playing.

"Stand up right now!" Bentley commanded. "I really hate this part," he said to O'Reilly, drawing his Glock and clicking off the safety. He motioned for O'Reilly to take the left side of the cart while he took the right. Simultaneously, they crept around the golf cart, leaping the final yard, their guns extended. But Do Kham was not there. O'Reilly dropped down on his stomach, weapon pointing under the cart.

"Jesus, Bentley, he's not here!"

"He's here, all right," said Bentley, holstering his weapon. "There's a false bottom in this thing. Cover me."

Bentley took off his suit coat and laid it on the ground. He drew a deep breath, took hold of both left wheel wells and with the yell of a power lifter, heaved the golf cart on its side with a crash. He jumped back and fumbled for his gun. Once the cart was on its side, he could see that there had never been room for a man to hide under there, false bottom or not. The fiberglass body of the vehicle was splintered from one end to the other. The right headlight was broken off and lying, shattered, beside the split right front fender. Battery acid was leaking and creating a sour smell as it hissed, melting the plastic.

Bentley sat down heavily. "Now you can call for backup."

O'Reilly stood with his gun out and his mouth open. "Where'd he go?"

"Well, he sure as hell went somewhere."

"A man can't just disappear," said O'Reilly.

"Then maybe you can point him out to me, because we didn't see him leave and he isn't here now."

O'Reilly holstered his gun and sat down next to Bentley. "How is this going to look in our report?" he moaned.

Bentley struggled to his feet and walked over to where Do Kham had been using his metal detector. He could not see any holes where the skewer poked through the sod, but there were several one-inch holes at various intervals. He knelt down and examined the holes. He stuck his finger in one. He dropped a penny down one and listened for it to hit bottom. "Hey, O'Reilly," he said. "You know what a core sample is?"

O'Reilly had been sitting with his head in his hands. He looked up, surprised by the question. "Yeah, I guess so. Geologists take core samples to classify rock layers when they look for oil and stuff."

"Well, why would anybody take core samples in a golf course?"

O'Reilly got up and brushed off his grass-stained slacks. He walked over to where Bentley was kneeling. "Do Kham was looking for something metal," he said.

"Yes, but why take a core sample unless he was looking for something in a particular layer?"

"Something that was buried a long time ago?"

Bentley nodded. "Something that was thrown away a long time ago."

"And now they've come back to dig it up."

"What's the name of the landfill company that used to own this place, Green Leaf? Green Twig?" Bentley asked.

"Greenstem," said O'Reilly. "They've got an operation in Downey. It's going to be a city park when it fills up."

"Well, get your cell phone out and call Greenstem up and find out if anybody has accessed their records for this place in the last three months."

O'Reilly dialed his phone while Bentley took out Do Kham's metal detector and waved it over the area. He then walked back to where their golf cart had become stuck in the hole. There, Bentley found numerous other small holes in the turf, along with a distinct footprint of a woman's dress shoe. All around the large hole where the sod had been removed, Bentley found dirt crumbs, heavily mixed with chunks and granules from green asphalt shingles. He pulled out a plastic bag and scooped in some of the soil.

O'Reilly came running up to Bentley, out of breath and excited about something. "Eleven days ago, Greenstem received an inquiry about a load of trash picked up five years ago. Something about a Dumpster full of green shingles. And guess who that was?"

"It was Zelda Conroy," declared Bentley.

O'Reilly stood gaping. "How'd you know?"

"I wouldn't be surprised if she has a pair of shoes with dirt on them that matches this," he said holding up the evidence bag. "And I think we can assume she found what she was looking for."

"And whatever she was looking for, Do Kham was looking for it, too."

"No shit, Sherlock," said Bentley. "Now we have to beat it back to town and get a search warrant for Zelda's place. And hope we get there before Do Kham does."

Chapter 40

Amy and Simon sat on the couch with Cayce sleeping between them.

"Now we've got that out of the way," said Amy, "you want to tell me about Chen?"

"You're such a romantic!" said Simon.

"And speaking of romance, maybe you should begin by telling me about Crystal."

Simon choked. "You must be frightening in a courtroom. I don't know what my former friend Kenny told you, but there was nothing between Crystal and me. Mr. Z invited me to dinner—"

"May I remind the witness he is under oath," Amy interjected.

"Honestly, I can prove my innocence . . ."

The phone rang and woke Cayce up. Knowing he'd have to get up anyway, he jumped to the floor. "Berk!" said Cayce.

"It's probably your girlfriend," taunted Amy.

Simon pantomimed a shushing sound and picked up the phone. "Hello?" he said. "This is Simon." The smile faded from his face as he listened intently. "I assure you that will not be necessary."

"What is it?" demanded Amy, getting to her feet.

"I understand," said Simon. "We'll be there as soon as we can. You know what traffic on the 405 is like this time of day. All right. All right. Yes. No police. We're leaving now."

"What the hell's going on?"

Simon took Amy by the shoulders. "J. D. Harriman has taken your mother hostage at the country club."

"What?" Amy said, incredulous. "Why would he have my mother? What are you talking about?"

"I don't know. Your mom has been hanging out in the lobby for the last few days."

"Why didn't you say something?" Amy practically shouted.

Simon started dialing the phone. "Harriman wants Kenny and me in exchange for your mother. Hi, Kenny? I don't have time to explain. Harriman has taken Sabrina hostage at the country club. He says he'll let her go if we meet him there right away. Yes, he said no cops or . . ." Simon glanced at Amy. "Or, you know. We'll think of something on the way. I'll meet you there. And Kenny? I'm sorry about this, pal. Yeah, you too."

Simon headed for the door.

"Hold on! I'm going with you," said Amy.

"Not a chance," said Simon reaching for the doorknob.

"She's my mother and you'd better not try to stop me!"

"Okay then, come on," Simon said and opened the door, only to find a large bearded man wearing an angry expression.

"Where do you think you're going?" the man said.

Simon stood there a moment, temporarily stunned. "Oh, Mr. Johnson. You'll have to excuse me. I've got an emergency."

Mr. Johnson stood still, blocking the doorway. "I know you do," he said. "And you're going to take care of it right now."

"What do you mean?" asked Simon.

"My toilet is backed up again and you're not leaving until it's fixed!"

Amy tried to push past Simon. "Get away from the door, you big idiot! Can't you see we've got a real emergency?"

Mr. Johnson put a beefy hand on Simon's shoulder. "Not so fast. You know, you've been slacking off around here lately. But you're going to fix my toilet before you do one other thing. Look," he said, appealing to their sense of reason, "it will be quicker to just do it than it would be to argue about it."

Simon turned to Amy. "He's right, you know. It will only take a minute."

"I don't believe this," Amy seethed. "You stay here and fix Mr. Johnson's goddamned toilet and I'll drive my car."

She slipped past Simon and Mr. Johnson and started running toward the parking lot.

"That won't do you no good, ma'am," Mr. Johnson called after her. "My truck's blocking the driveway. I figured he'd try to weasel out of it."

Amy came stalking back. "You better be the fastest plumber in California."

They drove all the way to the Going Platinum Country Club in silence. When they arrived, they saw Kenny waiting by the front door. "I would have been done ten minutes sooner if their little boy hadn't stuffed the Teletubby so far down the toilet," Simon explained.

Amy stared straight ahead. "I will never forgive you for this. Never."

"What kept you?" said Kenny.

"Don't ask," said Amy.

They opened the front door and stepped cautiously inside the empty lobby. The staff had gone home an hour before and the room was silent except for the drone of the pop machine.

261

"Maybe he got tired of waiting," Kenny suggested.

"We're not that late," Simon insisted. "Besides, it's us he wants."

They looked warily around the room and found no sign of Harriman or Sabrina. Suddenly, the intercom crackled. "I hope for the old lady's sake you came alone." It was Harriman's voice.

Simon walked up to the intercom and punched the talk button. "We didn't bring the police. Where are you?"

"We're in your office," said Harriman.

"They gave you an office?" asked Amy, surprised.

"It's a small office," said Simon.

They made their way to Simon's office, stood for a moment outside the closed door, and then knocked, uncertain of what to do next.

"Back through the door and close it after you," commanded Harriman.

They did as they were told. The blinds were drawn and the lights were off. They stood facing the doorway.

"Who's she?" Harriman demanded.

"Amy!" Sabrina cried.

Amy turned around. "What on earth are you doing here, Mom?"

Sabrina was duct-taped to Simon's swivel chair. A wall clock ticked out the seconds. She blinked a couple of times and tried to smile. In a small voice, she said, "They were stealing."

"Oh, Mom!" said Amy.

Harriman was pointing a sawed-off pump 12-gauge shotgun at them at about waist level. "The old bat was following me. Can you believe it? So are all you morons working together?"

"No," said Amy. "All of us morons were working separately."

"Well, it makes no difference to me," he said.

Harriman had Amy duct tape the others to wooden chairs while he covered them with the shotgun, then he taped Amy to a chair himself. When he had all his hostages lined up together, Harriman sat across from them, staring.

"Now what?" said Kenny.

"Well, fat boy, why don't you start by telling me who you really are?"

Kenny tightened his shoulders slightly and the joints of the wooden chair creaked. "My name is Kenny. I'm a friend of Simon and Amy, and I work as a personal trainer."

Harriman snorted. "No kidding? You show people how to get in shape? So are you telling me you don't work for Going Platinum and that business back in Century City was all an act?"

Kenny grinned. "Yup."

Harriman aimed the shotgun at Kenny's head. "I'm going to do you first." Kenny's expression did not change. Harriman turned his attention to Amy. "So besides being the old lady's daughter, what's your connection with this thing?"

"Her name is Mrs. Castor," said Amy. "And I'm Simon's attorney."

Harriman sneered. "And his girlfriend, too?"

Amy looked him in the eye. "I was thinking of hiring him to do some plumbing for me. He's very fast."

"Don't toy with me!" Harriman growled. "Tell me what you know about me and my operation. Your life may depend on the answer."

"I know you have a string of juvenile arrests on your record, including assault with intent, burglary, grand theft auto, and forgery. You've got two adult arrests for receiving stolen property."

"And no convictions—thanks to certain members of your honorable profession," he said.

"And I know," Amy continued, "that you have been named in a conspiracy to smuggle uncut gems in and out of the country. In fact, I have submitted your name to the State Department for investigation of possibly providing money-laundering to certain terrorist organizations."

Harriman pointed the shotgun at her. "You're lying!"

Amy shrugged. "I wouldn't try to get through airport security if I were you."

He aimed the gun at Sabrina. "Okay, Mrs. Castor, just what the hell were you up to?"

Sabrina started to sniffle. "It's all my fault," she said with a little sob. "Nobody else put me up to it. But if there was stealing, I had to stop it."

Harriman directed his gun at Simon. "I kind of hate to shoot you, Simon," he said. "We worked together so well. You were the kind of stooge I could really make some money with. Then you had to go and spoil it. So before I splatter your brains all over the wall, you want to tell me what you thought you were doing?"

"Actually, I wasn't interested in your smuggling operation," said Simon. "I was only trying to find out who killed Steve Merritt."

"And you thought I did it?"

"Steve knew about your diamond business and tried to shake you down. You had reason to kill him."

"But I didn't kill him," said Harriman. "He was greedy, but I can work with somebody like that. Not like you. You're not greedy. That's why I'm going to have to kill you. Personally, my money was on Yakov."

"But Steve and Mr. Z were two of a kind," said Simon. "Why would he kill Steve?"

A smirk appeared on Harriman's handsome face. "You really didn't know, did you? Some investigator you are! Ever since Zelda started working for Going Platinum, Yakov had this thing for her. Don't ask me why. She gave me the creeps, but Yakov thought she was hot. Anyway, after Steve applied for the job, Yakov found out Steve was boinking her. It had been going on for a month or so. Then when Steve turned up dead, it was clear to me that it was Yakov who did it. Crystal clear."

Simon and Kenny exchanged glances.

"Crystal," said Kenny.

"Why didn't I think of that before?" Simon said. "It was staring me in the face the whole time."

"What about Crystal?" demanded Amy.

"Who's Crystal?" asked Sabrina.

"You're not saying Crystal killed Steve Merritt, are you?" asked Amy.

Simon laughed. "Melanie said, 'The one you seek is near. And although the way is clear as glass, you cannot see.' "

"Crystal clear!" said Kenny.

"Who's Melanie?" asked Amy.

"And the nosy neighbor!" said Simon, getting excited. "The astrologer said there might be a nosy neighbor."

"But Crystal was the key!" exclaimed Kenny.

"Who the hell is Melanie?" demanded Amy.

"What the hell are you people talking about?" asked Harriman.

Simon chuckled. "The ironic thing to you, Mr. Harriman, is that if you hadn't gotten paranoid and put yourself in the middle of all this, you might have gotten to go on smuggling diamonds for years without getting into any trouble."

"I'd have caught him," declared Sabrina.

"But," Simon continued, "you were too aggressive and you raised suspicion. Now the local and federal authorities have been alerted to your recent activities."

"And now you're toast!" said Kenny.

"So who killed Steve Merritt?" asked Amy.

"Zelda did, of course," said Simon.

"Zelda?" said Harriman, genuinely surprised. "Why?"

"Because Steve was going to buy the Going Platinum Country Club."

"That dump?" said Harriman.

"And Zelda figured she had to own it herself if she was going to dig around in it."

"You lost me there, partner," said Kenny. "Why would Zelda want to dig in a golf course?"

"For buried treasure," said Simon. "And not just any buried treasure. But something that had once belonged to her and which, unwittingly and in a fit of rage, she threw in the Dumpster."

"And it ended up in the landfill," said Kenny. "Which eventually became the golf course."

"Right," said Simon.

"Was it stolen treasure?" Sabrina wanted to know.

"Yes, it was, Mrs. Castor. And it was worth more than the country club itself. More than a hundred country clubs. And only Zelda knew where it was."

"What was it?" asked Harriman, now fully enthralled with the story.

Just then, there was a knock on the office door and everybody froze. After almost a minute, Harriman called out, "Who's there?" But there was no answer. Harriman picked up his shotgun, which, during the excitement of Simon's story, he had laid on the floor. He crept to the door, slowly turned the handle, and then kicked the door open with a bang.

But there was nobody standing in front of the door. Harriman peeked to the left and then to the right and still he saw no one. The hostages were all facing the other direction so they didn't know what was going on.

"Anybody there?" Harriman called out, but without much authority in his voice. He stuck his head through the doorway and looked both ways again. There was nobody there. He jacked a shotgun shell into the chamber, as much to bolster his courage as anything else, and stepped out into the hall. He stood there waiting for someone to materialize. But nobody did. Finally, Harriman turned around and said, "It must have been the wind or something."

At that moment, there was a crash from above as Chen's men dropped through the suspended ceiling. Lin kicked the shotgun to the floor as he fell and Chow landed behind Harriman, who rapidly glanced back and forth between them several times like a judge at a championship tennis match. Then Lin stepped up, swept the shotgun aside with his foot, and delivered a quick, straight right hand to Harriman's jaw, rendering him unconscious. As he fell, Chow caught him and laid him gently on the tile.

The bodyguards strode into the room.

"I'm so happy to see you Lin, Mr. Chow," said Simon.

Lin bowed stiffly. "Please forgive us for letting this ridiculous business go on so long."

"But your story was very interesting," said Mr. Chow, with a thick Chinese accent.

Lin said, "By now, you doubtlessly know why we are really here and what we must do now."

"Of course," said Simon.

"We are very sorry," said Mr. Chow, addressing all the hostages.

"Yes," said Lin. "We are very sorry. But we cannot release you. We will be leaving your country as soon as we have collected the merchandise which belongs to us and we cannot risk having you call the authorities."

Mr. Chow spoke up, "But Mr. Chen would like us to express his deepest gratitude for what you have done for him." He bowed toward Simon.

"And out of that gratitude," said Lin, "we are allowing all of you to live. Mr. Simon, now we are—how do you say?—even." He smiled and bowed again.

"Thank you, Lin, Mr. Chow," said Simon. "Please convey my gratitude to Mr. Chen."

Lin said, "Might we borrow some of your tape? I fear when Mr. Harriman wakes up, he will be in a bad mood."

With that, the bodyguards trussed up J. D. Harriman securely, picked up his shotgun, and left.

"What were those two scary-looking men talking about?" asked Amy.

"Unless I am mistaken," said Simon, "they are, through Mr. Chen, freelancing for the Chinese government, recovering that buried treasure which is probably now in Zelda's possession. And unless we stop them, somebody is about to be killed."

"Should we yell for help?" Sabrina suggested.

Kenny, who had remained silent throughout their encounter with the bodyguards sat with his eyes closed, slowly taking deep breaths.

"Kenny, are you okay?" asked Amy.

Suddenly, he tensed and the oak chair creaked. He let out a shout and twisted violently. The back of the chair groaned and splintered and the chair's arms snapped free.

Kenny stood up, and peeled off the duct tape that held the shattered remains of the oak armrests to his wrists. He brushed the wood fragments from his clothes, leaving a pile of oak kindling at his feet. He suddenly looked like a giant. The other hostages were staring up at him, open-mouthed.

Kenny grinned. "What?"

"My hero!" said Amy.

After Kenny released him, Simon grabbed the phone and called the police. They connected him with Detective Bentley.

"Chen's men were just here and they're on their way to Zelda's. You've got to get there right away!" he said.

"Who's Chen?" asked Bentley, unwilling to get excited or to be told what to do by a civilian.

"Chinese Mafia, smuggler, assassin—that's not important right now. But his henchmen are on their way to Zelda's."

Bentley said, "We tried to get a warrant, but since we didn't know what we were looking for, the judge said it was no-go."

"Well, they're about to kill Zelda for what she dug up in the golf course. Would that make your trip worthwhile?"

Simon could hear O'Reilly's voice in the background.

"Hey Bentley," O'Reilly said. "We just got a call from a Mrs. Mertz who says she lives next door to Zelda Conroy. She says some stocky Chinese guy just kicked the door down and went in."

"Do Kham!" Simon exclaimed.

"We're on it," said Bentley and hung up.

Chapter 41

When they arrived at Zelda's house, the only way Amy could convince her mother to remain in the car was to explain that they needed a look-out in the driveway, in case Do Kham, a notorious thief, tried to escape.

Simon recognized Bentley's car, but there was nobody inside. There was also a black BMW parked in the street that he was pretty sure belonged to Mr. Chow. Lights were on in the house but no sounds were audible from outside. The front door was open and hung at an angle from a single hinge.

Simon, Kenny, and Amy advanced slowly to within fifty feet of the house. They stopped and listened. There was only the sound of the wind through the eucalyptus trees.

"Let's go in," said Kenny, and they started to move.

"Psssst! Go back you idiots!" It was Bentley, whispering from behind a tree. They could barely see his large profile in the twilight. "This is police business. I'll cite you!" he threatened. "O'Reilly has called for back-up. It's what he does best. So go home."

"By the time back-up arrives, it will be too late," said Simon. "We're going in."

"Don't you dare!" shouted Bentley. A flurry of automatic gunfire showered the area around Bentley's tree with splinters.

"They've got infrared sights!" O'Reilly whined. "Son of a bitch!"

Simon spoke to Kenny and Amy. "You heard what Lin told me. He said that we're even. That means if we interfere, they could shoot us. I think you should stay here. I'm going."

"Me too," said Kenny.

"I'm in," said Amy.

"Detective Bentley," Simon called.

"What is it now?"

"Cover us!" he shouted and ran for the front door.

Bentley cursed but fired a volley of shots from his Glock and O'Reilly chimed in with his .38. A punishing return of machinegun fire came from across the yard and Simon and his friends slipped in the front door.

Once inside, they could see that the house was mostly lit with candles. The shadows that danced to the candlelight posed a distraction as they scanned the room for human movement. They cautiously made their way to the living room. The stiff Victorian chairs were lined up against opposite walls. Along bookshelves were small statues of Hindu gods next to Precious Moments figurines. A photograph of Zelda's husband, Robert, in front of the great statue of Roshana stood next to a glamour photo of Zelda and Crystal. The brass mandala appeared to be in the same position as Simon left it. The room was empty as a church.

The kitchen was empty too, except for broken dishes on the floor and the chairs that had been tipped over. A cast iron skillet stuck surrealistically handle-first into the wall. Shards of pebbled glass and three roses lay next to the window. There was water running in the sink.

They stood silently in the kitchen, wondering what to do next. The smell of fresh cigarette smoke drifted down from upstairs. Simon strained to hear any sound of activity.

"You might as well come up," said the voice of Do

Kham. "Please, Simon. You and your friends are welcome and quite safe from me."

The three looked at each other and proceeded up the stairs. When they reached the top, they saw Zelda, huddled in the corner of the room, her green sheath dress torn at the shoulder, a lit cigarette in her hand. Candles flickered in the window.

Do Kham stood beside her holding the phurbu dagger. "Do not be alarmed," he said. "Zelda and I were just about to come to terms. She has something I want—oh, why be secretive? Simon, I'm sure you know what it is by now."

"The Scroll of the True Sidhis," said Simon.

"Kill him!" Zelda hissed to Simon.

Do Kham smiled. "Precisely. You might as well see this adventure to its conclusion, Simon. I feel I owe you that, because you were instrumental in bringing Crystal to my little shop when she showed us her anklet."

Simon said, "The anklet was part of the package that contained the Scroll."

"Yes," said Do Kham. "Although it is practically worthless, it was described in the shipping manifest that included the Scroll. Of course, Zelda's poor husband Robert did not know its value, although he died trying to protect it. I had studied to be a monk and specialized in Sanskrit and religious antiquities. After the Tibetan uprising, many precious relics were smuggled out of the country, including the Scroll. When Mr. Conroy was working in Nepal, he came across a box of relics and agreed to ship it to the United States and hide it until they could be safely returned to Tibet. The Chinese government hired me to locate and evaluate such relics. But when I found the Scroll of the True Sidhis, well, you can imagine what went through my mind! Even many of the best scholars believed the Scroll to be a legend. When I interrogated Mr. Conroy over the period of several days, he unwittingly revealed certain facts that led me to believe he had possession of something of great importance. I persuaded the Chinese to leave me alone with Mr. Conroy, at which time I used rather aggressive techniques that resulted in him telling me he had already shipped the package to his home."

"Then, you murdered him!" said Zelda.

"Of course," said Do Kham. "The Chinese suspected he had the Scroll, but thought he died under torture and his secret died with him. I resigned and moved to America."

"But by then Zelda had already thrown away the relics," said Simon.

"Incredible, but true," said Do Kham. "The Chinese questioned Zelda, naturally. But she claimed the items were stolen. There was a complete search, but nothing turned up. Zelda knew nothing of the Scroll, but she could see that it must be worth a fortune if the Chinese would go to such trouble and she was cunning enough to get a job with Going Platinum, at the site of the old landfill, to be close to her treasure."

"And the Chinese hired Chen to stay close to Zelda," said Amy.

Gunfire erupted outside and everyone flinched. "Forgive me if I must cut this short," said Do Kham, toying with the phurbu.

Kenny made a step toward him, but Do Kham held up his hand. "Please do not attempt anything foolish," he said. "I am an expert in the martial arts and I do not wish to kill all of you. In fact, I was rather hoping you would help me convince Zelda to give me the Scroll so I would not have to kill her and her daughter, who I believe is hiding in that broom closet."

There was a gasp from the broom closet.

"You know, the Scroll belongs to Tibet," said Simon.

Do Kham drew himself up to his full height. "I am Tibetan, after all. I promise to return the Scroll to the authorities at Lhasa."

"After you're done with it," said Simon.

"It's mine!" Zelda hissed.

"Very well," said Do Kham. "The police will soon be here. Who shall I kill first?"

"Give him the stupid Scroll," Amy urged.

"Thank you for finding the Scroll, Denba." An Asian man entered the room from Crystal's bedroom. "But it must go back where it belongs." Simon recognized him as the homeless man.

"You cannot stop me, Tenzin," said Do Kham. "I am too strong."

"That is why you must give it back. You, of all people, know of its overpowering temptations."

"Help me, Tenzin. With the Scroll, we could drive the Chinese out of Tibet. Our poor backward country would flourish. There would be schools, hospitals. We could rebuild the temples. Our people would rule the earth. There would be peace."

"Mao Ze Tung also had such a dream, Denba."

Do Kham's lip curled with hatred. "Enough talk. First, I will kill the daughter."

"No!" Zelda screamed.

"Where is the Scroll?" Do Kham demanded.

Zelda hunched down in her corner. "It's mine," she said.

Do Kham looked at the broom closet where Crystal was hiding and took a grip on the phurbu. Kenny stepped in front of the closet, blocking it entirely. Do Kham's eyes narrowed and he threw the ancient dagger.

There was a blur across the room and Tenzin caught the phurbu by its bronze handle. "You would defile this holy relic with murder?" His voice choked with emotion.

"I will have the Scroll!" said Do Kham. He placed thumbs and forefingers together, palms up. A curiously serene expression crossed his face. A moment later, Do Kham faded and disappeared.

Zelda moaned and fainted, collapsing on the floor.

"What happened?" Amy asked.

Tenzin held up his hands for silence and every one stood still and listened. Simon turned his head sharply and stared at a blank spot on the wall. Tenzin watched Simon's eyes.

Do Kham moved about the room as in a fog that shielded him from being seen by others. He stepped lightly, soundlessly, looking but not touching. For him, the world took on an unreal appearance, like a photographic negative. The others turned to listen. Tenzin extended his arms, feeling for air movement. Do Kham controlled his breathing and smiled. He entered the bathroom, looked into the open shelves that held towels and under the claw-foot tub. He looked into the heating duct.

Tenzin directed each person to stand at strategic points around the room and in front of doorways to maximize the chance of detecting Do Kham if he passed by. Outside, there was the sound of more gunfire and then sirens. The pulsating flash from the lights of the police cruisers hammered through the upstairs windows, washing out the candlelight with its bright strobe and making it difficult to see.

Simon was positioned in front of the door to Crystal's room, facing outward. Tenzin noted that Simon seemed to be watching something. On Crystal's bed, Muffy snored, oblivious to the tense activity all around him. Do Kham slipped past Simon with the silent grace of a spider. He looked in Crystal's cluttered clothes closet and under her bed. Muffy squirmed uneasily in his sleep. Do Kham lifted the large feather pillow and there was a shiny metal cylinder about eighteen inches long. There was a keypad on one end. He quickly punched in one series of numbers, and then another. Slowly, he twisted the top and there was a slight hiss from the escaping nitrogen gas, but the noise from the police bullhorns masked the sound. Carefully, he laid the top of the cylinder on the pillow. Then, he reached in and gently withdrew the ancient vellum Scroll.

As he started to unfurl the Scroll, something caught Do Kham's eye. The flashing police lights made him blink and look again. But there, hovering above the floor, was Ben Hogan, arms akimbo, white tam pulled down over his eyebrows and his bright-colored argyle socks which seemed to flash with the lights. He was looking directly at Do Kham. And he looked angry. "You cheat at golf!" he said.

Do Kham let out a gasp of horror and became visible. Muffy woke up and, seeing a stranger next to him on Crystal's bed, let out a loud bark and clamped his teeth on Do Kham's arm. Tenzin charged to the doorway, tossing Simon aside like a rag doll. Do Kham had the look of a cornered rat. He started to disappear and Tenzin threw the phurbu. The heavy, three-sided iron blade split Do Kham's sternum like a ripe watermelon and buried itself up to the Makara that formed the top of the handle. He gurgled and blood spilled out of his mouth. Do Kham slumped over and it was several seconds before Muffy realized he was no longer a threat and released him. The dog became unsettled at the smell of human blood and left the room.

There was gunfire, now near the house. Zelda came to and asked what had happened. Amy, Kenny, and Simon stood at the doorway to Crystal's room to find Do Kham expired on the bed.

"His real name was Denba Daja," said Tenzin. "We were fellow monks at the Tashilhunpo monastery in Shigatse. He could have been a great scholar, even a Siddha. He was the best of us all."

Having sufficiently recovered, Zelda pushed past the others to enter the room. She stood aghast at the bloody corpse of Do Kham. Her eyes fixed on the Scroll on the pillow.

"It will go back where it belongs now," Tenzin gently told her.

Zelda turned to face him with rage in her violet eyes. "It's mine," she seethed. "But if I can't have it, no one can!" She snatched up a glass jar of acetone from one of Crystal's art projects. She uncoiled her arm, hurling the jar against the wall near a burning candle. The room exploded in flame. In one motion, Tenzin reached in and pulled Zelda from the room and stepped into the middle of the conflagration. The others were stunned to see the monk standing in the fire with his arms outstretched, his clothes beginning to smolder.

Then, it was as if all the oxygen were removed from the room. The flames sank and dwindled. Soon, there was nothing left of the fire but the smell of smoke and acetone. Tenzin carefully picked up the Scroll. It was not even singed. He replaced it in the metal cylinder and screwed the top back in place.

"Everybody okay?" Bentley called from downstairs. He and O'Reilly ran up the steps, their weapons drawn. "We saw fire blow out the upstairs window. What happened?"

Zelda lay whimpering on the floor, her green dress smoking at the hemline, her dark hair singed. Nobody seemed able to speak. Muffy scratched on the broom closet door. Tentatively, it opened. Muffy barked wildly and Crystal cautiously stepped out into the room.

"Is it over?" she asked.

Bentley said, "Yes, ma'am. We have everything under control now. We have apprehended the gunmen outside and . . ." His voice trailed off, following Crystal's gaze to where Kenny was standing. Kenny, in turn, stood transfixed, staring back at Crystal.

"Kenny, this is Crystal," said Simon. "Crystal meet Kenny."

They continued to gaze at each other until Bentley broke the spell. "I'm sorry, Crystal, but we have an arrest warrant for your mother. Uniformed officers will be up shortly to secure the scene and take her away. Is there anything else we can do for you, ma'am?"

"Well," said Crystal, still watching Kenny, "why don't we all go downstairs and I'll fix us something to eat."

"I'm starved!" said Bentley, looking suddenly cheerful.

"I'll give you a hand," Amy offered.

O'Reilly holstered his gun. "I could eat," he said.

Chapter 42

Crystal and Amy became better acquainted in the kitchen while working out the details of a simple three-course snack, beginning with Gratineed Potato Gnocchi in sage cream, a nice light Lobster Bisque, followed by some reheated Chicken Dijonaise. They recruited Sabrina to set the table.

Tenzin told Detective Bentley that he would be happy to answer any questions regarding the Scroll and the body of Do Kham, but showed him his papers documenting his diplomatic status.

With Crystal's permission, Simon opened the mandala lock and revealed the hidden wall safe, which was opened by a specialist from the police department. Neither Crystal nor Zelda knew of its existence. Inside the safe were several ancient holy relics, along with a bronze mirror believed to date back to 1500 BC. There was also a letter from Robert Conroy explaining that the items, some of which he had purchased and some he'd smuggled out of the country at the request of the Tibetan government, were to be returned as soon as the political climate in Tibet allowed.

By the time the meal was prepared, everyone had been properly introduced and were ready to sit down together.

"So, Simon," said Bentley, forking down a huge mouthful of Potato Gnocchi, "O'Reilly and I spent hours on the computer tracking down Merritt's contacts and financial records to discover he had a gambling problem.

How did you find out ahead of us?"

Simon broke off a piece of baguette. "Oh, I just asked my astrologer."

Sabrina asked, "Why did Zelda kill Steve Merritt?"

Bentley jumped in. "Zelda was embezzling money from Going Platinum, ironically, so she could buy the place and dig around for the Scroll without anybody getting suspicious. But Merritt was planning to buy the golf course himself for his own reasons. While rifling through Going Platinum's books, he must have figured out that Zelda was embezzling and confronted her. She bonked him on the head with a golf club, then stuffed it down his throat to make it look like Simon did it."

"But you never really thought Simon did it, did you?" asked Crystal.

Bentley helped himself to some chicken. "Certainly not."

"Simon, how did you figure out that Do Kham—or whatever his real name was—had been looking for this Scroll of the True Sidhis?" Amy asked.

"Crystal, you remember when we were in Do Kham's office? I was looking right at the door when I saw him materialize in front of me. That's not a skill just everybody has."

"O'Reilly and I saw him disappear on the golf course!" Bentley interrupted.

"Right," said Simon. "I had read about the Scroll in college. Naturally, I assumed it was a legend."

"Originally, there were two Scrolls," Tenzin explained. "There were eighteen True Sidhis, or supernatural powers: ten minor and eight principal Sidhis. Some say the True Sidhis were written down by the Shaivite saint, Tirumular himself, in the eighth century. The existence of the two Scrolls has been a closely guarded secret, each hidden in a separate location. The man you knew as Do Kham had been privileged to read the minor Sidhis because of his remarkable scholarship and his pure devotion. But, tragically, the temptation was too great even for him and the desire for godlike power caused him to lose his way. The eight principal Sidhis are considered inappropriate for the eyes of the unenlightened and, to my knowledge, only His Holiness, the Dalai Lama, is permitted to look upon them."

"But don't the Chinese want the Scrolls?" asked Amy.

Tenzin smiled. "Curiously, times have changed in China and now, instead of destroying our temples, it has become politically expedient for the Chinese to be seen as helping us preserve our heritage. Also, it seems they do not wish to start a spiritual arms race with the rest of the world. So, at least until the political climate changes again, Tibet is to remain the guardian of the True Sidhis. Within an hour, a pair of your best fighter jets will take the Scroll and me to an undisclosed location where it will remain safe from the likes of Denba Daja."

"Where no one will ever steal it again," said Sabrina.

"And what about that thing you did, putting out the fire? Was that one of the Sidhis?" Kenny wanted to know.

Tenzin waved his fork dismissively. "That was a simple Tantric trick of no great importance."

O'Reilly spoke up, "But Simon, how did you figure out that Zelda had the Scroll?"

"When I felt myself enter the mandala in the living room, I encountered a dragon that hoarded treasures it could never use. It reminded me of Zelda—excuse me, Crystal."

"Oh, that's okay," said Crystal, serving Kenny another helping of Lobster Bisque. "I'm guessing when they give her a psychiatric examination, they'll figure out she's, like, insane. I've always thought so."

"Now that you're on your own, what will you do, Crystal?" asked Kenny.

She looked at him shyly. "Well, I was thinking of joining a health spa."

Kenny's eyes grew wide.

Tenzin said, "You may be happy to know that there is an international agency for the repatriation of Tibetan art treasures. The reward for returning the relics your father collected will be substantial. Also, as soon as it is permitted, we will be returning the stolen treasures from Denba's shop."

Just then, Ben Hogan appeared, hovering above the table. Simon tried not to give himself away, but Tenzin noted that he was watching something no one else could see.

"Well, I've played my eighteen holes," said Hogan, "and it's time for me to go. It's been fun working with you. But I'd still rather have been with Tiger Woods. I know you'll miss me. Don't say anything. You'll only embarrass yourself." And with that, Hogan wafted through the wall.

Tenzin leaned close to Simon and whispered, "Was that a spirit of your acquaintance?"

Simon nodded, his mouth full of Chocolate Mousse. "An old golfing buddy."

Amy turned to Tenzin. "Among all the people—Zelda, Do Kham, Yakov Zhelev, Mr. Chen—why did you choose to follow Simon?"

Tenzin shrugged. "I had a feeling about him."

"Me too!" said Bentley.

"What will happen to Mr. Z and his relatives at Going Platinum?" asked Simon.

"Jail, of course," said Bentley. "Along with that creep, J. D. Harriman, who our boys found hog-tied back at the country club."

O'Reilly chimed in, "We're making an audit of their assets. We found records of a Swiss bank account in Simon's name to the amount of two hundred eighty-six thousand dollars."

"It's not my money," said Simon. He grinned. "Well, it looks like I'm broke again."

Kenny got up from the table. He picked up the newspaper and tossed it to Simon. "I guess it's time you started looking for another job."

About the Author

Daniel B. Brawner is a humor columnist for the Mt. Vernon/Lisbon *Sun* in Mt. Vernon, Iowa. He studied English with an emphasis on mythology. Qualifications in hand, he landed numerous dead-end sales jobs, including telemarketing gold-plated golf putters to car dealers.

Dan's mother taught sociology and anthropology. His father is a retired housing contractor. His sister teaches Sanskrit at Maharishi School of Management in Fairfield, Iowa. Dan's older brother lives on a beautiful mountainside estate on top of what used to be a dump. His younger brother is a computer programmer and martial arts expert who raises giant killer dogs.

DATE DUE

SEP 0 2 2004		
SEP 1 0 2004		
OCT 0 9 2004		
OCT 0 4 2004		
DEC 2 2 2004		
GAYLORD		PRINTED IN U.S.A.